hottie

Jonathan Bernstein

razOr
bill

Hottie

RAZORBILL

Published by the Penguin Group
Penguin Young Readers Group
345 Hudson Street, New York, New York 10014, U.S.A.
Penguin Group (USA) Inc., 375 Hudson Street, New York, New York 10014, U.S.A.
Penguin Group (Canada), 90 Eglinton Avenue East, Suite 700, Toronto, Ontario, Canada M4P 2Y3
(a division of Pearson Penguin Canada Inc.)
Penguin Books Ltd, 80 Strand, London WC2R 0RL, England
Penguin Ireland, 25 St Stephen's Green, Dublin 2, Ireland (a division of Penguin Books Ltd)
Penguin Group (Australia), 250 Camberwell Road, Camberwell, Victoria 3124, Australia
(a division of Pearson Australia Group Pty Ltd)
Penguin Books India Pvt Ltd, 11 Community Centre, Panchsheel Park, New Delhi – 110 017, India
Penguin Group (NZ), 67 Apollo Drive, Mairangi Bay, Auckland 1311, New Zealand
(a division of Pearson New Zealand Ltd)
Penguin Books (South Africa) (Pty) Ltd, 24 Sturdee Avenue, Rosebank, Johannesburg 2196, South Africa

Penguin Books Ltd, Registered Offices: 80 Strand, London WC2R 0RL, England

10 9 8 7 6 5 4 3 2 1

Copyright © 2009 Jonathan Bernstein

Library of Congress Cataloging-in-Publication Data

Library of Congress Cataloging-in-Publication Data

Bernstein, Jonathan.
  Hottie / by Jonathan Bernstein.
    p. cm.
  Summary: When a power surge during experimental plastic surgery turns fourteen-year-old Alison into a
human flamethrower, she drops from popular Beverly Hills princess to social outcast, but with the help of
a comic-loving "geek," she becomes a real-life superhero.
  ISBN 978-1-59514-212-2
  [1. Heroes--Fiction. 2. Self-esteem--Fiction. 3. Supernatural--Fiction. 4. Popularity--Fiction. 5.
Stepmothers--Fiction. 6. High schools--Fiction. 7. Schools--Fiction. 8. Beverly Hills (Calif.)--Fiction.] I.
Title.
  PZ7.B4566Hot 2009
  [Fic]--dc22
                          2008021059

Printed in the United States of America

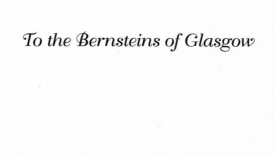

To the Bernsteins of Glasgow

ONE

If Alison Cole had any notion of how deeply her best friends detested her, she probably wouldn't have been smiling quite so brightly. But she had just been elected Beverly Hills High freshman class president in an overwhelming landslide and, as Alison prepared to accept her presidency and express her surprise and gratitude, her thoughts, in order, were:

1. *How she looked.* ("Like someone who wishes she were someone else. Someone shining with confidence. Someone with unblemished skin and obedient hair. Someone the exact opposite of me." This is what Alison Cole, who was prone to sporadic attacks of low self-esteem, was thinking. Her voting public thought otherwise. In

their adoring eyes, Alison was a stunning combination of artfully disheveled ash blond hair, ice green eyes, and suntanned skin. The absolute embodiment of privileged, blond, gorgeous California adolescent aristocracy.)

2. *How bizarre and unexpected it was that she'd been elected to a position of responsibility.* (Ridiculously bizarre! And it would never have happened if Alison had ignored the message on her Facebook wall from a name she didn't recognize. She was completely aware that any creep could claim to be an up-and-coming independent TV producer with an idea that was "just amazingly perfect" for her. But she had her father, Roger Cole, senior partner at Yarborough Cole McNabb Attorneys-at-Law, carry out an exhaustive check on the mysterious poster, and sure enough, the producer was everything she claimed. Which was how the Beverly Hills High election came to be co-opted to create the plotline for Alison's popular-girl-runs-for-office reality show, *Ms. President.*)

3. *How likely it was that she would sound dumb when she opened her mouth to speak.* (Fairly likely. "I always say dumb things when I get nervous," she fretted. Which didn't mean that Alison was, by any means, un-smart. It just meant that whenever she was rattled or stuck in a situation outside her comfort zone, words and sentences would fly out of her mouth without having first been verified by her brain.)

As much as good fortune dropped into her lap on a daily basis, Alison Cole sailed through school engendering no grudges. When conversation turned, as it did regularly, online and in person, to the subject of Ms. Cole, even participants secretly seething with lust, envy, or animosity found themselves unable to accuse her of being stuck-up, exclusionary, or having a mean bone in her body.

That's why no one resented Alison's superstar status. Not even when the presence of the cable TV camera crew that trotted obediently after her made it clear that the freshman class presidency was going to be a one-horse race. Sure, Brie Feltz (six votes) may have experienced pangs of regret that she'd never get to deliver the inaugural address she'd been rehearsing since the age of ten. Maybe Connor Mattacks (two votes) began involuntarily twitching as he anticipated his father's voice sighing, "Once again, you bring disappointment to the family." But neither rival hated her. Not when she seemed so sincerely overwhelmed by her win and not when she faced the school and prepared to deliver her acceptance speech.

Hanging on the gym wall behind Alison was a ten-foot blow-up of her campaign poster. It was a perfectly executed parody of a *Vogue* cover with the magazine title replaced by the word *Vote* and a shot of Alison that made her look nineteen. As Alison gripped the edge of the podium, she felt dwarfed by the huge poster. *That's not me,* she fretted. *I can't live up to that.* But every eye was on her and she had to say something.

"I don't know if any of you guys ever played the Fortunately/Unfortunately game," Alison said, looking up from her sheet of paper and glancing around the gym. "It was something my mother taught me." Alison paused. Mentioning her mother still affected her, still made her feel heavy with sadness. . . . She wasn't unique. She wasn't the only one in the gym to have to live with a loss. And it had been four years. *I can get through this,* Alison told herself, and continued her speech.

"My mom would start with something like, '*Fortunately*, it's a beautiful day.' And then I'd say, '*Unfortunately*, it's the end of the world.' And she'd say, '*Fortunately*, that means that we can shop all day and not have to pay for anything.' And I'd say, '*Unfortunately*, all the shops are full of mutant zombies.' And she'd say, '*Fortunately*, mutant zombies don't wear anything in my size.' We could go on like that all day. I guess it was stupid but . . . anyway, what I'm trying to say is, I can't play that game anymore. Partly 'cos my mom's not around to play it with me and partly because there is *no* 'unfortunately' about this. You've shown me you believe in me, you trust me, and you've got faith in me, and I can't even tell you what that means to me. I promise you I won't let you down. When I went into this, I didn't really have an ambition beyond being the best-dressed candidate, which—no disrespect, Brie, Connor, you guys both look cute in your own ways—I think I achieved. But now I want more, a lot more. Now I want to be the best freshman class president ever."

Alison stopped speaking. A split second of silence followed. *I sounded dumb,* she thought.

Then the gym erupted into applause and cheers.

That's right, make it all about you. Show them how desperate you are for attention, was what Alison's best friend Kellyn Levy was thinking at that moment. The only way Kellyn could rationalize

Alison's ridiculous popularity was to convince herself it was an act of charity, that the students of BHHS actually *pitied* Alison and all instinctively understood *Kellyn* was the cool one. That's why they kept a respectful distance. "If they knew me better, they'd like me more," she told herself, failing, as ever, to understand that the tart tongue, rolling eyes, and dismissive demeanor she'd acquired as part of her 24/7 resentment of Alison were what was stopping anyone from getting to know her better. Of course, Kellyn was up out of her seat, clapping, cheering, and whooping with everyone else as Alison accepted her position with a cute and completely spontaneous little victory dance.

Zat beetch. 'Ow can she 'ave so leetle self-respect? Oh, me and ma poor dead mamán, we zank you from ze bottom of ower 'arts. C'est pathetique! was what Alison's other best friend, Dorinda Galen, who, it should be said, was *not French*, was thinking. Dorinda affected a world-weary demeanor. She spoke in melodic Frenglish, occasionally lapsing into the mother tongue when English escaped her, and she made occasional mention of her glamorous life growing up in Paris. But Dorinda was *not French*. What she *was*, was scared to death of being invisible. Of being known, if at all, only as the other best friend of the lovely and popular Alison Cole. But even though she spent her school life consciously maintaining her fake accent, invented personality, and fictitious family history, Dorinda continued to be plagued by doubts that anyone at BHHS was actually aware of her existence. Of course, Dorinda was up out of her seat, clapping, cheering, and whooping with everyone else as Alison continued her cute and completely spontaneous little victory dance . . . .

★ ★ ★

Every dude in here would die to be me, was what Alison's eleventh-grade boyfriend, Warren Douglas, was thinking. He'd been popular before he hooked up with her. By rights, Alison should have been his arm candy, his dumb-but-fetching junior accessory.

But that wasn't how it worked out for Warren. It was like everyone steamrollered over him to get to her. Like his mom *lit up* every time Alison came over. Like his friends couldn't stop talking about her. When an anonymous text spread through the school claiming that Warren and Alison had broken up, all his so-called homeboys wasted no time coming up with excuses to show up at her door. Of course, when the text proved false, they crawled back to him, declaring their undying bro-yalty and swearing on a sky-high stack of Bibles that if—*if*—they'd gone anywhere near Alison, it was only to persuade her to reunite with Warren. (They seemed so sincere that Warren never let on he sent the text as a means of confirming his worst fears.) While everyone else was up out of their seat, clapping and cheering as Alison worked her presidential booty, Warren looked over at the only other person still sitting.

You can look, but you can't touch. Oops, did I say can't? I meant can. Can touch, was what Ginger Becker was thinking when she saw Warren dart what he imagined was a subtle glance in her direction. Quirky little anime chicks like her generally didn't end up with uncomplicated blond, buff surfer dudes like Warren Douglas. But she could see from the way that he stared at her ever-present sailor suit, taste in garish, glow-in-the-dark cosmetic products, and magenta hair that her presence annoyed and irritated him.

And this was her advantage over beautiful, blond, bland Alison. She could get under his skin. Meeting his gaze, Ginger batted her panda eyes and taunted, "Class president. Wow. That makes you, what, first lady?" Watching him struggle for a reply made her shiver with delight. Even though he was looking at his pretty little girlfriend accepting her accolades up on the stage, Ginger knew Warren was stuck with *her* Day-Glo image in his head. Ginger Becker was aware that Warren Douglas regarded her as a phony. She knew she bothered him. But somehow he always seemed to find himself staring at her. Ginger Becker grinned and readdressed her attention to the lollipop that was rarely far from her carnation-colored lips. Lick. Suck. Smirk.

This is when it happens. This is when it all changes. This is when the world learns the name David Eels, was what David Eels was thinking as he stood behind a curtain in the gym, listening to the applause and cheering that greeted Alison's acceptance speech and victory dance. *This is when people stop thinking* random geek *and start thinking* Class Clown, Most Unforgettable, Most Likely to Succeed. *This is when reputations are made,* David assured himself as he prepared to invade the stage and say goodbye to his years of middle school obscurity.

And yet . . . it was so nice behind the curtain. Nice and warm and dark and comforting. Couldn't he just stay there for a few more years? "Snap out of it!" David told himself. "You've spent your whole life huddled in the dark. Now it's time to be noticed." He then burst out from behind the curtain.

And that's when the sudden, shock appearance on the gym stage of a random geek in a homemade superhero costume caused

Alison's victory celebration to dwindle away into stunned silence. *Good. I've got their attention!* thought David. Clad in boots, tights, red underpants, and a blue T-shirt with an *E* Magic Markered on the chest where the legendary Man of Steel *S* would normally be, he positioned himself in front of a surprised Alison. "Excuse me, ma'am," he said politely before grabbing the mic and addressing the ninth grade. "It's a scary world out there," proclaimed David. "Danger lurks around every corner. No one's what they seem. It's getting harder to tell good from evil. You need someone on your side, but who do you trust? Who's really looking out for you? This school needs more than a president. This school needs . . . a hero!"

Whack! A Fiji bottle boinked off his temple. "You define sucking!" barked an annoyed spectator. More missiles followed. Textbooks. Phones. Sneakers. Panic started to set in. *Maybe this isn't how reputations are made.* Resolving not to crumble in front of the scornful mob, David attempted to act as if he were modestly acknowledging the thanks of a grateful nation. And even though he could see his few friends hiding their heads in their hands, he punched a fist proudly into the sky and kept it aloft as two teachers and a janitor forcibly removed him from the stage.

The celebratory atmosphere that followed Alison's acceptance speech seemed to have dissipated. She looked out into the audience, sensed the unrest, and, with perfect timing, broke back into her cute and completely spontaneous little victory dance, and, within seconds, everyone had forgotten the random geek and were out of their seats, clapping, cheering, and whooping.

TWO

After school, the cameras filmed the throngs of students gathered around Alison brandishing copies of her campaign poster. Like Beyoncé at an after-show meet-and-greet, Alison smiled and signed. Every Vote poster received a scrawled signature and a brief burst of a smile so dazzling it was like standing too close to the sun.

"Wow," gasped a stunned student. "Your smile is devastational."

Alison accepted the compliment modestly. "Dr. Chung on Wilshire. He's like a god of teeth-brightening. Make an appointment. Mention my name."

Warren, relegated, as usual, to standing by her side and holding her ridiculous elephant-shaped Commes des Garçons bag, wasn't having such an exciting day. The sea of students approaching Alison showed no signs of drying up. Even though Warren made a big deal out of yawning and checking his watch and whining, "No, we're *still* here," into his iPhone, she continued handing out hugs and promises to all her admirers.

Asked by starry-eyed devotees how they could be like her, Alison was about to recommend her wizard of a nutritionist. Instead, she said, "Be a good person and good things will happen to you."

"I'm gonna get Alison Cole to autograph her stupid poster. *If* she can even write," announced David Eels. Unscarred by his removal from the gym, David stood on the school steps with his small, select crew, who—if anyone had ever noticed them or cared enough to ridicule them—would have been cruelly nicknamed Phlegmy, Tiny Head, Toenail, and Odor Eater. He watched Alison Cole holding court. His companions immediately launched into spasms of eye rolls and derisive nasal, phlegmy snorts.

"What can I do? It's on the list," replied David, pulling a crumpled sheet of paper from inside his red underpants. Phlegmy, Tiny Head, Toenail, and Odor Eater took a collective grossed-out step back. David read from the sheet of paper: "'Things I Promised Myself I'd Do To Make Freshman Year Bearable. Numero ten: Quell the robot uprising.' Done. When was the last time any of you were menaced by robots? Don't thank me; it's my job. *'Numero nine: Mess with the empty head of the most popular chick in school.'*"

David shrugged at his friends. Unlike him, they had accepted their lowly place in the universe and only wanted to get through high school unscathed. "It's out of my hands," he told them.

★ ★ ★

Alison couldn't get over "Be a good person and good things will happen to you." It had just flown out of her mouth and it wasn't even dumb. She scribbled it on every Vote poster, adding, "I really believe that," because she really did. Alison had her pen poised when she noticed the poster in her hand already had a written message. *Superhero at your service* was what the message said.

Alison looked up from the poster and saw, standing in front of her, a smirk playing around his mouth, the same, clearly emotionally damaged, superhero geek who had been dragged from the stage. Alison stared at David, baffled.

But all David had was the smirk. His sudden close proximity to the Incalculably Popular Alison Cole had caused his brain to lurch into complete shutdown mode. And then Alison laughed. "Love the outfit."

"Versace," said David, his brain, thankfully, rebooting.

Alison looked genuinely stunned. "Is not!"

"You didn't get an invite to the private sale? At Barneys?"

For a second, Alison looked like she was about to hyperventilate.

"I shouldn't have mentioned it. It was only for a few selected customers."

"Selected?" repeated Alison, eyes widening in shock.

"Special," he amended.

"*I'm* special," she insisted.

"Would you say you have special needs?" asked David.

"Yes, I have *very* special needs."

David looked over at his friends to see if they were watching his masterful mockery of the new president. Then he looked back at Alison. Was that actual distress shining in those deep, green liquid eyes? Could *he*, the guy behind the curtain, have actually caused *her* a moment's distress? And if he had, how come he wasn't enjoying it more? How come he wanted to make that moment go away?

"Just kidding," he said. "I'm a kidder. You might say I was like the class clown."

Alison touched him lightly, reproachfully on the arm, making her the first female who wasn't a relation, an aged neighbor, or a nurse to ever make physical contact with David Eels. Her tap on his arm disoriented him so much it triggered his most feared reaction to stressful situations.

"Hic . . . hic . . ."

You're not hiccuping in front of Alison Cole? Seriously, you're not?

With his mind reeling, David almost missed hearing Alison say, "Are you really at my service? 'Cos if there's one thing I need, it's a superhero."

David nodded, unable to speak without unleashing a volley of high-pitched *hic*s.

"Anytime I need you, you'll be there to save me from danger?"

All he had left was an obedient nod.

"Well, I'm in danger of failing English. Maybe you can take care of that for me?"

The combination of her looks, her absolute ease in her own skin, his hiccupping problem, and his peripheral view of his friends pointing in his direction and hanging themselves from imaginary nooses left David mute and scarlet-faced. Alison wrote a sentence on her Vote poster and pushed it back into David's hands.

As he was about to slink *hic*-ing away, she held up a finger, commanding him to stay as one would a trained Labradoodle, and then gestured to Warren to pass her the ridiculous elephant bag. Opening it, Alison removed a scrap of paper and a pen. Then, as she carefully drew a line through some typing, she smiled. *Number ten: Mess with the head of the most tragic loser in school.*

David stared at her, agog and aghast. She grinned back, revealing the artistry of Dr. Chung. *His* empty head had been successfully messed with by the most popular chick in school! Before he could fully process what had just happened, David was swept aside by Kellyn and Dorinda, who embraced their triumphant friend. "Fabinet meeting!" yelled Kellyn, who needlessly went on to explain, "We rule the school and we're fabulous, so now we're called the Fabinet."

Alison rolled her eyes. "We're not calling ourselves the Fabinet." Kellyn had a "*But . . .*" on her lips, which she grudgingly bit back. She hated how much she needed Alison's approval and hated even more that it was so often withheld.

Warren was done being Alison's bag boy. He was about to shove the ridiculous Commes des Garçons elephant back at her when Winter Wertzky—the producer of Alison's TV show—pushed past him, juggling a Caramel Macchiato, her BlackBerry, two copies of *Allure*, and a yoga mat.

Hugging her star, Winter, who had so many half-finished thoughts ricocheting around inside her hypercaffeinated head that she rarely managed to finish a sentence, said, "That was just. You could not have been more! I'm *so* excited! And wait till Josh. He's one of my best. I've known him for seriously like. And this is just the. Tonight! The party's gonna be so. And I've asked. And they all said!"

Kellyn stared at the scene unfolding in front of her. *Alison's* party, *Alison's* presidential celebration, *Alison's* producer, *Alison's* TV show. Kellyn couldn't take it. Her temples throbbed. Her eyes stung. Her acid reflux returned. She grabbed Dorinda's arm. "We're going," she said curtly, dragging her friend toward the long, gleaming line of Cadillacs, BMWs, and Maybachs waiting to whisk the departing BHHS students back to their palatial homes.

"Ow!" bleated Dorinda. *"You are bweaking zee skin. Ah weel 'ave a 'eedeeous woond!"*

Warren was already waiting in his car. He honked the horn of his H4 and gestured to Alison to take her rightful place by his side.

But Winter hadn't finished with Alison. "You're knocking at the door of diva-osity. You're almost a diva. You're a pre-va! There's so much we've got to. We need to start thinking about the and how we're going to." So saying, she gestured for Alison to board *her* H4.

Alison looked at both of her prospective chauffeurs and caught them shooting competitive glares at each other. The sound of a plane passing overhead as it made its way toward LAX caused her to look up.

"Three forty-eight. American Airlines. Arriving from Monterey Peninsula Airport," she said to herself.

"Hic!" hiccuped David. Alison had forgotten he was still

there. David lowered his eyes, embarrassed. He had allowed himself to become mesmerized by Alison's hectic, exciting whirl of a social life. He'd hoped that his stage-invading superhero stunt would help him wind up with a life like that. He'd hoped that once the school saw what an unpredictable prankster he could be, his buddy list would finally extend beyond Phlegmy, Tiny Head, Toenail, and Odor Eater. But then a few members of the BHHS lacrosse team spilled down the school steps and yelled their congratulations to Alison. And, a moment later, the Madrigal Singers did the same. So did the Mental Dental Collective, the school's dominant street dance crew. In less than sixty seconds, members of three wildly divergent social units had paid their respects to Alison and none of them had so much as noticed him. It became clear to David that no matter how hard he tried, Random Geek was as high as he'd ever climb at this school.

Correction: Random Geek with chronic hiccups.

Honk. Warren's H4. "You coming or what?"

Honk. Winter's H4. "Ally. I've got a call in to the editor of. You're so right for the cover of their."

Alison ignored both honks. She pulled a water bottle from her elephant bag and passed it to David. "Swallow it all in one gulp. Good advice from your president. See, I'm making a difference already."

As David began to gulp down the water, she walked away from him, waved goodbye to Winter and Warren, and hurried after Kellyn and Dorinda, who were climbing into the limo provided by Kellyn's rarely present mother.

"Fabinet meeting," muttered Kellyn to herself as she saw

Alison approach.

"Know what we are?" she demanded of Dorinda.

"Um . . . um . . ." Dorinda always panicked when she saw the storm clouds pass across Kellyn's face.

"We're dogs. We're the loyal devoted companions Alison turns to when she needs a break from the latest fantastic thing to happen to her."

"Hey, sexy ladies," trilled Alison, climbing into the limo.

"Woof, woof," barked Kellyn.

"Woof, woof," Alison barked back happily, thinking her clever friend had come up with a secret code that only they could understand.

Within moments, the cars, the throngs of admiring students, and the TV cameras had all disappeared, leaving David standing alone, dressed in his homemade superhero costume and clutching Alison's Vote poster. He'd actually talked to her and, to his surprise, she'd proved unexpectedly cool. He gazed down at her face on the poster. *Be a good superhero and good things will happen to you.* She'd taken the time to personalize a message to him! She knew who he was! He'd made an impression! And not just his usual horrible first impression. Not only that, he'd swallowed the water in one gulp and was no longer *hic*-ing! She *was* a good president! He reached a hand into his red underpants, pulled out his list, crumpled it into a ball, and threw it away. He didn't need it anymore. Freshman year had just become bearable.

"What an incredible triumph . . ." snorted Phlegmy, immediately making it unbearable again. ". . . is what I would have been saying if you'd been able to get a word out without drowning—*hic!* in—*hic!* a pool of—*hic!*—flop sweat."

"She was actually not un-nice," insisted David.

"Yeah, right," mocked Tiny Head. "Not un-nice, like the supermodel's not un-nice to the Make-A-Wish kid who paints with his feet."

David should have remained coolly mute. Instead, he blurted, "We had chemistry."

Amid the snorts of high-pitched laughter, Toenail sneered, "Of course you did. 'Cuz doucheburgers like you and bips like her are such a natural fit."

David, irked, replied, "Don't call her a bip."

"Why not?" demanded Odor Eater. "It's not like she knows anything about you."

"That's where you're wrong," said David, brandishing the Vote poster with its personalized motivational message that he realized, just a moment too late, she'd made out to "David Ellis."

THREE

Alison's father, Roger Cole, the high-powered defense attorney, didn't pull out all the stops for the inauguration party he threw Alison at their sprawling Brentwood estate. She wasn't lowered by helicopter onto a waiting red carpet. She wasn't greeted and serenaded by Chris Brown. There was no special Cirque du Soleil performance in the backyard. She didn't get to cut the ribbon tying up her special present, a powder blue Bentley with the license plate AL1SON. Roger was saving *those* particular surprises for Alison's sweet sixteen. He had promised his daughter that her victory party would be a low-key affair. That meant catering by In-N-Out, Southern California's calorific-but-irresistible burger franchise; it meant hot local band of the moment, Lozenge, playing in the backyard. And, as Alison discovered to her horror at 6:15, a mere forty-five minutes before the party was scheduled to begin, it meant personalized DVDs issued to every guest, chronicling every recorded second in the history of Alison Cole.

It took Alison another fourteen minutes to search the house's two stories, six bedrooms, four bathrooms, sauna, screening room, gym, and guesthouse before she had rounded up every one of those offending DVDs. Well, almost every one.

"Low-key. Do you even know what low-key means?" snarled Alison seconds before she wrenched open the living room door and found Roger in floods of tears. He was watching the final highlight on the last DVD.

". . . I can't play that game anymore," said on-screen Alison."Partly 'cos my mom's not around to play it with me . . ." Her anger immediately expired. She went up to her father and entwined her little finger around his in a ritual they'd carried over from childhood.

"I'm so proud of you, honey," he gasped through tears. "And I know your mother is too. I know she was up there, watching."

Alison tried to hold it together. "I hope so, Daddy. And I want you to know something. Once tonight is all over and everyone's gone, I am going to kill you. Literally kill you. Bury you under a big pile of DVDs."

"Too much?" Roger smiled.

"No, that ice sculpture by the door's too much. Oh, sorry, Carmen, I didn't see you come in. . . ."

Roger glanced over at his stone-faced second wife, Carmen St. Cloud-Cole, then back at Alison. The pleading look on his face was, he hoped, obvious to both of them. "Not tonight," it begged. Not another night of barely hidden hostility between his daughter and her stepmother. Carmen turned her subzero gaze to the TV screen and Alison's cute, spontaneous victory dance.

"Oh, you look so cute begging for attention like that."

"Thank you *so* much," replied Alison, oozing insincerity. "I wish you could have been there, but I understand why you had to stay away. The lighting in the gym is *so* harsh. It plays up every little imperfection."

Carmen remained fascinated by Alison's performance. "These TV people are real miracle workers. Look at how polished and professional you are. They've gotten you to stop twitching and chewing your hair. Who knows, with a little more work, they may even stop you from spitting when you talk."

"I only ever do that when I'm around you, Carmen," shot back Alison, filling the room with her warm smile.

Not waiting for Carmen to construct a comeback, Alison aimed the remote control at the CD player. Ancient music emerged. Road trip music. The Rolling Stones. "Wild Horses." Alison didn't know anything about The Rolling Stones, but she remembered this song from all the sleepy drives home from Malibu Beach with her mom's head resting on her dad's shoulder. Alison smiled at Roger, grateful that he still remembered when they were a *real* family. She took his hand, pulled his arm around her waist, and let him dance her around the room. Just like they used to when she was a little girl.

Alison loved that the music had the power to make her feel close to her father, that it brought back memories of those summers, and that it completely shut out Carmen.

Looking over at her stepmother, who remained standing in

the doorway, Alison asked innocently, "Did you dance to this when *you* were a teenager?"

Carmen barked, "That song's forty years old!"

Alison smiled back at her, the picture of innocence. Attempting to regain her composure, Carmen murmured, "Well, I hope you enjoy tonight. Your father's gone to a lot of trouble to make it perfect."

Still dancing with Roger, Alison looked at the gaunt woman who lived in her house, shared her father's name, bed, and bank account, and who, though only fifteen years her elder, had already begun to resemble a department store mannequin that was about to melt.

"Tha-a-a-anks," replied Alison, drawing out the word to such an extent that it was obvious she didn't mean it. "So, I can't wait to see what you're gonna wear tonight. You always look *so* stylish."

This might have seemed like an olive branch generously extended between estranged stepparent and stepchild had Carmen not taken the time to frame herself in the doorway to show off the satin Gucci gown for which she'd spent all day being fitted.

"*This* is what I'm wearing!" was what Carmen was about to hurl back in her stepdaughter's smug, ignorant face when she realized that Alison was well aware of that fact.

Flushing and unable to conjure up a suitably stinging retort, Carmen was reduced to simmering silence.

Just remember, I didn't start this, thought Alison, remembering how sweet Carmen had been to her when Roger first introduced them. She'd wanted her father to be happy. She'd wanted to believe he'd found someone who could help him get over her mother. Then she'd overheard Carmen on the phone, gloating, "He's got a brat, but I'm making sure she's shipped off to boarding school." From that moment, it was war.

Alison might not have been able to make Roger see Carmen in her true skanky, lying colors, but she *was* going to do everything in her power to make her evil stepmother's life miserable. So she kept dancing with her father and enjoying the anger in Carmen's eyes. Seconds before "Wild Horses" faded away, Roger seemed to get tangled up in his own feet. He took a couple of staggering steps backward.

"So you think you can dance?" Alison smiled. Her smile faded as she saw her father about to fall backward into the glass coffee table.

"Dad!" she yelled.

Roger flailed around like he was fighting to regain control of his limbs. He barked his shins off the edge of the coffee table. He lurched forward and grabbed at the first solid object that was loose enough to break his fall. The closest solid object was a fruit bowl. Roger's hands gripped two oranges, which exploded under the strength of his grasp.

"Dad, are you okay?" gasped Alison.

Roger pulled himself upright, caught his breath, and attempted to regain some semblance of dignity. Which was difficult since orange pulp was dripping from his hands. "I'm fine," he said.

"You might consider acting your age in the future," murmured Carmen.

Alison stared at her stepmother, appalled at the lack of sympathy and also that she'd laid herself *so* wide open to a stinging retort.

"I think I hear guests arriving," yelped Roger, rushing from the room, leaving his wife and child to make death eyes at each other.

Alison's victory party should have been the absolute high point of her year. Instead, it had rapidly become a seeping, sucking nightmare for four reasons:

1. *Winter Wertzky.* And her ever-present cameras. And her executive decision to pepper the party with celebrity cameos. "Treasure Spinney! Five minutes away!" she announced every fifteen minutes. Treasure Spinney? Alison was terrified of Treasure Spinney! As far as she was concerned, America's most lovable, huggable little teenybopper tomboy TV star was the embodiment of evil. She didn't want the embodiment of evil showing up at her victory party.

2. *The Shine Down Love on Those Who Need Love Foundation.* It wasn't enough that Carmen St. Cloud had deviously wormed her way into the affections of a grieving widower who couldn't be held responsible for his actions. It wasn't enough that she had the organs of dead cows injected into her forehead, cheeks, and chin on a regular basis. No, Carmen craved respectability. She was desperate to be seen as an equal part of an LA power couple. She wanted to throw A-list Oscar parties. She wanted designers falling over themselves to get her to wear their new lines. She was ravenous to be featured in

glossy Los Angeles magazines. That's why her publicist pitched Carmen to the press *not* as the new trophy wife on the block but as a tireless philanthropist whose every waking moment was devoted to making a difference.

"To," as Carmen emphasized when extracting promises of hefty donations from Alison's guests, "shine down love on those who need love." And then she described her vision of a lavish, extravagant Christmas ball where the invitees would be a mixture of the very rich and the very poor, with each member of each economic group learning the true meaning of Christmas by purchasing presents for the other. With Winter's cameras watching her, Alison couldn't let her frustration show, but she wished one of the guests would summon up the nerve to ask Carmen, *"What does that Shine Down Love stuff even mean? Who does it help? Where does the money go?"*

3. *Warren.* Alison wasn't always aware of how insecure and overshadowed Warren felt. But there was a moment tonight when, stress getting the better of her, she said, "Here, hold my bag," only to realize she didn't *have* a bag with her. The look on his face told her everything. Alison reached for his hand. "This is all so crazy. I'm happy you're here to help me through it. . . ." But then Winter came bounding breathlessly up, dragging some fitness guru that Alison just *had* to meet. She saw Warren's face harden and knew that this was an excellent opportunity to prove to him that she was aware that he was feeling neglected and she was going to go to great pains to include

him. "Hiiii," said Alison to the fitness guy. "Thanks for coming. Have you met my boyf—" But she never got to the last syllable because Warren had already pulled his hand away and walked off.

4. *Christian Bale.* Or at least the lean and chiseled teenage version of the actor who seemed to be inhabiting the body of Beverly Hills High junior president Tommy Hull. (Or T, as he was more commonly known.) Alison was a one-guy girl. She loved Warren. All her carefully constructed future plans involved Warren (although they'd now been modified to remove bag-carrying duty). Even though her star outshone his in the eyes of all who beheld them, in her mind she was part of a blissful merger called "WarrenandAlison." *That said*, there was something about T that made her heart beat faster, her mouth lose its moisture, her mind empty of all coherent thought, and her feet and hands lose their power to perform any function beyond fidgeting. And all of this aberrant behavior that T—with whom she'd barely shared more than a passing "hiii"—brought out in Alison was suddenly in full effect now that T was here *in her house, in her lovely illuminated, tented backyard,* striding toward her, fixing her with a gaze that made everything suddenly slide into slow motion. T stood in front of Alison. Taken separately, the components—five-foot ten, broad shoulders, sandy hair that he kept brushing out of his brown eyes—were hardly remarkable. But put them all together and she was left breathless. T extended a

hand. She watched the hand make its achingly unhurried progress toward her. And then he had his hand in hers. *Not clammy,* she mused. *Engulfing. Warm. Like being at the beach. And I like being at the beach.*

"Congratulations, Alison. I really want us to work together. I think we can accomplish a lot." T was talking, but Alison had trouble following what he was saying. She concentrated harder on his mouth. It seemed like he was saying something about cleaning up poo. Did he want *her* to clean up poo? Had someone made a mess that needed cleaning up? Maybe Carmen had irritable bowel syndrome? That would be excellent. "As long as every student takes responsibility for their pet's poo," intoned T, "I don't see why we can't bring our dogs and cats and hamsters to school. It's a documented fact that students suffer separation anxiety when they have to leave their animals at home. I know I feel more relaxed when my meerkat's within stroking distance. The Bring Our Pets to School initiative was one of my big election platforms, and now the principal's acting like it's a bad thing, like it might be disruptive." T smiled. "We should liaise on this, put our heads together. I know, I'm up on my soapbox, but this is a biggie for me. We'll talk about it more in school. The party's great, by the way. Congratulations again."

With that, T walked away. *I handled that pretty well,* thought Alison, unaware that she had failed to utter a single word.

Warren didn't know Alison hadn't said a single word to T. He stood in the shadows, watching his girlfriend bask in the attention of an assembly line of admirers. Suddenly, an empty glass was pushed into his hand. "I'll take another Diet Coke when you've got a minute," said Ginger Becker, who had suddenly material-ized beside Warren, smirk and lollipop in their usual positions. "Oops." She giggled. "I thought you worked here." As usual, she had succeeded in irritating him. As usual, he didn't know how to voice his irritation. "But you're not the waiter," taunted Ginger Becker. "You're just waiting."

Lick. Suck. Smirk.

FOUR

"*Banoodles party, baby* girl. You did your thing," proclaimed Marvelette Bridgewater-Rivington to Alison as she made her exit.

"Thank you *so* much for having me to your lovely home and allowing me to be a part of your inspirational victory. I hope to one day follow your example," gushed Cinnamon Quon to Alison as she headed home.

"You worked it and you looked fierce, which is all that matters," hissed Nino Nixxon, triple air-kissing Alison as he flounced into the night.

Alison, operating on autopilot, dutifully handed out good-bye kisses, hugs, smiles, and nods to her departing guests, all the while scanning the house for signs of Warren's presence. He couldn't have just left without saying goodbye, she assured herself while trying his iPhone for what, she hoped, wasn't the tenth time in the last hour. "He can't be mad at me. I didn't do anything wrong."

Warren, as it turned out, *had* left the party without saying goodbye. He was extremely mad at the lack of attention and consideration he received from someone who'd barely even existed before he plucked her out of obscurity. But Warren wasn't the type of guy to carry a grudge. He knew Alison knew she'd been neglecting him. He knew she felt bad. She'd called him fourteen times in the last hour. Warren knew it was fourteen because the last time the iPhone in his pants pocket vibrated, Ginger Becker, who was making out with him in the backseat of his H4, shrieked with delighted laughter for the fourteenth time that hour.

As Winter's camera crew clocked off for the night and the catering staff returned the Cole garden to its original splendor, Alison relished the termination of her smiling hostess duties. Did she really want a TV show? Did she really want to be freshman class president? Did she just want to be liked because she remembered how it felt to *not* be? Did she really have a clue what she wanted? A plane passed overhead and she looked up, watching it make its way toward LAX.

"Ten-oh-six. British Airways. Flying out of Heathrow," she said to herself.

"Wouldn't you love to just jump on the next plane and fly right out of here?" said a wistful voice.

Alison was surprised to see Carmen standing by her side. The older woman kept her gaze skyward. "Air travel must be so much easier for you. Now that you don't need two seats."

Alison said nothing. Where was Carmen going with this?

"I saw the pictures," Carmen said, looking down from the dark sky and grinning straight into Alison's face. "The ones from when you were a little girl. Well, I say *little* . . ."

As if she hadn't hammered the point home hard enough, Carmen puffed out her cheeks and extended her arms around an invisible-but-enormous belly.

"Have another drink, Carmen. Don't worry about embarrassing yourself," replied Alison through gritted teeth.

"That's *big* of you," said Carmen, who walked away, bubbling with laughter.

Alison's face betrayed no emotion. Fair enough. Score one point to Carmen. One point compared to the unbeatable high score Alison had notched up insulting and decimating Carmen. Except . . . *why did she have to go there?* It was a low blow and it wasn't true. But Alison was a lot more the girl in that picture than she was the high school popularity icon. And Carmen had just stabbed straight into the heart of the girl in the picture. This was a bitter end to what was supposed to be a celebration of All Things Alison.

Then an explosion of shrill girlish giggles filled the back garden. Kellyn and Dorinda. *So* cute. *So* fun. *So* supportive. Alison laughed out loud and suddenly knew exactly what she wanted. She wanted to be with her girls. She wanted to be silly and loud with people who loved her unconditionally.

There they were, her best friends in the world. Kellyn, who had been by Alison's side before the summer when she grew two inches, her skin cleared up, she shed a few pounds, and her features realigned in such a way that everyone who had previously ignored her suddenly acted like she was giving away free money. Dorinda, who was so glamorous and exotic and loyal and sweet.

There they were, a little bit buzzed on Red Bull, giggling and paddling their toes in the Coles' floodlit pool. In the months following her mother's death, Alison had felt completely isolated, like she meant nothing to anyone. Now everyone acted like they loved her, but how could they when they didn't really know her? All Alison needed and all she wanted was a small tight circle of friends who cared about her. And there they were, competing to see who could spit ice cubes the farthest into the pool. Alison rushed to join her friends.

"Fabinet meeting!" she yelled, squeezing between Kellyn and Dorinda, missing the bitter "so it's okay if *you* say it?" look that briefly clouded Kellyn's eyes.

As midnight drew near, the three girls let their emotions flow free.

"I love you," said Alison to Kellyn.

"I love *you*," replied Kellyn, brimming over with sincerity.

"You are ma best frenz in all ze worl," slurred Dorinda.

"You're the best," said Kellyn to Alison.

"No, you," replied Alison.

"You!" exclaimed Dorinda.

"You're so gorgeous," insisted Alison to Kellyn. "You're like a little porcelain doll. I feel like this big clumsy mess next to you." Kellyn responded to Alison's effusive endorsement of her beauty with a tight smile. "Little porcelain doll" felt less like a well-intended compliment and more like a stinging slap across the face.

Before the summer when everything changed, *Kellyn* had been the one telling Alison how gorgeous she was, promising that her skin problems would soon be a thing of the past and assuring her that there would come a day when guys would take one look at her and forget how to spell their names. Never once thinking that those pulled-out-of-thin-air predictions would ever for a second come to pass.

"And you," gushed Alison to Dorinda. "That shiny black hair, those crazy pouty lips. I'm Erica Generica compared to you. . . ."

This is *exactly* what Kellyn had thought three years earlier when she more or less abandoned shy, spotty Alison for shiny, pouty Dorinda. Never once thinking that *she'd* have to crawl her way back to the suddenly stunning Alison. And *certainly* never once thinking that Dorinda would be so intimidated by her first glance of their new mutual friend that she'd adopt a bogus accent and identity.

Outraged by the cruel trick nature had played on them and blazing with the conviction that just beneath Alison's beauteous exterior lurked a pimply loser painfully aware that her popularity could evaporate as rapidly as it had appeared, Kellyn seized control of the conversation.

"Tell her she's the most beautiful," demanded Kellyn of Dorinda.

"Exqueeeseet. Like a bébé foal nesting een the boozoom of its mamán," said Dorinda, fluttering a hand over her heart for emphasis. *"'Ow could you zink ozerwise?"*

Alison stared down at her reflection in the pool. Then she splashed her feet in the water, breaking up her image. "Because

Warren was weird. Because having my Step-Misery around makes my face break out. Because I've got cameras on me every second. And Winter Wertzky's all, "You'll forget they're." But I *don't* forget! What if I look dumb and people laugh at me? What if I look, I don't know . . . *squishy?*"

Kellyn and Dorinda swapped glances. They'd been friends long enough and had harbored deep-seated resentment long enough for them to recognize an opportunity and, without words, exploit it. Kellyn shuffled close to Alison and took her hand.

"Listen," commanded Kellyn. "You girls know how I feel about Rihanna, right?"

All three nodded reverently. Rihanna was *flawless.*

"Well, Rihanna's squishy next to you. End of discush."

Alison was moved. "I love you, K."

"I love you, A," said Kellyn.

"I love all of you," added Dorinda.

"You're the best," said Kellyn, waiting just the right amount of time before she gave voice to the thought that had been marinating inside her head, ". . . but if you're *really* worried about it . . ."

Alison responded just as her best friends hoped she would: "*Should I be?* Oh my God, you think I should be? You think I'm squishy!"

"I'm just saying," soothed Kellyn, playing her hand perfectly, "there's this guy I read about . . ."

"Not one of the butchers who hacked up Scarmen . . . ?"

The girls all cackled at their pet name for Alison's stepmom.

"No, this guy's supposed to be a genius."

"Zey're all supposed to be jenioozes." Dorinda grimaced, recalling the travesty that was her second nose job, before Kellyn silenced her with a *"not* helping" glare.

"He is, though. I read about him in *Flaunt* magazine."

Attempting to redeem herself, Dorinda leapt in, *"Yes, hees theeng ees that beauty is about, 'ow you say, seemetree. . . ."*

Alison looked puzzled. Kellyn shook her head impatiently at Dorinda's linguistic facade.

"She means symmetry. You need the perfect dimensions to have a classically beautiful face."

Alison flushed with excitement. "I've always thought that! This guy *is* a genius!"

"I know!" said Kellyn.

"And," added Dorinda, dialing down the Frenglish just a smidgeon for maximum comprehension, "he's been working for years on a technique that can—"

Alison was already there. Jumping to her feet, she yelled, "Give me symmetry!" Overjoyed, she grabbed the nearest Red Bull can and, finding it empty, leapt up to snag a refill.

Kellyn and Dorinda watched her scamper back to the house. Then they turned to look at each other.

Kellyn was *glowing* with warmth, happiness, and excitement.

"Uh . . . what joost 'appened?" asked Dorinda, who had her suspicions but needed them confirmed.

"We just persuaded our friend to undergo experimental cosmetic surgery."

"Zat she doos not need?"

"Exactly."

"*Boot what eef she gets 'urt or, 'ow you say, maimed?*"

"She won't. Dr. Bracken is like the Picasso of plastic sur-geons. I mean that in a good way."

"*Boot what . . .*"

Dorinda was growing more anxious by the second. Which made Kellyn more irritated.

"*. . . what eef she emerges from ze opairaishon even more gorgeous?*"

"Oh, be less average, Dorinda!" snapped Kellyn.

Dorinda bit her lip and stared into the water.

Kellyn, who tended to divide the world into two categories, (1) Herself and (2) People Who Are Stupid, knew she'd been too abrupt.

Taking Dorinda's hand, she continued in softer, more mea-sured tones. "We were never not cute. That's the difference be-tween us and Alison. Dr. Bracken may well make her even more beautiful and stunning. But that's not what she'll see when she looks in the mirror."

Kellyn could see comprehension creeping across Dorinda's face. She continued, "Alison doesn't need surgery. She needs our approval."

"*So she weel do anyzing we ask?*"

Kellyn nodded.

It was the end of the night, but for them, it was a new begin-ning.

"I love you, Dorinda."

"*I love you too, Kelleen.*"

Kellyn gave Dorinda a cold stare. "It's just you and me."

Dorinda swallowed hard. "I love you, Kellyn," she said again, but this time in her natural thin, reedy Valley Girl voice.

FIVE

Đr. Bracken looked like a gift that had
yet to be unwrapped. More specifically, he looked like he was
still factory-sealed inside a protective coating of plastic. As Alison sat on the luxurious soft white leather couch in the famous
plastic surgeon's plush, all-white office, she couldn't help but
stare at the man who was supposed to wipe away all her imper-
fections. He was *shiny*. His face wasn't just free of any imperfec-
tions, it was almost free of any features. He was like one of the
Blue Man Group. Except he was pink. And a doctor. Maybe he
was part of the Pink Doctor Group? She began to wonder if this
operation was a good idea. As if picking up on her panic, the

doctor looked up from his notes and smiled a shiny smile.

"I know what you're thinking," he intoned smoothly. "What am I doing here? Is this right for me? Who is this guy anyway?"

"No, no, no," gasped Alison. "I'm beyond thrilled to be here."

"A little trepidation is only natural at this stage. You're worried about what you're getting into. Let me try and put your fears at rest."

Dr. Bracken clicked a folder on his PowerBook. A female face filled the screen. Average. Perhaps less than perfect. Weak jaw. Eyes a little squinty. Blobby nose. Dr. Bracken looked at Alison. She looked at the doctor, then at the screen and, feeling like the onus was on her to appear intelligent, pulled out her notebook and wrote the word *face*. She looked back up at the doctor. He smiled at her, then began to speak.

"Many formulas have been used in the attempt to calculate the perfect dimensions for what constitutes a beautiful face."

The doctor paused, looked at Alison again. Unsure whether he was ready to take questions, she looked back down at her notebook and once again wrote the word *face*.

Dr. Bracken continued, "The most famous formula . . ."

Then he stopped talking. Alison had noticed the huge oval mirror on his office wall. She was shooting little sidelong looks at it, touching her hair and examining her teeth.

Pulling herself away from the mirror, Alison smiled at the doctor. ". . . the most famous formula. I'm listening. . . ."

"Was developed by the Greeks. It was known as . . ."

Alison's hand shot up like she was back in class. "The Grecian Formula?"

"No."

"Chic by Greek?"

"No."

"That would be good, though, wouldn't it?"

"I don't know. May I continue?"

Alison held up her pen to indicate her readiness.

"It was known as the golden ratio. It's a ratio of 1 to 1.618. This numerical association has been used in great works of art and architecture for centuries. Take, for instance, Michelangelo's *David* . . ."

As Dr. Bracken talked, Alison tried not to glaze over, tried to pay attention, but the lure of the mirror was proving hard to resist.

The doctor caught her little shifty looks and picked up his pace. "Many of my colleagues have been using the golden ratio as a guide for their work, but that can be messy and the results are not always guaranteed. I've taken it a step further and, I can assure you, a step *safer*. . . ."

Alison wrote the word *safer* beneath *face* and *face*.

"I use noninvasive radiation technology to soften the underlying bone structure. I then reshape the structure to give the face perfect symmetry. . . ."

The moment Dr. Bracken uttered the word *symmetry*, the picture on the desktop began to change. A grid of rectangles appeared over the woman's face.

Alison yelped in fright and covered her eyes. "You never said this was gonna be scary!"

On the desktop, the rectangles were absorbed into the woman's face.

"They're *eating* her face! Gross!"

As they faded from view, the woman looked sort of the same but also subtly, inexplicably *different*. Suddenly, she was *beautiful*.

And Alison was barely capable of breathing. "That's the greatest invention of all time. You *are* a genius. *Flaunt* was right!"

"Some of my comments were taken out of context," said the doctor modestly.

"I want it. I want symmetry."

"I believe you're a suitable candidate, and once the procedure has been fully tested, my office will be in touch to make an appointment—"

"I want symmetry *now*," she emphasized.

"I'm attending a conference in Geneva in a few days. I believe we're close to a breakthrough."

Alison was by no means a spoiled brat, but on the occasions she resorted to whining, the recipients of her brattishness generally waved the white flag within seconds.

"I need symmetry. I'm gonna be on TV! You said I could have it!"

"I don't recall specifically saying . . ."

This guy was made of stone. Shiny stone. Alison amped up her attack.

"It's not fair," she said in a tremulous voice. "Everyone gets what they want. . . ."

She started sniffling and flapping at her moistening eyes.

The shiny doctor started to exhibit signs of surrender! "Well . . ." he said, giving in.

Alison immediately reverted to her previous good nature.

"When do I get symmetry?"

"This is, as I said, a very new procedure."

"When do I get symmetry?"

"I want to emphasize, it's never been tested on actual human subjects."

"So I'd be the first? I could get on *The View*!"

"You'd have to sign a waiver absolving this practice from all liability from unforeseen side effects."

Alison scribbled her name on the notebook, ripped out the page, and thrust it at Dr. Bracken.

Helpless in the face of her unbridled enthusiasm, he took one more shot. "The costs will be *substantial*."

This was of so little significance to Alison that she abandoned all pretense of paying attention. Gazing at her reflection in the doctor's big oval mirror, she imagined what she would look like after the rectangles had sunk into her skin. A shiver ran through her. She was going to be *devastational*!

SIX

Carmen was never home. She was always at her shrink or her hair guy or her nail team or her colorist or her nutritionist or her tennis guy or her charity committees or at her joke job as life coach. It was perfectly possible for Alison to avoid her stepmother for weeks on end. Except today. The day when she needed to ask her father for the money to pay for her symmetry. She instinctively knew that no amount of whining or waterworks or even dead-mom-ing (an absolute last resort to which Alison had never—and hoped she would never—descend) would suck so much as a cent from him if he knew she wanted it for something he'd see as insane and unnecessary. If Alison had been alone with her father, she would have felt confident in her abilities to extract the check without embellishing the truth to an outrageous degree. *Especially* if she was alone with him in the kitchen, where they'd bonded over their shared inability to put together even the simplest recipe. The mornings they spent getting under each other's feet and eating food off each other's plates kept them from becoming strangers in the big empty house.

But Alison wasn't alone with her father in the kitchen. Carmen was there, nibbling like a hamster at her tiny serving of flaxseed and blueberry. Why was she arching her eyebrow? Why was she sneering ever so slightly? Why did she have that insufferable "I told you so" expression on her immobile face when Alison nervously broached the subject of Roger giving her the money?

"Daddy, I need it, it's so important," pleaded Alison, adding wildly, ". . . for the future of world peace."

Stone Face spoke up. "This is just another of your things."

With wounded dignity, Alison replied, "No, it is not one of my *thing*s, thank you very much; it's the Greeks."

Roger looked lost. "The Greeks?"

"The penniless but brilliant Greek boyfriend. First of many parasites to come." Carmen yawned.

Alison choked back a "You're a parasite, you parasite!" She summoned inner peace and focused on lying to her father.

"The Greeks have a ratio of 1 to . . . 1.532 . . . or 3? . . . No, I'm sure it's 2, and it's affecting their art and their architecture. I mean, look at *David*. . . ."

"Who's David?" asked Roger, more lost than ever.

"Michelangelo's *David*. He needs the money."

Something close to comprehension appeared on Roger's face.

"Are you talking about art restoration? Is this a school project?"

"Yes!" proclaimed Alison. Things were going her way again!

"This is something you feel passionate about, isn't it?"

"Completely, utterly, and totally passionate. You don't even know."

Could the moment get any more perfect? Yes, it could! Roger gave Carmen a disappointed shake of the head, clearly chiding his wife for underestimating his lovely daughter as she blossomed into responsible maturity.

"I see the young woman you're becoming," said Roger lovingly.

"Does she have symmetry?" asked Alison before covering her blunder with a perky "So you'll write the check?"

Roger took a moment to slice up some strawberries, a banana, and a kiwifruit. He dropped them into the blender and added milk.

"Dad?"

Roger nodded happily. Noting Carmen's open disgust, Alison squealed with pleasure and hugged her daddy extra hard. She could *feel* her stepmother's eyes boiling over with anger. *Excellent.*

"Thank you *so* much. I can't wait to tell all the guys on the, uh, Greek art restoration field trip I'm going on."

Roger smiled and flipped the blender switch.

"Dad!" yelped Alison. "You forgot to put the—"

She didn't get a chance to say the word *lid.* The blender exploded a wave of mushed-up strawberry, banana, milk, and kiwifruit all over Roger.

Alison couldn't help it. "You *dork!*" she howled, red-faced with laughter as she passed Roger a roll of paper towels.

Carmen watched her husband sponge up the stains from his shirt and shook her head in disapproval. "I can't believe how clumsy you are."

"He wasn't before he married you," Alison retorted. "I'm not saying there's any connection. I might be thinking it, though."

Before Carmen had the chance to reply, Alison skipped out of the living room and scampered upstairs to lie to the other significant male figure in her life.

Lying on her California queen-sized bed, a framed poster of Audrey Hepburn in *Breakfast at Tiffany's* watching over her, Alison called Warren and said, "I can't tell you where I'm going this weekend. It's a secret. It's about national security. All I can tell you is when I come back, I'm going to be different. That's all I'm allowed to say at this point. Will you still love me if I'm different?"

Warren got out of his car and walked up the driveway of his Malibu home. "Yeah, sure," he mumbled before hanging up.

"Hey hey, you you, I don't like your girlfriend," sang Ginger Becker to herself in a self-amused whisper as she wriggled her way out of Warren's H4 and followed him up the driveway.

SEVEN

"*Was that Mischa* Barton?" said Kellyn.

Alison wasn't quick enough to see the face of the willowy figure in the hospital gown who was stepping into the elevator. But then again, every patient and staff member of the discreet and exclusive Schute-Bruggemann clinic in Beverly Hills looked like they might be someone famous. As Alison sat in the spotless, antiseptic reception area of the clinic, waiting for her name to be called, she found herself increasingly unsoothed by the hospital's ambient music and sky blue color scheme. She clutched the white Jimmy Choo Saba bag bulging with her many choices of overnight wear. Her feet tapped the ground with increasing rapidity.

The plan had been conceived and executed with military precision. She'd breezed out of her Brentwood house and jumped into Kellyn's waiting limousine, then she'd called the school coughing, which gave her all of Friday to undergo the operation. She'd have the weekend to heal up, which meant she could head home with no one knowing the difference on Monday. *Brilliant!*

Except that now she was *here*. In a *hospital*. Was this an amazing, spontaneous decision or had she been rash and thoughtless?

"You're not nervose, are you? Zere's no need to be nervose," said Dorinda, reading her friend's thoughts.

"You're not scared. You're excited," Kellyn assured her. "'Cuz when you get out of here, you're going to make Emily Blunt look like a bucket of turds. Oh, hi, Emily, I didn't see you there."

Alison followed her friend's gaze and wondered, for half a second, if the pale stunner in the wheelchair was the icy British actress. Then Kellyn cackled with laughter. Dorinda joined in. Alison relaxed her grip on her bag and stopped tapping her feet. She reached for her friends' hands, grateful for their support and happy in the knowledge that they'd always be there for her.

"Alison Cole?" said the receptionist.

Alison stood up. "That's me."

"I think it's going to rain," said a radiologist.

"Feels like a storm on the way," predicted a nurse.

The small talk faded as Alison, fully made up, hair perfect, clad in a silvery hospital gown (from Jean Paul Gaultier's Scalpel Couture collection), was wheeled into the operating room. She smiled at Dr. Bracken's team as they lined up in front of the CAT scan machine. Then her face fell.

"Stop!" she said, and motioned to be wheeled out by her confused attendant.

Dr. Bracken's team nodded in resignation. When it comes to the crunch, no one really wants to be the first guinea pig.

Less than a minute later, the attendant wheeled Alison back into the operating room. This time, she was wearing a black hospital gown, which went much better with the room.

Alison tried to focus her thoughts on matters of vital global importance so she wouldn't focus on the fact that her face was completely obscured by a plastic mold with holes at the nose for breathing. "Shouldn't I be shopping at Surly Girl right about now?" she mused. "They promised they were going to hold on to that pink leather tote for me. But if I don't show up, they'll give it to Hayden Panettiere, and she won't even pay for it. She'll get her publicist to swear she'll carry it on the red carpet. So not fair!"

She started to feel like she was drowning. *I wish they would have let Kellyn and Dorinda into the room with me,* she thought.

"Don't worry," said Dr. Bracken, no stranger to jitters. "I haven't lost a patient yet."

Positive that he had allayed all her fears, Dr. Bracken prepared Alison for the procedure.

"As we discussed, this may feel a little constricting at first, but over the course of the process, the symmetry mask will gently shape your bones as they soften under the cathode rays."

Here's what Alison remembered from the rest of the afternoon:
1.   She remembered the sensation of sliding inside the

machine's dark tunnel.

2. She remembered the initial wave of claustrophobia passing and changing into something pleasantly womb-like.

3. She remembered Dr. Bracken's voice saying, "If you're okay in there, Alison, wiggle your feet."

4. She remembered wiggling her feet.

5. She remembered her mother looking down at her and saying, "You don't need to do this. You're beautiful just the way you are." Except it wasn't her mother, it was Nicole Kidman. And who did Nicole Kidman think she was? Telling Alison what to do, with the amount of work *she'd* had done!

6. She remembered the doctor telling a pair of nurses to keep watchful eyes on Alison's progress.

7. She remembered the doctor telling her, "In five hours, we'll see what we've got. But so far it's looking good."

8. She remembered the doctor returning to the operating room and telling her, "You can stop wiggling your feet now."

9. She remembered that random geek in his homemade superhero costume. What was he doing in the hospital? Was he still hiccuping? She *told* him to swallow the whole bottle.

10. She remembered the cute junior president who'd come to her party and held her hand. Wasn't that nice of him to show up here? *But I'm a one-girl guy . . . a one-guy girl . . .*

And then everything went black. After the anesthetic kicked in, Alison had no idea that the two nurses were discussing her with disapproval.

"Fourteen," hissed the first nurse. "Fourteen, with all that money and all that face. And that's not enough for her."

The second nurse sucked air through her teeth. "What she oughta be doing is donating that face to someone who doesn't have one. That's the only business she's got being here."

Alison slept through the nurses' trash-talking, and she continued to sleep when the storm they'd earlier predicted not only manifested itself but proved severe enough to knock out the electricity for the entire block.

Shrugging in the darkness, the nurses waited for the clinic's fail-safe power supply to kick in and restore the hospital to normal functioning.

Ten seconds turned to twenty, then thirty. Outside the clinic, thunder rolled and crashed. Rain lashed the roof and the windows.

Then Dr. Bracken ran back into the operating room. His shiny features were creased with consternation.

"Wake her up! Get her out of there," he gasped. "The backup generator's off-line! We've got no power."

No sooner did those words fly from the flustered doctor's lips than the room was bathed in light.

"The power's back," chorused the nurses. "Everything's fine."

But everything wasn't fine. The operating room lights were blinding. It was like the generator was making up for its period of inactivity by creating a power surge. The lights got brighter until the bulbs shattered.

The unflappable nurses finally registered fear, clinging to each other as shards of scorching glass exploded across the room. Bursts of lightning from outside the hospital sent a strobe-light effect into the operating room.

The sudden power surge fried the clinic's elevators, its phones and computers. But most urgently, it caused Alison's CAT scan machine to go haywire.

It started with the rumbling. Then the rumbling got louder. The machine started shaking with such ferocity it seemed like invisible chains were trying to wrench it free from its moorings and drag it through the clinic roof. Then the room got hot.

"What's happening?" whispered the first nurse. "It's like a furnace in here."

The source of the sudden intense heat was the machine. Smoke, sparks, and quick bursts of flame spat from inside the CAT scan machine.

"Oh my God," breathed the second nurse. "Doctor, do something. Pull the plugs! She's getting barbecued in there!"

Dr. Bracken cursed his stupidity at allowing the fourteen-year-old daughter of a high-powered attorney to bamboozle him into taking her on as a client. Now they were both doomed!

The doctor approached the machine, and waves of heat suddenly caused his glasses to go moist with condensation.

The door flew open. A hospital technician entered, recoiling from the heat. "We had a power surge."

"That's why you make the big money," muttered the first nurse.

"But it's stabilized. We're back to normal."

"Not all of us," said the second nurse.

The nurses watched Dr. Bracken as he approached the now-silent, docile machine. No more rumbling, no more smoke or sparks.

He looked down on Alison's still, masked face. His shiny face was slick with sweat. One of the nurses rushed forward to wipe him down. His career was about to go up in smoke. His professional life was over. He let loose a moan of despair.

"She signed the waiver," he whispered repeatedly to himself. Then he watched and waited.

"Mmm," came the sleepily contented sigh from beneath the mask. "It's all toasty warm and snuggly in here."

EIGHT

Alison sat in Dr. Bracken's office the next day, her face swathed entirely in bandages except for tiny slits around the eyes, the two breathing holes at her nose, and the giant Chloe sunglasses she thought would divert attention away from her procedure. But even though she couldn't speak and her vision was limited, she still thought the doctor was acting a little odd. He was sweating. He was twitching. He couldn't sit still. Plus, he wouldn't stop staring at her. And not in an "I Am An Artist Proud Of My Creation" way. He was gawking and blinking at her like he couldn't believe what he was seeing! But for all his strange behavior, the doctor maintained a soothing, pleasant tone.

"How do you feel?"

Alison wiggled her toes in reply.

"That storm didn't shake you up too much?"

Alison had no memory of the storm, let alone its aftermath.

"It sounded a lot scarier than it really was. You can take the bandages off . . ."

Alison's hands leapt toward her face.

"In two days!" said the doctor hurriedly. "Just rest up in the meantime. I have to leave for Geneva tomorrow, and I don't mind telling you what we've accomplished here is going to be the talk of the conference. This time next year, people aren't going to be lining up asking for symmetry." The doctor left a slight dramatic pause before continuing, "They're going to be begging for The Alison Cole Procedure."

From deep beneath her bandages, Alison emitted a shriek of pure delight.

NINE

"Ze Aleesong Cole Pwoceedyuh? Zat's what
eet ees to be called?"

Alison, who was spending the remainder of her recupera-
tion laying low in Kellyn's Hollywood Hills home, nodded. Her
friends were appropriately impressed.

"Your own procedure. Your own procedure named after
you. That's major," said Kellyn.

*"Leensee Lohong 'az no pwoceedyuh. Veectoriuh Beyckuhm 'az no
pwoceedyuh. Reehonna . . ."*

Kellyn shot Dorinda a warning look.

Dorinda mumbled, *"Rehonna could 'ave a pwoceedyuh eef she
wanted. . . ."*

Kellyn gazed at Alison. "What do you need? What can we do?"

Alison pressed her hands against her cheek to indicate sleep. Then she pointed at the phone and shook her head to indicate no contact with the outside world.

"You got it." Kellyn nodded. "My mom's having her toxins pumped out. You can stay here as long as you want."

"Wawwen's going to die when 'ee sees 'ow good you will look," said Dorinda.

Kellyn shook her head. "Girl, the first thing the new you's gonna do is trade up. I like me some Warren, you know, but this is The Alison Cole Procedure. *Yesterday* that dude."

Dorinda stared at Kellyn for two reasons:

1. Because she'd suddenly broken into Homegirl. This made no sense. Now one of them was going to be faux French and the other fake ghetto?

2. Because Kellyn had obviously let her newfound power over Alison go to her head and decided that if *she* didn't have a boyfriend, then Alison could not be allowed to have one either.

"Ready?" said Kellyn and Dorinda in unison two days later.

Alison nodded. She'd slept the entire weekend. Now it was time to put Dr. Bracken's genius to the test. The girls were gathered in the majestically overdecorated master bedroom that was rarely used by Kellyn's mother. Kellyn and Dorinda lounged on the enormous California queen-*mother*-sized bed that was roomy enough to park a pair of SUVs. Alison sat in front of the dresser mirror. Her hands traveled to the back of her head, and she prepared to remove the bandages. Kellyn, with a sense of occasion, pointed the remote control at her iPod dock. James Blunt's "You're Beautiful" swelled through the room.

Working quickly, Alison unwound the bandages until her face was bare except for the plaster strips covering her eyes. She removed them, blinked her eyes open, and attempted to focus on the room and her friends.

Kellyn came into focus. She was staring intently at Alison's face, which looked *absolutely identical* to the way it had looked before the entirely unnecessary procedure.

Dorinda came into focus. She was staring intently at Alison's face as if it didn't look exactly identical to the way it had before the entirely unnecessary procedure.

Both girls looked at Alison as if they were seeing her for the first time.

"Well?" breathed Alison.

"You look . . ." began Kellyn.

"Amazeeng," said Dorinda.

"But she always looked amazing," said Kellyn.

"Zat's true. I thought zeir may perhaps be more amazingness."

"Oh my God, you *guys!*" wailed Alison.

"No, no, no! You look stunning. Beyond stunning. Stunsational," said Kellyn quickly.

"I 'ave nevair seen anyone zo, 'ow you say, eencandescent!"

"It's just gonna take a little time to get used to how amazing you look."

Dorinda held up a picture of the three girls together at the Beverly Center. She folded it so that only Alison remained visible in the picture and held it up against her friend's new face.

"Before," said Dorinda, pointing to the picture.

"And after," said Kellyn, pointing to Alison's *absolutely identical* face.

"It's better, right?"

Alison was floundering here. She'd wanted immediate affirmation. She'd wanted Kellyn and Dorinda to shriek and weep and fall to the floor like they were in the presence of a miracle. She wasn't getting the kind of validation she wanted.

"Mooch bettair." Dorinda nodded.

"Night and day," added Kellyn. "And there's probably a follow-up procedure that'll take you to a whole new level."

"Ze Aleesong Cole Pwoceddyuh Part Deux!"

Alison nodded, visibly deflated.

"We need to celebrate!" proclaimed Kellyn, referring not only to the entirely unnecessary procedure but also to the fact that their friend's security and self-esteem was, from now on, entirely in their hands.

Dorinda and Kellyn exchanged brief, treacherous smirks that Alison interpreted as a gesture of caring and support from her two best friends in the world. Suddenly, she understood! They loved her symmetry! They thought she looked amazing. They were simply allowing her to come to terms with her new look at her own pace.

Alison beamed. "This is a very special, life-changing moment," she said. "When big things like this happen, there's a place where I go to give thanks and reflect."

TEN

Kellyn's limo service pulled up outside Barneys on Wilshire Boulevard. Seconds later, Alison flew up the staircase to the second floor, leaving Kellyn and Dorinda gasping in her wake. Friends were friends. Procedures were procedures. But the second floor at Barneys was where Alison snapped up her first Marc by Marc Jacobs dress. It was where she found her semi-sheer Zac Posen.

Alison's eyes flicked speedily and expertly across the second floor. She didn't know exactly what she was looking for. But like a lion knows its prey lurks trembling in the brush, she could sense the presence of an item destined to be hers. And there it was. A taffeta trench coat by Stella McCartney. Twenty percent off. Alison tried not to betray her excitement. She didn't cry out with pleasure; she didn't noticeably quicken her pace. She simply made her way toward the rack where her prize hung.

What she didn't see was the shopper coming out of the changing rooms and heading for exactly the same rack. Then instinct kicked in and Alison was aware of the intruder with eyes on what was clearly, *legally* her property.

It was Treasure Spinney, the thirteen-year-old lovable, huggable teenybopper tomboy who played Sunday Mundy on the hit show *Signal Hill.* Alison's heartbeat increased. Her stomach lurched. Her mouth went dry. Treasure Spinney could kill with a smile. Her compliments were bombs set to detonate days later when you started to question whether she'd actually insulted you to your face. Alison had been introduced to her at a party and found herself reduced to tongue-tied embarrassment. ("How fabulous are you?" enthused the pocket-size star. "Look at all these poseurs in their million-dollar designer outfits and you just throw a few old things together and you look better than all of them!" It wasn't until long after the party was over that Alison remembered she was wearing her brand-new floral yellow sundress!)

That wasn't going to happen this time.

Man up, Ally, Alison thought. *Treasure Spinney is not getting her tiny hands on that coat.*

But Treasure Spinney was moving faster than Alison, and she looked more determined than Alison, and she was seconds away from reaching the rack. Their eyes met.

"Hi," said Treasure Spinney. The angelic features. The petite frame. The tumbling chestnut curls. She was America's favorite little sister. She was the cutest thing in the world.

Alison thought she was about to wet herself but instead managed to blurt, "How are you?"

"Supreme," said Treasure Spinney, smiling with practiced malice.

Suddenly, it was a standoff. Alison kept smiling. Treasure Spinney kept smiling. Neither removed their eyes from the other. *Then they both reached for the coat!*

Alison grabbed a sleeve. Treasure Spinney grabbed the collar and, for someone so microscopic, she had a grip like a pit bull. Alison pulled back. It was still a standoff.

Kellyn and Dorinda pushed through the crowd of shoppers who were gawking at the tug-of-war. They couldn't believe what they were seeing. Treasure Spinney was being dragged by her heels across the Barneys sales floor by Alison.

"Let go," gasped Treasure Spinney.

"You let go," countered Alison.

"Alison, *let go*," called Kellyn.

Alison looked over at her friends and at the other shoppers and realized she was making an embarrassing spectacle of herself. And on Barneys' second floor, the closest thing she had to a second home.

"This is ridiculous," said Treasure Spinney, her baby face scarlet and blotchy, her forearms trembling with exertion. "It's just a coat."

"I know. I'm sorry," said Alison.

"Count of three, we both let go," suggested Treasure Spinney.

Alison, looking impressed at Treasure Spinney's maturity

and diplomacy, nodded and let go.

But Treasure Spinney didn't.

She grabbed the coat and hugged it to her chest and laughed.

That's when Alison lost it. Wasn't it enough that the little star had the adulation of millions? Did she have to have *everything*? Alison felt her face redden. Her breathing turned hard and ragged. There was a roaring in her ears. She felt a prickling sensation growing at the end of her fingers. The sensation grew stronger, and as it did, she let out a gasp of surprise and anger. Alison lunged forward to grab at the coat, and as she did, the coat burst into flames!

Treasure Spinney screamed and threw the blazing item away. It landed on a pile of Jil Sander T-shirts.

Suddenly, there were flames everywhere. Treasure Spinney was screaming. The other shoppers were screaming. The sales assistants were screaming. Kellyn and Dorinda were screaming. The fire alarm drowned out their screams. Then the sprinkler system went into operation.

Once a haven of high-end fashion, the second floor at Barneys was now engulfed in chaos. Skeletal sales assistants tried to save sale items as they were soaked by the sprinklers. Devious shoppers tried to stuff dresses into their bags as they ran for the stairs. A model slipped on the wet floor and tumbled to the ground. A stylist tried to take shelter under a pile of cashmere sweaters. A makeup artist slumped to the floor and wept.

In the middle of the madness, Alison stared at her hands. Were her fingers *glowing*?

And what was that wafting from her fingertips? Was that *smoke*?

ELEVEN

SHE'S HOT! TREASURE SETS BARNEYS ON FIRE was the headline of the story running on TMZ.com approximately three minutes after the blaze began (thanks to the due diligence of a spy at the Kiehl's counter). Shivering, shell-shocked evacuees from the second-floor inferno found themselves set upon by a swarming mass of paparazzi, freelance gossip leeches, cops, and firemen. Alison, feeling the beginnings of a panic attack, stood close to Kellyn and Dorinda, praying the strength and support of her friends would calm her down.

"Are you high?" demanded Kellyn.

"Why would you try to set Treasheur Speenee on fire?" demanded Dorinda.

"I don't know what happened," gasped Alison. "One minute

I was grabbing the coat, which I was *quite* within my rights to, by the way; I saw it first. Shopper's law."

"And then you torched the place!" said Kellyn unsupportively.

"Why me? Why does it automatically have to be me? Why couldn't it have been bad wiring? Why couldn't it have been someone on the third floor tossing a cigarette downstairs? Maybe it was Courtney Love; ever think of that?"

This was a fair point, but Kellyn and Dorinda were looking at Alison like she belonged in solitary confinement. So was Treasure Spinney. *Signal Hill*'s little sweetheart was, at that moment, being questioned by LAPD officers and was summoning up fake tears as she glanced and gestured in Alison's direction.

I have never felt more alone or misunderstood, thought Alison. She would have collapsed even deeper into an abyss of self-pity had her full attention suddenly not been taken by the totally hot firefighter walking toward her.

If Alison hadn't been a self-professed one-guy girl, she might have entertained a fantasy featuring the fireman walking toward her in sexy slo-mo, Nelly's "Hot in Herre" playing in the background, his protective clothing falling away like wet paper, his rippling torso . . .

"Alison?" inquired the fireman, suddenly standing, fully clothed, non-sound-tracked, directly in front of her, an expression of concern on his face, which, the closer she looked, seemed to bear a disturbing resemblance to her secret crush, Junior President T. Hull. "Are you okay?"

"Uh, I . . . uh . . ." (*How does he know my name? And how come he looks just like T. Hull? And why can't I speak?* she panicked internally.)

"What's up, T? How come you're dressed like a fireman? Are you going to a party? Can we come?" said Kellyn.

"I volunteer with the LAFD. We all need to do what we can. Southern California's like a tinderbox," said T.

"'Ow beeg 'ees your 'ose?" asked Dorinda.

Kellyn gave her a look of shocked delight, chiming in, "Is it a sprinkler or does it squirt out a big spray?"

Amazed at their comic invention, both girls collapsed in fits of giggles. T dismissed them as immature infants and returned his attention to Alison.

"You didn't inhale any smoke, did you?" he said, gazing at her, concerned.

Staff from the nearby Escada boutique descended on the damp crowd still milling around outside Barneys, patting them down with fluffy towels and entreating them to come to their dry store. Kellyn and Dorinda gradually stopped laughing and found themselves watching the way T was treating the soaked and still-shocked Alison. He was smoothing down her hair! He was wiping water from her face! And the way he was talking to her, so close, so intimate! *So unfair!*

Alison watched T head back to the fire truck, wondering if she'd successfully maintained her record of never actually uttering an entire word in his presence. Kellyn and Dorinda swooped on her.

"Somebody told me that you had a boyfriend," sang Kellyn in a mocking, accusatory misuse of the Killers song.

"What are you talking about? Nothing happened," protested Alison.

"Nuzzing 'appened? Nuzzing except you offairing your tendair young flesh to 'eem and saying, 'Bon appétit!'"

"I did not! I didn't say anything!"

"You didn't have to. It was written all over your face."

"What was?" demanded Alison.

"Your brilliant decision. You took Auntie K's wise advice and decided to de-Warren your life. And with the Junior President of Cuteness!"

Dorinda marveled at her friend's ability to stay on track. In the middle of this celebrity meltdown, Kellyn was still focused on sabotaging Alison's love life.

"You loooove him! You have loooove for him."

"Shut up! I do not!"

"He makes you all tingly down in your jingly!"

"I don't even know what that means!"

Alison just wanted to get away from the store and the crowds of onlookers. "I gotta get home. Can we go? Now? And listen, not a word about any of this to Warren. Okay?"

"A word about what? Who's been talking about me?" said Warren. Alison gasped, surprised by the sudden appearance of her boyfriend pushing his way through the Barneys evacuees now being fought over by employees from the Bebe and Ferragamo stores.

Warren! He was here! He'd come to see her. She *was* a one-guy girl! She rushed to greet him. Seeing her soaked clothes and hair, Warren took a step back.

"Don't get that on me," he said.

"What are you doing here?" asked Alison.

"Uh . . . *the sale*?" replied Warren in disbelief.

Failing, as she so often had, to recognize the hostility in his tone, Alison gushed, "I missed you so much."

"What's all the stuff with the people and the wet?" said Warren, noticing the moist populace milling around Wilshire Boulevard.

"Treasure Spinney tried to burn down Barneys," said Alison.

"I heard that, you monster!" screamed Treasure Spinney. "That's slander. Slander added to personal injury. See you in court!"

"Let's get out of here," whispered a shaken Alison, pulling Warren away from the crowd and signaling Kelly and Dorinda that she'd call them later.

"Tingly jingly!" bawled Kellyn after her.

"So. I've been gone awhile. Do I seem different?" asked Alison. As they drove down Sunset Boulevard, Warren shot her a sidelong glance, aware that his reply was of vital importance.

"You've done something to your hair?"

Alison's day was going from bad to worse. "No." She sighed.

"You've had your upper lip bleached?"

"No." And then her hand flew to her lip. "*Should* I?"

Warren's gaze fell down toward her boobs.

"No! You're not even trying!"

She looked up at the giant Guess billboard towering over Sunset. The Guess girls never had to deal with this level of neglect and indifference!

Warren pulled up at a red light opposite Chateau Marmont, the famous hotel that played home to a hundred celebrity breakdowns. He gave her his full attention.

"Colored contacts?"

"You got it . . ." Alison smiled.

Warren relaxed, interrogation over.

". . . *wrong!*" barked Alison, enraged. "You got it wrong. You don't even know that my eyes are green. I know *everything* about you. I know you didn't speak till you were three, and here, look, I've still got the first picture we ever took together. . . ."

Warren closed his eyes. This was going to get ugly. Alison opened her bag, anger and impatience causing her to dump its contents in her lap. Then the light turned green. The H4 started moving.

All the items on Alison's lap ended up on the floor. With increasing bad humor, she bent forward to scoop them up and then stopped moving. A second later she sat upright, clutching something that wasn't among her possessions.

"What's *this*?" said Alison, trying to keep her tone even.

Warren kept his eyes on the road.

"Warren?"

He looked at Alison and saw the half-eaten lollipop in her hand.

"Gross. Throw that away."

She felt, at that moment, like the Guess girls were laughing at her.

"Is this Ginger Becker's?"

"What. That? No. It's one of the guys'."

"Has she been in this car? Have you and she . . . ?"

"What? Have we been what? You're crazy!"

Alison couldn't let it go. "You're right, I am crazy. Crazy to think I could go away for a weekend and the only guy I've ever gone out with, the guy I'd planned on spending my entire life with, wouldn't immediately hook up with some lollipop-gobbling whore!"

No sooner had the final "whore" exploded from Alison's open, angry mouth than her fingertips began prickling again. She started breathing hard. She felt a jolt in her stomach. All her nerve endings seemed like they were alive. And then Ginger Becker's lollipop burst into flames. Alison stared in disbelief. Twice? Flames *twice* in a matter of minutes? Was Treasure Spinney behind this?

Alison didn't have any more time to devote to conspiracy theories. The lollipop was burning her fingers. She screamed in fear and hurled it at the dashboard, where it immediately began burning a hole in Warren's expensively customized mohair interior. Warren grabbed the latest *Maxim* and began beating at the flames. The magazine caught fire. Warren hit the brakes. The car screeched to a halt. The car behind slammed straight into the H4.

Warren and Alison were immediately engulfed by air bags.

A moment later Warren said, "You *sure* you didn't do anything to your hair?"

TWELVE

"*Warren's the best.* He's so calm and composed. I can't even remember what we were fighting about. This is going to make such a funny story. It'll get wilder the more we tell it. And it'll be so cute because we'll be talking over each other. That's what makes us such an awesome couple: we've got history, we've been through stuff, and we've been there for each other. . . ."

This was what Alison was thinking as Warren's burning car brought Sunset Boulevard traffic to a halt. Amid the chaos and accusations, she stood by an ambulance and watched Warren give his statement to the LAPD officer. She couldn't believe his confidence. Look at the way the cop was smiling and nodding, totally disarmed, laughing now. What could Warren be saying?

She couldn't even remember what had happened in the car beyond her yelling and then a tingling sensation in her fingertips and then the dashboard catching fire. As soon as she recalled the tingling sensation, Alison remembered a similar feeling in Barneys just before the sprinklers went off.

Suddenly, more cops were laughing. And the cops were approaching the firemen and the ambulance crew and *they* were laughing.

"What's happening, Officer?" yelled a driver to a cheerful cop who was walking past Alison at that moment.

"Clingy ex-girlfriend couldn't believe she'd been dumped, set the dude's car on fire." The cop chuckled.

The driver shook his head. "Yeah, *that's* gonna change his mind."

The cop and the driver swapped sympathetic "chicks—they're-all-crazy" looks. The cop was suddenly aware of Alison's close proximity. She smiled at him and scrunched her face up into the exact same expression. She didn't realize they were talking about her! She didn't realize Warren had blamed the accident on her. Then she saw the expression on the cop's face: he saw her as every one of his psycho ex-girlfriends. So did the driver. So did all the drivers and all the cops and all the ambulance crew. And all the *women* drivers and the *women* cops and the *women* ambulance crew. None of them wanted to be associated with a gender-disgracing psycho brat. And they were all sympathetic to Warren.

She looked over at him. He was shaking hands with the LAPD officer! And as he shook hands, Alison was, once again, aware of the tingling sensation in her fingers, the one that preceded the last two sudden fires. She looked down at her hands. The tips of her fingers were glowing an increasingly deep dark red. Sparks were flying from her fingertips.

Her heart was racing. She was sweating. She could barely breathe. "What's happening to me?" she gasped.

"You're on fire," said T.

The sight of the junior president, who had just walked up to her, still in his volunteer fireman uniform, filled Alison with panic but managed to divert her attention from what seemed to be happening to her body. She jammed her hands in her pockets and winced. She could *feel* her fingers. They were *scorching*.

"Getting caught up in two emergencies in less than an hour. That's some sort of record."

"I know!" gasped Alison. "You must be thinking I'm some sort of nymphomaniac."

"I . . . uh . . ." was all T could manage.

"But I swear I'm not the sort of girl who goes around starting fires for fun."

She smiled at T, partly because it was hard *not* to smile at him, partly because she'd just realized she'd managed to complete two whole sentences around him, and partly because she could feel her fingers cooling off.

"Bummer about your boyfriend's H4. So many unknown factors can start a fire like that. Leaking gas lines, head gaskets, cracked radiators . . ."

Out of the corner of her eye, Alison could see Warren still shooting the breeze with the cop and yukking it up with the other drivers.

"Wrong," snapped Alison.

"I'm just a volunteer," replied T defensively.

"He's *not* my boyfriend."

"Oh. Okay."

They gazed at each other for a long, charged moment. And amid the chaos that brought Sunset Boulevard to a halt, T found himself looking at Alison Cole as more than just the new freshman class president. Now *she* was the one who seemed to be moving in slow motion. Now he was at a loss for words.

THIRTEEN

Military precision, thought Alison as she walked toward the front door of the Coles' Brentwood mansion. She'd tapped Brie Feltz and Connor Mattacks to send her links to reputable Greek art restoration websites so she'd be able to drop a few credible names into conversation. She'd be vague but enthusiastic, which would be all her dad really needed to hear. The best-possible scenario would be that he'd be so taken aback by how radiant she looked and attribute it to her newfound passion for the Greeks and their ancient art. The already-repressed memories of the afternoon's events receded even further into the distance. She opened the front door and saw Carmen standing in the hallway, waiting for her. And even though her face wasn't capable of many expressions, Alison recognized the one presently there was saying, "Gotcha!"

"No bags?" inquired the stepmother, keeping her voice even and amicable.

"Nope. And unlike you, I didn't need a surgeon to suck 'em out."

"How was your weekend? Work on any interesting old relics?"

"Funny, I remember asking my dad that question. And then he brought you home."

Carmen wasn't composed enough to hide her irritation. Alison smiled, savored her superior bitchery, and walked upstairs. The sound of Carmen's high heels clattering behind her indicated she wasn't ready to admit defeat.

Bring it on, Botox, thought Alison. *'Cos I could do this all day.*

"I called your school on Friday. They said you were sick."

"Well, they know I have to live with you."

"Do you mind telling me where you've been for the past four days?"

"My support group. Stepdaughters of Gold Diggers. We shared our stories. I feel so much less alone now."

Carmen's calm had almost entirely dissipated. Crimson spots marked her cheeks and neck. She was pissed. This made Alison a little bit giddy.

"I ain't sayin' she's a gold digger, but she ain't messin' with no broke lawyer," she freestyled cheerfully.

"I've had some interesting phone calls this afternoon," said Carmen, sounding shrill.

Alison kept "Gold Digger" going as she headed to her room, anticipating the force with which she was going to slam the door in the old crone's face. Maybe she'd chip off a bit of that pointy nose.

"From attorneys representing Treasure Spinney. And from your boyfriend's insurance company."

Alison stopped rhyming. The repressed memories of the afternoon started to reassert themselves.

"Those fires weren't my fault," she muttered.

"Nothing ever is. Alison never does *anything* wrong *ever*. And anyone who says she does is just *mean*," retorted Carmen, enjoying the reversal of power.

"I didn't say that. When did I ever say that? They were *accidents*," said Alison, aware she was starting to sound whiny but unable to do anything about it. "And anyway, what's it to you? Daddy will take care of it."

"Like he always does." Carmen nodded, as if she'd finally summed up Alison. "You're selfish, spoiled, thoughtless, and irresponsible. Your father trusts you implicitly and you abuse that trust. He's put you first his whole life and you lie to him and steal from him. You treat him like he's there to pay your bills and clean up your mess."

Alison was beyond shocked. They normally battled with veiled insults. She'd never been talked to like this. And it wasn't true! It *so* wasn't true. But someone who didn't know her, who didn't know all the facts, someone just hearing Carmen's side could maybe be forgiven for thinking it *was* true. Groping for a retort, she stammered, "And you treat him like . . . a thing . . . that thing that's built into the wall . . . that gives you money when you press the right buttons . . ."

Alison was flailing. In her distress, she'd forgotten what an

ATM was called, she'd ceded the moral high ground, she'd mislaid her armory of killer comebacks, and worst of all, she'd let Carmen crush her.

Don't cry. Don't let her see you cry, she told herself. But it was too late. Tears started to sting the corners of her eyes. She began to feel her fingers prickling and quickly hid her hands behind her back.

Carmen didn't even try to mask the pleasure she took in her stepdaughter's distress. "Things are going to change around here, Alison," she said. Then she turned and walked calmly, victoriously away.

"Does that mean you're going up a boob size?" Alison shot back.

Which might have wounded Carmen, except that Alison said it ten minutes later when she was alone in her room and she'd finally stopped crying.

FOURTEEN

"*Please, please have* Dr. Bracken call me the minute he gets back from Genoa," said Alison urgently. She gripped her Sidekick tightly and listened for a second before continuing. "Okay, *Geneva*. It's vitally important and of the utmost urgency. It's about national security. Alison Cole. Of The Alison Cole Procedure. He'll know. Just have him call me back."

She fell miserably onto her California queen-sized bed. Everything in her life had gone hideously wrong since she'd had that operation. Even if there was no direct connection, she needed to have whatever she'd done to herself reversed. But she couldn't go on like this. Carmen had made her cry. She had potentially alienated her father. And as for Warren . . .

Knowing it was a bad idea, she clicked the WarrenandAlison

file on her Sidekick. There they were: all the good times, all the happy times, all the funny times, all the romantic times. Their whole relationship history was preserved on her phone, and he hadn't even bothered to call her. He'd just deleted her from his life.

(And Winter Wertzky had left her something like twenty-three messages, none of which contained a coherent sentence.)

Alison felt herself plunging into despair, and as she plunged, her fingers glowed and sparked. Within seconds, the Sidekick in her hand was a bubbling chunk of melting plastic. She screamed and hurled it across the room. The ex-Sidekick landed in a pile of stuffed animals, which instantly went up in smoke. Gasping in horror, Alison still possessed the presence of mind to drag the sheets off her bed, wrap the burning bunnies, puppies, and pigs inside, and hurl the package out of her bedroom window, where, luckily for her, it landed in the swimming pool.

Alison watched the sheet containing the toys she'd clung on to since childhood sink to the bottom of the pool. Within seconds, her friends Mr. Snuffles, Fizzy the Pig, and Happy Puppy Sprinkles bobbed back up to the surface, charred and smoking. She gazed at them for a moment, then turned away from the window and stared at herself in the bedroom mirror. She looked red-faced, wild-eyed, and entirely freaked out. She couldn't call Dr. Bracken again. But there was something she *could* do.

She dug out her landline, dialed Kellyn's number, and, before her friend even had time to utter the first syllable of "hello," barked: "Highest heels. Shortest skirts. We're going out tonight."

FIFTEEN

Alison wanted to feel invulnerable. She wanted to link arms with her two best friends, swan past the LA losers in line outside Wet Wipes, the most happening and hard-to-get-into club on Sunset Strip, and smile at the bouncer as he lifted the velvet rope to usher them inside. She wanted to feel the "who's-that-girl?" stares from the hipsters lining the bar and the banquettes. She wanted to dance with her friends and lose herself in the music. She also wanted—and this was something she would not admit to her friends or even to herself—Warren to show up at the club and see what a fabulous time she was having and how amazing she looked and what a devastational effect she was having on all the assembled scenesters. She wanted him to understand what a gargantuan mistake he'd made and she wanted him to *ache*. And when Alison, Kellyn, and Dorinda walked into Wet Wipes, Warren *was* aching. But not for the reasons Alison hoped.

Warren hadn't revised his opinion of Ginger Becker. She was still phony, she was still irritating, her anime affectations still grated, but she had her good points. Or, at least, she had one good point. Ginger seemed to lack even the most basic inhibitions, and as he gripped her waist on the dance floor at Wet Wipes while she energetically made out with him, he reflected on how one good point could compensate for all the negatives.

Kellyn and Dorinda scanned the club for evidence of the usual allocation of C-list celebrities. In Kellyn's case, she was trying to hide her excitement about possibly enjoying a one-on-one encounter with Nick Stygian, the seventeen-year-old, tattooed train-wreck heartthrob currently on extended hiatus from *Signal Hill* but rumored to be out of rehab and back in circulation.

While Dorinda helped Kellyn search for Nick, they failed to see Alison watching, grim-faced, as Ginger Becker guided Warren toward the privacy of the VIP room. But they snapped to attention as they heard Alison yelling in a piercing voice, loud and angry enough that it sliced over the thud of the music.

"WARREN! HEY, WARREN. HI!"

Warren turned around and winced.

"I'VE JUST GOT ONE THING TO SAY TO YOU. ONE LAST THING."

One thing. At least it would be over fast, he hoped.

"HOLD MY BAG!"

Alison hurled her ridiculous elephant-shaped Commes des Garçons bag at him. It wasn't until the bag had left her hand that she realized, for the fourth time that day, that her fingers had burst into flames. Standing under the flashing lights in the middle of Wet Wipes' dance floor, Alison stared, fascinated and horrified, at her hands.

"Fire!" screeched one of the clubbers.

"Duh!" retorted Alison. Then she realized the panicked clubber wasn't referring to her hand but to her Commes des Garçons elephant, which was now a ball of fire flying straight at a stunned Warren. Alison was horrified. "Everything I own is in that bag! My credit cards, my makeup, my iPod, my fake ID, my keys, my lip balm! *And my lips chap so easily!*"

Warren threw himself down on the ground to avoid the fireball headed straight for his head. Ginger fell on top of him and tried to continue making out. Alison rushed forward, pushing past dancers and trying to grab at the bag with an outstretched hand. A further surge of flame jetted from her fingers, propelling the flaming elephant across the club and into the DJ booth. It landed on a crate of rare and expensive vinyl, which, within seconds, was an inferno of melting plastic.

The DJ stared in disbelief. The collection that had taken him years and cost him thousands to amass was belching black smoke. *"My twelve inchers!"* he howled, beating at the flames with his leather jacket, which quickly caught fire.

The Wet Wipes dance floor was now packed with cheering clubbers holding their camera phones aloft. The DJ might not have put together the most seamless sets, he might not have been the most technically adept scratcher, but he knew how to put on a show! As the cheering continued, the sobbing DJ threw his blazing jacket out of the booth, where it landed on a tray of drinks.

The waitress carrying the drinks exhibited the coolest head of anyone in the club. She dropped the tray to the ground and started stamping out the flames. Unfortunately, she was wearing thigh-high PVC boots, which turned out not to be the most sensible footwear in the middle of a fire.

Closed-circuit surveillance showed blurry footage of Alison throwing the bag that started the fire. But no one was able to definitively say that she was actually responsible for setting the elephant alight. And since the owners of Wet Wipes didn't particularly relish having to explain why fourteen-year-old girls seemed to be regular visitors to their premises, they declined to press charges. So the night ended happily. Except that Alison had to spend a few miserable hours waiting for her father to come and collect her from the Hollywood Community Police Station. After he finally appeared, Roger refused to say so much as a word to his daughter as he drove her back to Brentwood.

"It wasn't my fault," she said on several occasions during the ride home. But all she got in return was silence.

This is so unfair, she thought.

Alison had almost convinced herself of her complete innocence by the time she returned home. Carmen was standing in the doorway, holding a laptop, and greeted her stepdaughter with the usual arctic stare. "What's on the computer?" breezed Alison, determined to never again betray a moment's vulnerability in front of Carmen. "Someone leak one of your *private* tapes?"

Carmen shook her head and enlarged the computer image to full screen. Camera phone footage of Alison throwing the bag that ended up setting Wet Wipes on fire.

Fortunately, she was a YouTube phenomenon, having notched up over a hundred thousand views. *Unfortunately*, her reputation had just gone up in flames.

SIXTEEN

"*She's going to* be out of school for the rest of the week," breathed Kellyn, relaying to Dorinda the principal's reaction to Alison's Wet Wipes incident, her stay in the police station, and her YouTube notoriety.

The door to the girls' toilet opened. Kellyn sent a glare of ice at the intruder, who quickly reversed her steps.

"It's time. Introducing Operation Ding Dong."

"What ees thees Opairation Deeng Dongh?"

Kellyn sighed. "Ding, dong, the wicked witch is dead? From *The Wizard of Oz*? Or don't they have that in Not France?"

Dorinda ignored the jab. *"But Aleesong ees not zee weeked weetch. She ees our fren."*

"Listen to yourself, Doodles," said Kellyn, using Dorinda's

much-loathed pet name. "You're a joke. And I say that as someone who loves you. You may end up talking like that your whole life. Think about that, my little phony: a joke your whole life. There's something to look forward to. Don't look at this as something we're doing *to* Alison, look at it as something we're doing *for* us. To save our self-esteem . . ."

The toilet door opened again. "Private meeting. Leave, ugly fat girl!" snapped Kellyn.

The door slammed shut. Kellyn took both of Dorinda's hands in hers.

"Opairation Deeng Dongh." Dorinda nodded.

"This is the way the world works. For us to feel good about ourselves, Alison has to feel *bad* about herself, which means that we have to make everyone who once looked up to her turn against her."

"'Ow do we do zat?"

"We do that with four little words."

SEVENTEEN

I always knew I'd be in therapy, thought Alison as she glanced around the waiting room of noted psychologist Dr. Kim Mee. *But in a cool way. The way that Drew Barrymore or Katherine Heigl sees shrinks. To unburden themselves about how happy and successful they are, how great they look, and how rich they are. And the therapist tells them not to feel guilty because they deserve all the good things that happen to them.*

But this wasn't cool therapy. This was surrender.

Alison had allowed Carmen to make the appointment with Dr. Mee "because it would make your father happy. It would say to him that you recognize there's a problem and you're taking steps to correct it. That would mean a lot to him."

Alison still didn't care about Carmen, but she cared about

what her father thought. As long as he continued to act like
he was disappointed in her, cooperating with Carmen seemed
the only way to repair their relationship. But Alison hated being
there. Hated that people saw her as some sort of out-of-control
teen trouble magnet.

Why couldn't Shia LeBoeuf walk through the door? she wondered.
Why couldn't they strike up a spontaneous conversation and discover that they had a million things in common and then make
plans to meet up? They couldn't because, knowing the grim turn
her life had lately taken, the next person to walk into the waiting
room was more likely to be an unstable weirdo with serial killer
potential.

And that's when the waiting room door opened and David
Eels walked in early for his weekly appointment with Dr. Mee.

If David had known he was going to encounter Alison in his
therapist's waiting room, he might have prepared an ironic and
appropriate entrance line. He might have given her a nod and a
nonjudgmental smile that said, "We're all just works in progress."

But he didn't know she was going to be there. When he saw
her, he felt his stomach lurch. He felt the red rise to his cheeks.
He didn't know whether to make eye contact, whether he should
say something, or whether he could just do the Cool Guy Nod.
Instead, he walked into the magazine rack, knocking it to the
ground. He felt her eyes dart pained looks at him.

I can still save this, he thought. He began returning the scattered titles to their rightful places and, while doing so, threw out
the casual inquiry, "So . . . uh . . . how was the . . . uh, party?"

Alison, having no recollection of her previous and only
interaction with David, stared at him blankly, ready to scream if

he looked like he was going to turn violent.

"Last time we met, I had a big *E* on my chest. *E* for *Eels.* You'd just been elected president and . . ."

Alison nodded. "Right. How are you?"

"I immerse myself in comic books as a means of divorcing myself from reality, and I've got a problem socializing with others due to mixed feelings of superiority and self-loathing. How about you?"

Alison looked wary.

David shrugged. He understood that the unlikely connection he'd thought he made with Alison was symptomatic of his ongoing delusional problems.

"None of my business," he said, sitting several seats away from her.

If I'm going to say something, I might as well say it here, she thought. So she said something.

"None of my friends will talk to me," she said. "My boyfriend cheated on me, then dumped me. Treasure Spinney's suing me. I was in a police station with a bunch of crackheads. My dad won't even look at me. My stepmother's probably made arrangements to send me to military school. . . ."

Dr. Kim Mee stepped out of her office and into the waiting room. She smiled at David, then looked at her new client.

"Alison?"

Dr. Mee gestured for Alison to follow her. As she trudged toward the office, Alison glanced back at David.

"Oh yeah, and flames shoot out of my fingertips . . ."

With that, she disappeared behind the door of Dr. Mee's office, leaving David staring after her.

EIGHTEEN

"*I had a plan.* I had the *best* plan. I was gonna marry Warren, who would be a partner in my dad's firm by then. After that, I was gonna poop out a couple of super-cute kids, Troop and Briar, then me and Kellyn and Dorinda were gonna open a spa. . . ."

Alison had found herself surprised by how fun therapy had turned out to be. She just had to talk about herself. She could do that all day. Except that suddenly, her voice was trembling.

"And now, none of that's gonna happen. And it was gonna be a *fantastic* spa; you'd have loved it, Dr. Kimmy. . . ."

"It's Dr. Mee. Or Kim, whichever you prefer . . ."

"We would have served you champagne cocktails while you got your seaweed wrap. We would have gotten the *gre* spread in *InStyle*. Eva Mendes would have picked us as her favorite relaxation oasis on her rare days off. 'No one pampers me like the girls at Aldoke,' she'd've said. Ask me why it was gonna be called Aldoke."

"Why was it going to be called Aldoke?" asked Dr. Mee patiently.

"*Al*ison, *Do*rinda, *Kel*lyn. So cute! But now Eva Mendes is never gonna come, and neither is Eva Longoria. . . ."

"You can still open a spa, Alison."

"No, I can't. You think Rihanna would come near my spa? What if I burned her hair off?"

Alison stared hard at Dr. Mee, waiting for a reply. Dr. Mee wasn't sure how to respond.

"And my dad." Alison sighed. "We were *so* close. Now we're like strangers. It's all *her*."

"Your stepmother?"

"I just wanted him to be happy after Mom died, so I didn't throw the kind of tantrum I was legally entitled to when he married her, but I *knew* she'd be bad for him. Those fake fundraisers of hers . . . The only charity she's interested in is the one called *Carmen* . . . unless there already is a charity called Carmen that's for a good cause, maybe global warming or the destruction caused by Hurricane Carmen, that's nothing to do with her, but . . . what I'm trying to say is that she's plastic and artificial and shady. And she knows I'm on to her. She knows she'll never win my approval. And that's why she's poisoning my father against me. . . ."

"So what's the new plan?" asked Dr. Mee.

"There *is* no new plan," sulked Alison. "There's no Warren, there's no Kellyn or Dorinda or Dad. They were part of the old plan, and they don't care about me anymore. Now I don't know who I'm supposed to be."

"Can't you just be Alison, who's fourteen, who's lost her mother at a young age and maybe hasn't fully dealt with all those issues . . . ?"

Alison started to zone out. *This* was what she expected from therapy: a bunch of clichés delivered by a soft-spoken quack trained to beam "tell-me-everything" eyes into her brain. She made an effort to look like she was paying attention as Dr. Mee droned on.

". . . is it possible that there's an Alison Cole inside who hasn't allowed herself to express all her emotions, to let go of everything she's feeling? Do you think *that* Alison Cole is the one who takes control of you and says, "Hey, look at me, I'm not perfect!'"

Alison worked hard to choke back her sudden urge to laugh. *Nice* Signal Hill *audition, Kimmy. We'll definitely be in touch.*

"'I'm in pain and I need you to respect my pain and that's why I'm accusing my stepmother of poisoning my father against me, that's why I'm setting things on fire. . . .'"

Alison felt her fingers start to heat up.

"Wait. Hold up. You think I'm deliberately starting fires?"

"I think you're crying out for help."

"You're right, I am. I *want* flames to stop shooting out of my fingers. Can you help me with that, Kimmy?"

"We can work through this. We've made a great start here. . . ."

"I don't think we have. I don't think you believe me. Well

watch this. . . ."

"I understand, Alison. The rage. We all have it. But we can find ways to put our rage in a peaceful place. For me, that place is music."

And then, Dr. Mee reached under her chair, pulled out a ukulele, and began strumming. As she played, she bobbed her head and smilingly encouraged Alison to clap along.

Alison might have been beyond mortified, but Dr. Kimmy's methods were effective.

If I'm not angry or upset, maybe I won't keep burning things down! she thought. *Fortunately,* the oncoming heat had faded from her fingers. *Unfortunately,* she was now unable to set fire to the uku-lele, which meant that Dr. Mee was free to play Jack Johnson songs for the entire last half hour of the session.

NINETEEN

While the rest of Beverly Hills High's student body remained under lock and key, Alison was at liberty, following her worthless session in Dr. Kimmy's House of Pain and Ukuleles to wander the glittering, glamorous streets of Beverly Hills.

Which is why Alison hopped out of a cab and trotted happily up, as she had so many times before, to Kitson, the overpriced, overpublicized fashion black hole of Robertson Boulevard. And they wouldn't let her in. The door closed in her face as she left the cab. The salesgirl who'd sucked up to her a hundred times in the past made a "sorry" face as she slowly backed away from the locked door. The other salesgirls and the manager and the store's gullible tourist clientele all stared openly and disapprovingly at her.

Let them stare, thought Alison defiantly. *I've got every right to be here. I can wait here all day.*

Then she felt the heat rush through her fingers.

This could be good or bad. She could burn her way through that locked door. She could raze Kitson to the ground. But then word of her pyro-freakishness would spread like . . . like wild-fire.

Ten seconds later, she walked away, red-faced and embar-rassed. *Fine,* she thought, *I'll go to Lisa Kline instead. I love Lisa.*

Lisa Kline wouldn't let her in either. Lisa Kline had a buzzer entrance. Alison buzzed and buzzed. This salesgirl had the same "sorry" expression on her face, but she wasn't sorry enough to release the lock and let Alison in. Her reputation as a fire starter had preceded her.

Alison found herself thinking back to when she was six and her best friend, Bee, had suddenly decided she wanted some new best friends. If only Bee had *told* her. She might not have liked it. She might not even have understood. But she wouldn't have gone to Bee's birthday party. She wouldn't have trundled up to the front door and buzzed and buzzed and wondered why no one would let her in even though she could see through the window that they all knew she was waiting outside. Alison shuddered at the memory. Then she pulled her finger away from the buzzer, which was now a glob of molten metal.

"*Fine.* I'll go to Anya Hindmarch. I *love* Anya."

Alison walked away, hoping the evil salesgirls were shamed by her dignified exit, and found herself staring at David Eels, who was leaning against a nearby parking meter, immersed in a comic book.

If I'm quick, he won't see me, she thought.

"Hi," said David, looking up from his comic at that exact moment.

"So I've got a stalker now?"

David looked flustered.

"No. No, I wasn't trying to. I mean, I cut out of my session early and I thought I saw you heading in this direction. . . ." David trailed off. He had bailed on his therapy session to follow a girl. There was no way to make that seem like acceptable behavior.

"'Cos if I do, that's okay. At least it means *someone* still likes me. . . ."

"I like you," said David, cringing at how that must have sounded. He quickly continued, "But what I really wanted to talk to you about was that thing you said before, you know, about shooting flames from your fingers. . . ."

Alison laughed dryly. "Pretty crazy, huh? Probably sounded like I needed *to see a therapist!*"

"That's the thing. It didn't sound crazy. There was no reason for someone like you to say something like that unless it was true. Is it?"

Alison saw a cab pull up. She started to walk toward it. "I gotta go."

The girl in the cab paid the driver and went to climb out. Then she saw Alison. Fear flooded her face. She jumped back in and locked the door. The cab drove off. Alison closed her eyes and concentrated on breathing deeply. In with the good energy. Out with the bad.

"Is it true? Can you do it? Can you shoot flames?"

She opened her eyes. "I don't wanna talk about it. I'm focusing on staying positive and healthy and making time for me."

"You're like Zoe Falconer," said David.

"I usually get Kate Bosworth. Who's Zoe Falconer? Is she cute?"

David held up his comic book. "Darqmoon. She could harness the power of the night. She could black out the sun."

"Oh, her," muttered Alison, losing interest.

"But she didn't want it. Not at first. She wanted to be normal. But what she didn't realize was that she was different, special. That she'd been chosen to fight evil, to right what was wrong and bring justice to a corrupt world because . . . the darkest hour is just before the dawn. . . ."

Alison said nothing for a moment, then looked David in the eye.

"See you in therapy."

TWENTY

"Four little words." That was Kellyn's prediction. With four little words, she and Dorinda would break their shackles and free themselves from the oppression of Alison's friendship and popularity.

Of course, they didn't say the four words right away. They let a few days go by. They let rumors circulate. They let interest simmer. They let every BHHS demographic form its own opinion. And then, on Friday at lunch, when representatives of every clique, tribe, and subset made their usual inquiries as to Alison's health, state of mind, and estimated time of arrival back at school, Kellyn looked at Dorinda. Dorinda looked back at Kellyn. They both sighed. They both looked a little sad and a little hurt. They both looked like they'd learned a hard lesson. Then

Kellyn said: *"Alison's not that nice."*

Four little words. But it was all about Kellyn's Oscar-winning delivery. The expression on her face when she said them and on Dorinda's face as she reacted to them planted seeds of suspicion throughout the cafeteria and, soon, the school.

"Blondie's been talking smack about me?" inquired the head of the girls' soccer squad, whose suspicions that Alison was too good to be true suddenly bubbled to the surface.

"Perhaps her friendship was merely a facade meant only to guarantee my support for her campaign. Well played. I will remember that strategy. It will help me in later life," reflected the captain of the chess club.

"Oh, she wants to throw shade at me? Well, I know all the deep dark dirty about her, all the scandal she wants to keep buried. And if I don't, I'm going to make it up," plotted BHHS's anonymous gossip blogger.

Kellyn had gambled, brilliantly, that she and Dorinda weren't the only ones who resented Alison's popularity. Her four little words didn't incriminate Alison, and they certainly couldn't be used to accuse Kellyn of stabbing her best friend in the back. All she'd done was allow her fellow students to draw the conclusions they'd previously been keeping to themselves.

"Alison's not that nice." Of *course* she isn't! Why would she say hi to dorks and goths and foreign exchange students if she wasn't secretly sneering at them? And if her BFFs think she's not that nice, what kind of monster must really be lurking behind that bland mask of blond gorgeousness?

"Another freshman headed for a meltdown," clucked a gaggle of junior girls disapprovingly. "At least we don't have to be ashamed of *our* class president." T was aware of the negative buzz concerning Alison. Somehow, though, he couldn't reconcile the girl who still moved through his thoughts in slow motion with the self-destructive mental case whose exploits were the talk of the hallway.

"See?" crowed Tiny Head, Phlegmy, Odor Eater, and Toenail in triumphant unison. "Your little bip's not the dream girl you thought she was!"

David knew better than to give his friends any indication that they were getting to him. So he said nothing. But as they continued to mock him, he thought, *Her popularity's collapsed. Her reputation hangs in tatters. She's an outcast, an underdog. This is how every great superhero story begins. This is* classic*!*

TWENTY-ONE

Alison flipped through the preset radio stations in her father's Rolls-Royce Corniche convertible, stopping at a familiar song, one that reflected her newly restored optimism.

"You like Nina Simone?" asked Roger.

Alison had no idea who Nina Simone was, but she knew this song from a million commercials, remixes, and *Idol* auditions, the one with the chorus that went, "It's a new dawn, it's a new day, it's a new life for me. And I'm feeling good."

That song's a sign, Alison thought. A sign that everything was going to be okay, that her descent into hell was over, that she'd been given the opportunity to make a fresh start, and that her relationship with her father had been repaired. After all, he'd offered to drive her to school. Alison couldn't wait to get back to BHHS. Not only was she going to properly begin her class presidential duties—and the first thing she was going to do was delegate her class presidential duties to the two runners-up in the election—but she'd *finally* get to see her friends again. It was weird that Kellyn and Dorinda hadn't called or texted or come to see her. Weirder still that they hadn't replied to any of her messages. But Alison had a sneaking suspicion Carmen was behind that. She wouldn't put it past her stepmother to try and cut her off from the world.

You lose, *old crone.* Alison smiled to herself. *I'm getting my girls back just like I got my dad back.*

So there they were, father and daughter nodding in time to Nina Simone's "Feeling Good," the rift between them healed to the extent that Roger broke into his deliberately bad impression of a tone-deaf singer.

"Nooooo. Stop! You're embarrassing everyone in the world!" Alison wailed, acting embarrassed but secretly relieved that he had forgiven her.

"I've been gone a week and Lego accessories have exploded," marveled Alison as she joined the wave of students making their way toward the school. As she looked at the Lego earrings, bracelets, and rings adorning the limbs of her classmates, Alison realized how much she missed being part of BHHS's never-ending runway show. Kellyn might have labeled their fashion-addicted peers "style monkeys," which was just like her—*so* mean, *so* funny— but Alison's brief absence confirmed to her that she finally fit right in.

"Brie Feltz!" Alison yelled, excited at spotting her student council minion. Some of the other students shuffling to their classes broke into malicious imitations of her. That was weird. What was also weird was the way people she might not have known by name but had never previously ignored were reacting to her. The lacrosse team seemed to be averting their eyes. The Madrigal Singers shot her cold, challenging stares. The Mental Dental Collective curled their lips. Other students shook their heads sadly or they whispered to their friends while staring her straight in the face. *Weird.* But she didn't dwell on it, preferring to catch up to Brie Feltz, who didn't look completely pleased to see her.

"Hey, Brie. You look cute. So what have I missed, presidentially speaking? Is there anything outstanding that needs my attention?"

Brie couldn't meet Alison's eyes. She shuffled nervously, darting furtive glances around the hallway in hopes of salvation.

"I don't know," she finally muttered. "I haven't heard what's happening."

"About what?" Alison had no idea what Brie was talking about. She wasn't a clear communicator. No wonder she'd lost the election.

A passing student glared at Alison, then yelled at Brie, "You telling Psycho Barbie she's impeached?"

Brie turned bright red and stared at the floor. Alison's immediate thoughts were that she'd contravened some sort of arcane color code. She even looked down at her outfit to make sure that she wasn't in peach.

"You haven't been impeached, *exactly*," said Brie. "It's just that with all that's happened—and I don't even know what's happened—people just thought it would be best if . . ."

Alison suddenly got it. "I'm not allowed to be president anymore? That's not fair."

Brie prayed for an earthquake, a really big one that would shake the school to its foundations and stop Alison from staring at her with those hurt, angry green eyes.

"Does Winter Wertzky know about this? I bet she doesn't. There's no show without me. You *know* that, don't you?"

Alison's indignation almost equaled Brie's discomfort. A small crowd gathered around as Alison called her TV mentor and waited and waited. No message. Nothing. It just kept ringing. And now she knew there was no show anymore. But that crowd was watching her every move, suspicion in their beady, unfriendly eyes. She wasn't going to give them the satisfaction of watching her fall to pieces.

"*Hiii*, Winnie," she drawled into the phone, "how are *youuuu*? Sorry it took me so long to get back to you, I'm *soooo* busy, but I *looove* what you were saying about doubling my clothing budget for the show. Fabulous. Hit me back whenever. *Byeeee*."

Brilliant performance! She waited for the crowd to melt away with the usual awed looks on their stupid faces. But they didn't seem awed; they seemed very un-wowed by her. And then someone broke the silence, letting out a nasty, sneering imitation of her "*byeee*." And then everyone laughed and high-fived. It was an awful, endless moment that only stopped when she was told to report to the principal's office.

Nina Simone was still stuck in Alison's head as she wandered disconsolately through the empty hallway. She was now half an hour late for her first class of her first day back. "Taking the best interests of the parents and the board of governors into consideration . . ." was what the principal had said. He'd tried to soften the blow. He'd said something about her running next year. *"Once it all blows over."*

He talked some more about not penalizing her over one mistake. He was trying to be nice, she knew, but the more he talked, all she really heard was, "No more president. No more show."

Her return to school might not have been the triumph she was expecting, but she was still Alison Cole, and she could still make an entrance. This was how it was going to go: she'd walk into math class like she was walking past the LA losers in line at Wet Wipes.

She wouldn't apologize to the teacher for her tardiness; she wouldn't even acknowledge him. She'd drink in the envious stares of the rest of the class, and she'd make her way toward her regular seat at the back of the room, where her two best friends in the world waited excitedly for her. The Fabinet was about to be in session.

Raise your chin, she told herself. *Toss your hair back. Focus your eyes dead ahead and smile like you're in on the most hilarious joke ever told.* Alison followed her own instructions and *almost* made an awesome entrance. *Almost.* She came through the door and into the classroom like she was walking the runway on Fashion Week. She could feel the envy in the air. Even the teacher didn't have the nerve to tell her she was late. Then she turned her ankle. Some supermodels can pull off losing their footing. Alison couldn't rise above her stumble. She cried out with pain and shock when she went down and reached out for the nearest desk to steady herself. And just like that, the envy that had filled the room was gone.

"Have a good trip?" chortled a student.

"Where's the fire?" countered a more topically inclined comic.

Then a mock-concerned voice sang out, "Troubled teen," and that was the one that caught on. Within seconds, half the class were coughing, "Troubled teen," into their hands.

"Find a seat, Alison," said the teacher wearily. Easier said than done. Marvelette Bridgewater-Rivington was sitting in *her* seat, the seat everyone knew was hers, looking like she couldn't *wait* to see Alison try to move her.

And where were Kellyn and Dorinda? Her friends weren't there! In their places, in the seats that everyone knew were theirs, sat two overdressed, overcosmeticized pre-vas with fake tans, fake noses, and fake imperious attitudes. Who were these newcomers with their Chanel sunglasses on their heads and their matching bobs energetically texting each other and laughing at the messages that showed up on their respective Sidekicks?

The teacher raised his voice. "Kellyn. Dorinda. Put your phones away and pay attention or I'm splitting you up. I mean it."

Wait a minute. *What?* Those were her *friends?* But why were they sporting new looks and new hair? Why were they staring at her with no affection but with something that looked more like defiance? And why were they raising their hands to their mouths? She got the answer to the last question when Kellyn and Dorinda joined the rest of the class, who were coughing, "Troubled teen," into their hands.

Alison stared at her two best friends in the world. Not a trace of affection in their faces.

"What's going on, Kel?"

"Alison, sit *down*," said the teacher.

"Doodles?"

Dorinda flinched. She *hated* that name!

"Why did you never come to see me or return my calls?"

"Alison, I'm not telling you again. Sit down!"

"Troubled teen," hand-coughed Kellyn.

"Troubled teen," hand-coughed Dorinda.

"Alison!"

"If I've done something wrong, just tell me," she begged her friends. "But don't do this."

"She hasn't done anything wrong, has she, Dor?"

"Nuzzing. She nevair puts a foot wrong."

"A foot wrong!" howled Kellyn.

"She's funny," said Marvelette.

Alison saw the admiring looks flying between Kellyn, Dorinda, and Marvelette.

"So *she's* your friend now? What does that make me?"

Kellyn stared back. "I don't know, Alison. What *does* that make you?"

"Alison, you can sit down or you can get out of my class!"

The teacher was yelling at her. Her supposed friends were stabbing her in the back, *only they were doing it in her front!* The rest of the class were eating this up.

She could feel her face burning. Worse, she could feel her fingers heating up. Alison turned and fled the classroom, slamming the door behind her so hard the glass cracked. It wasn't much of a consolation, but her exit proved far more unforgettable than her entrance.

TWENTY-TWO

Alison sat on the toilet, drying her eyes. "And now I'm no one again. The same pimply, friendless loser I used to be," she mourned. "Except now I don't even have a mother who can make me feel better. Now there's nobody." She checked her watch. Twenty-three minutes of sobbing, self-pity, and smeared makeup. Her return to school had been a nonstop marathon of betrayal and humiliation. "So what do I do now?" she wondered aloud. After another forty-five seconds of combined sniffling and nose blowing, she considered her options:

1. Stay in the bathroom.
2. March proudly and defiantly into the cafeteria at lunchtime. Select an empty table, sit down by herself, radiate strength and self-confidence, and strike shame into the shallow hearts of

her enemies.

3. Consider the possibility she'd been the victim of an elaborate prank. Walk into the cafeteria to be met by cheers and applause and marching bands and Winter Wertzky and her camera crew and even Treasure Spinney, who would present her with a bouquet and thank her for being such a good sport.

The longer she dwelled on option three, the more hopeless it seemed. The longer she considered option one, the more tempting it became. Then a fourth option occurred to her:

4. Avoidance. "I wasn't ready for this. It's way too soon for me to be back in school. I need at least a double session with Kimmy before I'm mentally prepared to deal with all this negativity."

Dr. Mee had been super-nice about slotting Alison into her busy schedule on such short notice. As she approached the office, Alison started to think about the upcoming session. She had a lot to talk about. The students, the principal, the teacher, her best friends: they'd all turned against her. Was she really ready to discuss this with Kimmy? What if the shrink tried to blame *her* in some way? And what if she had a whole special repertoire of ukulele favorites ready for just such an occasion? Before Alison could get ready for Dr. Kimmy, she needed a refreshing fruity beverage. Which is how she came to be entering the Jamba Juice on Rodeo Drive at the exact moment it was being robbed by a pair of inept but imaginative petty criminals.

Two minutes earlier, the juice girl had smiled at the only two guys in the store. "What can I get you?" she'd asked.

"Everything in the register," one of them growled dramatically, opening his jacket enough for her to see the butt of the gun sticking out of his waistband.

The juice girl gulped, thought about stalling the guy till the manager got back from lunch, then thought about how much she was making per hour and began counting out bills.

As she did this, the second part of the petty criminal tag team freaked her out by jumping behind the counter. The juice girl gasped, but the second guy ran past her and began to unplug one of the juice machines.

She stared at the first guy, who just shrugged. "He always wanted a juice machine."

The juice girl nodded and went back to emptying the cash register.

That's when Alison breezed in.

"Medium orange carrot explosion, one ounce of wheatgrass, burner boost, oh, and a multiboost too. I *really* need it today."

The juice girl didn't even look up!

"Oh, okay. So *you're* gonna ignore me too? So now I'm a city-wide nobody? What am I supposed to do, join a nunestry?"

Then Alison realized there was another customer in the shop. The guy smiled at her. "What you're supposed to do is keep your mouth shut and get down on the floor."

Once again, he revealed the gun in his waistband.

"Do what he says," whispered the juice girl.

Alison nodded, shaken. Then, as she started to sink to the ground, the guy reached for her bag.

"Let me take that off your hands."

"What?" gasped Alison. "My Yves Saint Laurent Muse? Are you *mental*?"

"Don't make him mad!" pleaded the juice girl.

Too late. The guy grabbed for Alison's bag. She felt the familiar flicker in her fingers. Then she thought, *There's not a minute goes by I don't miss my Commes des Garçons elephant. I'm not losing another bag.*

She held the bag firm. He tugged at it. "Give it up, princess," he snarled.

"You give it up, *princess*," she said.

Then the strap broke. Alison inhaled sharply. She watched the YSL Muse fall—broken, *sullied*—to the ground. *Another bag lost!* She pointed at the guy. He didn't have time to fully process that a fourteen-year-old girl seemed to have a hand made of flesh-colored candles.

All he could see was a thin line of fire shooting toward him. He scrambled backward, grabbing for his gun.

Alison was faster. The bad dude wrapped his hand around the butt of a gun that was suddenly red-hot. He snatched his hand away from his waistband and staggered backward.

Alison advanced, two flaming index fingers pointing like gun barrels straight at him. His mouth opened and closed; his eyes widened.

Then the juice girl jumped up and bopped him over the head with a big steel spoon.

The guy with the gun was unconscious. The police had been called. This was going to completely reverse Alison's bad reputation. She'd be on the news! She might get a medal! She'd be a role model! Those losers who'd shunned her would be groveling to get back in her good graces.

* * *

"You were awesome," said Alison to the juice girl.

"*You* were awesome," said the juice girl to Alison.

"So can I get a medium orange carrot . . ."

The juice girl squealed in exasperation and pointed at the space in the middle of the line of juicers.

"He stole the machine!"

Monday was turning out to be the worst day ever.

"Option five!" snarled Alison.

"Huh?" said the juice girl.

"I don't know what it is, but it's the only one I've got left," Alison explained as she jumped over the counter and ran past the startled juice girl and out the back of the store.

The second bad guy was in the process of dragging the big juicer to his truck in the parking lot behind Jamba Juice. When he'd heard his buddy scream in pain, he decided that being part of a two-man team was holding him back.

He jumped in the truck, gunned the engine, and looked in the rearview mirror, where he saw Alison standing a few feet away with her arms folded. That's all she was doing, standing, staring at him. *Scared little schoolgirl,* he thought, tickled.

Backing the truck out of the parking lot, he popped his head out the window and gave her a friendly little wave goodbye.

Alison waved back.

"Hey, dude!" she called out. "I've had a bad day. Which I'm sure is something you can identify with. I'm thirsty and I'm angry."

"Boo hoo," he sneered back. "Run home and tell Mommy all about the bad man."

Alison kept waving. But now her fingers were on fire.

The guy blinked a couple of times. Was the sun in his eyes? No. Definitely a schoolgirl with a hand full of burning fingers. Make that two hands. Two hands shooting out flames! The truck lurched. The back window shattered. He felt the heat licking around the back of his neck. He yelped in terror, lost control of the truck, and slammed into a parked car in the lot.

The juicer-loving guy staggered out of the truck and looked behind him. Alison wasn't running, wasn't breaking a sweat, but she was headed toward him. He shook sense into himself. He was a big guy. He'd been around. He could handle himself. She was a schoolgirl. She looked like she'd rather slit her throat than smudge her makeup. Then he turned and ran.

"Bet you don't make it," Alison told the guy. He was a gasping, wheezing mess of fear-fueled adrenaline. He had run wildly and with no clear sense of direction. Now he found himself facing a chain-link fence.

"You're out of shape. You sound like a smoker. You're all sweaty and gross. You're never gonna get over that fence."

The guy turned and stared at Alison. He felt half dead. His heart was beating in his ears. She hadn't broken a sweat. She pulled out a twenty-dollar bill.

"Bet you."

The guy stared at Alison. More than anything in the world, he wanted to get away from that little blond devil doll. He gave her the most intimidating glare he had left and made a run for the chain-link fence, which was now on fire. He reared back before he made contact with the flames. His shoulders slumped. He knew she'd make a big show of putting the twenty dollars back in her pocket, and as he turned around, that's exactly what she was doing.

Then, putting her hands on her hips, she said, in a cold, clear, commanding voice, "Take the juicer back to the bar."

Option five totally rocked, thought Alison. Not only had she received a voucher entitling her to fifty percent off her next month's worth of Jamba Juice purchases but she felt *great.*

Suddenly, she didn't care what *anyone* thought of her, she didn't care that her best friends, the Shunning Sisters, had conspired to puncture her popularity, she didn't care that she wasn't president or that she wasn't going to be on TV or that her bag strap was broken . . . actually, she really cared about her bag strap but was determined not to let it ruin her good mood. She didn't know why her fingers did what they did, but for the first time, she didn't feel like a freak, she felt *special.* She didn't need any more sessions with Kimmy and her stupid ukulele. Alison had a super-sexy secret, and nobody knew but her. And the juicer-loving guy and his buddy. And the juice girl. But they didn't count. For the first time in her life, she felt like she knew who she was.

As Alison walked past Saks on Wilshire Boulevard, another retail paradise that she'd thought of as a home away from home, she barely gave the lavish window displays more than a brief longing glance. Then she looked away and began singing to herself. "It's a new dawn, it's a new day, it's a new life for me. And I'm feeling good."

TWENTY-THREE

"*Why not make* the boobs bigger?"

David Eels was so engrossed in his evening activity of Photoshopping Jessica Alba's head onto Jessica Biel's body that for a second, he sort of thought the voice offering such a smart morsel of constructive criticism had come from his own subconscious mind. Then he saw a reflection in his computer screen and became aware that Alison Cole was standing by his bedroom desk, watching him work. He scrambled to hit the Delete button, swiveled around in his seat to face her, and attempted to look less freaked out than he was feeling.

"Your mom let me in," she explained. "I told her we were in a book club. We're not really."

Awkward silence followed as Alison fully took in her surroundings. *Boy's bedroom,* she thought. *Ewww.*

David's thoughts were substantially similar. Suddenly, he wished he hadn't been so pleased when his mother announced she was done picking up after him and he could drown in a sea of discarded clothing, comic books, and software packaging.

David could see Alison appraising the room. *Maybe,* he hoped to himself, *she's a fan of Japanese action figures. She might be impressed by my collection. And she's probably noticed the twelve-pound weights that I use to work out. That I will use when I start working out . . .*

He could see her nose wrinkle in distaste. His eye fell on the Kleenex box poking out from the bottom of his bed.

"I wanna talk to you about something," she said.

"Uh-huh," he mumbled. Maybe she wouldn't see the box. Or if she did, maybe she'd just think he had sinus problems. Wow, that was a big box.

The teetering piles of comics swam in front of Alison's eyes. Then she found what she was looking for, the reason she'd made the spontaneous journey to David's Fairfax Avenue condo.

"I wanna be like *her,*" she said, picking up the copy of Darqmoon that David had shown her earlier that day. "I wanna be like Zoe Falcon . . . stein . . . whatever."

"But she's a superhero."

"Right."

"And you . . ."

". . . stopped two perpotatoes robbing the Jamba Juice on Rodeo. One of them had a gun, but I had *this!*"

Unable to stop the grin from spreading across her face, Alison pointed the fingers of her left hand in a menacing fashion.

"And *this*!"

Right hand.

"I mean, I don't know exactly how I did it. But I did it. And it was *awesome* . . ."

David's rapt expression betrayed not a shred of doubt. It wasn't desperation or stupidity that made him invade the stage during her acceptance. It was *fate*. It wasn't problems with reality that made him visit the same therapist as Alison. It was *fate*. It was the *fate* of a true comic book believer like him to wind up with an actual, life-size superhero in his bedroom.

"Show me," he said.

"I just did. Remember I went like this with the left hand and this with the right?"

"No, show me what you did, show me how it works."

"In here? I'll burn all your . . ."

The words died in her mouth. Torching his room would only be an improvement.

"We need somewhere better suited to target practice," said David.

He began to walk out the door and gestured for Alison to follow.

"Good idea," she said as she left his bedroom. "I wouldn't want to cause an accident and leave you without any *tissues*. . . ."

TWENTY-FOUR

Alison's Monday had been more memorable than many people's entire lives.

She'd lost her friends, she'd lost her boyfriend, her popularity, her presidency, and her TV show. She'd gained amazing superpowers, she'd brought juice bandits to justice, she'd been in a geek's bedroom, and now she was jostling for space amid empty pizza boxes and beer cans in the back of the dented, foul-smelling secondhand Honda Accord driven by Designated Dean.

Double D, as he encouraged Alison to call him, was David's neighbor, a chubby, stubbly, hygienically challenged nineteen-year-old who'd bailed on college and moved back to the home—or, to be exact, the garage—of his sorrowful parents. Double D now had no ambitions or means of support, which meant that he and his reeking Honda were permanently at the paid disposal of the underage and the hard-partying.

"You slippin' shawty the big eel?" Designated Dean had inquired of an embarrassed David when Alison clambered into the junk heap that was his backseat.

"It's not like that," mumbled David.

"That's what I thought. 'Cuz that little honey's giving me the green light."

"I can hear you, Double D," Alison had replied as she attempted to avoid the rusted springs poking through the seat.

She quickly got over her initial distaste for Designated Dean and began to fixate on the fact that she was voluntarily being driven into the middle of nowhere.

"Where *are* we?" asked Alison with mounting discomfort. Huge dark anonymous office building blocks. Empty storefronts. Deserted alleyways. The farther the car drove, the grimmer the surrounding environment grew.

"Downtown," replied David.

"Downtown LA?"

"You're telling me you've never been downtown before?"

"Downtown LA in America?"

A bustling hive of business activity by day, downtown LA was something of a ghost town after dark. Without warning, the Honda pulled up at the side of one of these big, empty buildings.

David got out. Alison, unsure of where she was or how secure she felt, didn't move.

"Yeah, I knew I felt somethin' goin' on between you and me." Designated Dean smirked, switching on the tape machine—the

Honda was still in the cassette era—and cranking some old-school booty rap.

Less than a second later, Alison was on the downtown sidewalk next to David, who nodded at her to follow him as he snuck around the back of the building.

"Downtown's full of office buildings getting torn down and turned into loft spaces and loft spaces getting torn down and turned into office buildings. They couldn't decide what they wanted this to be, so it's stayed a big old empty bomb site forever. They walked away from the job before they even finished clearing it out."

"So you thought of me and my obvious construction skills?"

"Yes," said David, surprised once again by Alison's sense of humor. "And then I thought some of the things they left behind might turn out to be useful for our superhero demonstration."

He pulled open the door of the loading dock. "You coming?"

Alison chewed her lip. What was it she'd predicted in therapy? The next person to walk into the waiting room was likely to be an unstable weirdo with serial killer potential? And in had walked Eels. And now he'd lured her to some post-apocalyptic hellhole he *claimed* was downtown LA when she'd never seen any kind of concrete evidence that such a place actually existed, and here he was inviting her into a big old empty bomb site. *Perfect* end to a perfect day.

"Okeydoke," she said, following him inside.

David positioned the last of the mannequins they'd dragged from the floor of the never completely demolished women's department of the never completely demolished department store and positioned it carefully against the wall at the back of the building.

Six of them stood in a row, all naked, pink, and plastic.

"Fire away," he said.

Alison stared at the dummies.

"They're naked."

She disappeared back into the store, emerging ten minutes later carrying armfuls of garments. David watched as she carefully dressed each of the mannequins. *I'm making it work. I could totally be on* Project Runway, she thought, standing back to admire her styling prowess.

"Fire away," said David again.

"But I just dressed them. I made it work! They look so nice."

David glanced at his watch. Designated Dean charged by the hour.

Alison knew what he wanted to see. She inhaled, pointed a finger, aimed it at the middle mannequin. She squeezed her eyes shut.

"Is it starting? Do you feel it happening? Can you describe what it feels like?"

"Shut up!"

"Sorry."

She refocused her energy.

Nothing happened.

"Is it starting now?"

"I can't do it with you watching. You're putting me off. Don't look."

"You're kind of missing the point of the whole superhero

demonstration process."

"Go stand inside the big empty building and watch through a crack in the door."

David, understanding that she was self-conscious, did as he was told.

"Fire away!" he yelled moments later from behind a crack in the door of the big empty building.

She pointed at the middle mannequin, and once again, nothing happened.

"This is stupid," she snapped, embarrassed and annoyed.

"Don't be so hard on yourself," said David, emerging from behind the door. "If it takes a while, then that's how long it takes. We'll go get something to eat, then we'll come back . . ."

Alison stared at him. "Are you trying to turn this into a date?"

David stared back. "What?"

She couldn't help herself. She was awkward and embarrassed and miles out of her comfort zone and the only way she could shift the focus from her shortcomings was to pick a fight.

"I get it. Designated Dean's spreading the word. We leave here and all your loser friends'll be lurking in doorways with their cameras clicking away. Look, it's our hero David Eels out on his big date with . . ."

David shot back, ". . . the most unpopular girl in Beverly Hills."

Alison pretended to clutch her heart in pain. "Still makes me *something*. Still means I'm noticed. I'm not a nobody. But in case I ever want to get into that line of work, tell me, what's it like?"

"It's great."

"I bet it is."

How had the situation suddenly turned so tense? They barely knew each other and now they were at war.

"I want to go home now," Alison demanded. "And I'm not setting foot in that fat freak's car. Call me a cab. And don't ever try to talk to me again."

With that, she started to walk away.

"Don't be such a bip," David muttered after her.

She whirled around. "What did you just say? Did you call me a bitch?" Her eyes were flashing.

"I called you a bip. *BIP.* Because I'm Pretty. That's what we call girls like you."

"Girls like me?" The quiet calm with which Alison uttered the words was in reverse proportion to the anger mounting inside her.

"The world revolves around girls like you. Because you're pretty. You get everything you want. Because you're pretty. Everything's easy for you. Because you're pretty . . ."

Alison blinked hard. This was how Carmen had made her feel, but she wasn't going to cry again. She especially wasn't going to cry in front of this random geek. But he wouldn't stop.

"We laugh at your jokes when we know they aren't funny. Because you're pretty. We treat you like you're smart even though you act like a retard. Because you're pretty. And the moment you stop being pretty, your daddy, or whoever's taking his place, will pay for you to be pretty again. . . ."

Alison screamed, *"Shut up!"*

Her face was red, her eyes were wild, and her fingers were ablaze.

"Now! Do it now! Fire away!" yelled David, pointing at the row of mannequins.

Alison, barely aware of what she was doing, ground both burning fingers into her palm. She shrieked in horror and surprise as she saw two balls of fire in her palms. *"Go!"* shouted David. Alison hurled one ball. *"Go again!"* She threw the second ball. They smashed into the heads of the mannequins flanking the middle dummy. Both heads exploded into flames and began to melt.

Alison breathed hard, trying to control herself. Her hands hung by her sides, her fingers still sparking and glowing.

David looked from the melting dummy heads to Alison's hands. Then he looked back to the dummies. Then back at her hands. His superhero fantasies hadn't just been realized, they'd been *exceeded*.

David ran up to her. "I didn't mean it, you know that, right? I just had to get you going. And you were amazing. The way it just *exploded* out of you . . ."

Alison didn't look at him. She didn't respond in any way. She just turned and began to walk away from the burning, melting mannequins. He hurried after her.

"You were fantastic. Whatever I imagined after what you told me, it was nothing next to seeing it up close."

She said nothing.

"I've never seen anything like that. What does it feel like? Does it hurt?"

She still wouldn't look at him.

"Alison?"

"Say you're sorry," she said quietly.

"I told you I didn't mean it. I was just trying to get you to react."

"Say you're sorry, using the word *sorry*."

"I'm sorry."

"And you're a jerk."

"I am a jerk," he conceded.

"And you will never use the word *bip* around me again."

"*Bip* will never cross my lips again."

"You know what me and my friends call you and your geek buddies?"

"What?"

Alison stayed silent. After a moment, she said, "That's what we call you. Nothing. We don't ever think about you. You don't exist to us."

"That's clever," said David. "See, an actual bip would never think of that."

Both of them were now aware that something momentous had just happened. As they walked back onto the now-darkened, desolate downtown street, they were quiet, absorbed in their own thoughts. Then they saw Designated Dean frantically flapping his raggedy jacket at the flames that were burning the roof of his Honda.

"That wasn't me, right?" hoped Alison.

"A stray spark, a gust of wind?" David shrugged. "Anyway, I always said he needed a sunroof."

TWENTY-FIVE

Marvelette Bridgewater-Rivington's permanently raised eyebrows almost shot off the top of her head as she opened her locker door and a black envelope bearing the white symbol +1 fell out.

A few feet away, Kellyn and Dorinda peeked out of the girls' bathroom door, observing Marvelette's reaction. She seemed intrigued. She was taking out her Treo. Both girls beamed. Kellyn, in particular, felt vindicated. She'd conceived the Plus One Party last Christmas. "If you want to come to the coolest party of the year, you have to bring a Plus One of our choice," she'd explained breathlessly to Alison, only to see her former friend's attention wander away before she'd even finished hyperbolizing what a devastational effect the plan would have on its invitees. Typical

Alison. Shooting down a genius notion, and why? Because *she* hadn't thought of it. Because *she* didn't think it was fun. Because *she* thought it was mean. How had Kellyn wasted her time on a fun-squasher like Alison all these years? *God*, the Plus One Party was an *incredible* idea. It hit every button. Competition. Jealousy. Fear. Everyone would be scrambling to snare sexy seniors, movie stars, and models. Whoever Kellyn commanded them to bring, they'd have to bring or else they wouldn't be allowed admittance to the one party they dared not miss. They'd all be aquiver with excitement and intrigue, just like Marvelette Bridgewater-Rivington currently was. Kellyn exited the toilet and sauntered up to the recipient of the black envelope.

"M B-R."

"Miss K."

"I'm hoping I'm gonna have the pleasure of your company at Chez K next Sat."

"You never know, I may find myself swinging by your chateau. You want me to bring anything special? Doritos? Funyuns?"

"I'd be delighted if you'd bring one particular snack."

"It's a tall order."

 "You're a tall girl."

Both girls smiled, raised their eyebrows at each other, and went their respective ways.

Dorinda scuttled out of the toilet and hurried up to Kellyn.

"What'd she say? Is she gonna do it? Is she in?"

"Oh, she's all the way in, baby." Kellyn grinned.

The Plus One Party's success was instantly assured. Kellyn had piqued the interest of Ms. M B-R, who possessed an effortless cool and who, most important of all, had become a custody hot button in the ugly divorce of her parents. There was nothing the soon-to-be-dissolved Bridgewater-Rivingtons would not do to prove to their daughter how much less she was loved and indulged by one than the other. And one of her warring parents worked at the talent agency that still counted Nick Stygian as a client.

This was beyond brilliant. Kellyn was going to have the whole school scrambling to follow her whims. She was going to have the TV bad boy of her dreams show up at her house and, most important of all, Alison was going to hear about it all. She was going to realize what a hideous mistake she'd made underestimating Kellyn, and her whole life was going to be devoted to wishing she had one of those coveted black envelopes. Kellyn allowed herself a moment to savor the beauty of her scheme. Then she turned and briskly clapped at the waiting Dorinda.

"Don't just stand there. Busy, busy, busy. Updates. Progress reports. RSVPs. Who's coming? Who's stalling? Who's faking? Get your hustle on, girlie!"

As Kellyn shooed her off, Dorinda was struck by the feeling that maybe, *just maybe*, she had abandoned the wrong friend.

TWENTY-SIX

This is what my life adds up to, thought Alison, shaking her head sadly as she looked at the fence at the far end of the empty skate park. She was bidding symbolic farewells to items that reminded her of dead friendships. Her pink iPod nano sat on the fence next to her Uggs, the remains of the bouquet Carmen had gone out of her way to make sure Alison caught at the wedding reception, the mementos of fun times with Kellyn and Dorinda: it was a pantheon of betrayal!

"Okay, so in our previous enthralling installment we saw the raging fireballs that exploded out of you when you were expertly manipulated into losing control."

Alison couldn't help smiling at David. He was *so* into his sensei role. He was like the Superhero Whisperer.

"And we learned that your amazing powers are tied to your emotions."

"Emotions," she repeated.

"You know, like emoticons? But real."

"I know what emotions are."

"Well, that's how you catch fire. You get angry, you heat up. But we can't go through life acting purely on emotion. We need to learn to control our powers."

Alison made an impatient "get on with it" gesture.

"You've got to be able to *use* emotion. Summon it up when you need it. Then shrug it off the moment you have no further use for it. But *how*, I hear you ask, how do I just switch my emotions on and off?"

"Tell me how, Mr. Spielnerd."

"I'd like to refer to a recent, moving speech by one of our former presidents and a surprisingly powerful orator. In her address, Ms. Alison Cole made reference to the 'Fortunately/Unfortunately' game. . . ."

Alison stared at David. Was he trying to mess with her again?

"Play it with all these souvenirs and presents you brought. Let the memories wash over you, think of all the good things and all the bad things. . . ."

Alison stared at the pink iPod nano. She remembered how cute Warren could be.

"Altoid?" he'd said, offering her the tin. She'd shaken her head, but he'd insisted, pressing the container into her hand and grinning with delight as she'd opened the lid and found the iPod nestling inside.

Fortunately, *Warren was the sweetest, most considerate boyfriend ever,* she thought. Unfortunately, *he cheated on me with a renowned slut and sold me out to the cops.*

The flames shot out of her fingers and reduced the iPod to a dribble of pink metal.

Fortunately, *we were the closest friends ever,* thought Alison as she turned her attention to a framed picture of Kellyn, Dorinda, and herself dressed as witches a few Halloweens ago.

Unfortunately, *they secretly hated me and couldn't wait to stab me in the back and shun me!*

The Halloween memory went up in flames.

"From red-hot to stone-cold in seconds. Impressive," said David.

Meshing her superhero training with the bedroom catwalk sessions she, Kellyn, and Dorinda used to enjoy after *Top Model* marathons, Alison placed a hand on her hip, then lashed out a finger and torched the Uggs Warren bought her for their three-month anniversary.

She started to walk away, then looked over her shoulder and set fire to Carmen's withered bouquet.

Looking around for another scorchable target, Alison saw a squirrel run up the base of a nearby palm tree. She shuddered. Alison nursed a terror of squirrels, fearing that they hid in palm trees, biding their time until the moment they could fall onto her head and wreak havoc with the gnawing and the biting. But did they deserve to be barbecued? Didn't some people even think they were cute? Although it was impossible for her to imagine how anyone could summon up affection for the bushy-tailed tree rats, Alison made the mental leap from squirrels to Bring Pets to

School champion junior president T.

Excitement coursed through her. She raised her arms in the air and two jets of flame rocketed upward.

"Wow," she gasped, breathless.

Moments later, two charred pigeons plummeted from the sky.

Sipping an Ice Blended outside the Wilshire branch of California's popular Starbucks competitor, the Coffee Bean & Tea Leaf, David tried to console Alison with the thought that some homeless guy was enjoying an unexpected pigeon feast at that very moment. She wasn't listening. A plane passed overhead.

Without looking up, Alison said, "Eight fifty-one. Delta flying in from Salt Lake City."

"How do you know that?" asked David, hoping she might be developing another superpower.

Alison stared down at her pomegranate and blueberry elixir, thought about changing the subject, but then said, "I memorize all the flights coming into LAX."

David grinned. "The cool kids all try to hide it, but sooner or later, their secret geek comes out of the closet."

Alison took another sip, then looked at David and felt like she trusted him enough to be honest.

"When I was nine, my mother spent New Year's with her family in London. She was supposed to be flying back to LAX on the ten-oh-six flight, British Airways from Heathrow. We waited for hours, but her plane never made it back. They found most of the bodies, but not hers. I kept thinking she must have gotten on another plane. I checked the flights every day and it just stuck."

David was aware that Alison had just shared something very

personal with him. He knew that their relationship had just turned a corner. He understood that his reply was an important indicator of his caliber as a confidant. He pulled his straw out of his Ice Blended and sucked at the fruit clogging the end. Alison was looking at him, waiting for some kind of reaction.

Weighing his words, he said, "Hey, did you hear about how many planes have faulty waste disposal systems? Supposedly, big balls of frozen poo fall out every day and crush people to death. That would be a gross way to die, wouldn't it?"

Alison stared at him for a long moment.

"I just shared something very painful and traumatic from my past and you . . ."

Then she understood. He liked the superhero side of her. *Fortunately*, they'd made a real connection. *Unfortunately*, he didn't want to deal with the personal stuff. She felt sadness collapse around her. *Could someone just care about* me? she thought. But then, Alison reasoned, she and David were just getting to know each other and under the weirdest-possible circumstances. Maybe they'd get closer over time. She changed tone.

"Tragic backstory. That definitely qualifies me for the super-hero club. Or league."

David grinned, grateful for the conversational detour.

"Almost," he said. "You need a name, a costume, a healthy sense of injustice, a split personality, a never-ending conflict be-tween your two diametrically opposed identities, a tendency to brood, and some cool catchphrases."

Alison gulped down the remainder of her Ice Blended and stared at David, suddenly bursting with excitement.

"Did you say *costume?*"

TWENTY-SEVEN

"Đon't laugh," warned Alison from outside David's bedroom door.

Laugh? He could barely stand up. For the past two days, Alison had sent him a steady stream of attachments chronicling her journey through her vast walk-in closet in search of clothing items that might constitute an acceptable superhero costume.

He'd made a screen saver out of the picture she'd sent of herself clad in pink leather hot pants, high-heel boots with flames running up the sides, bikini top, and cutoff silk bomber jacket. Now she was in his bathroom, preparing to model her final selection.

When Alison kicked open the door, growled, "The heat is on!" and hit a Charlie's Angels all-guns-blazing pose, David initially thought there was serious danger his blood might start pumping so vigorously it would cause his head to pop off the top of his body. But it didn't. She hadn't gone with the screen saver look.

"What, you didn't get my cool catchphrase? *'The heat is on'?* I thought of it myself. Well, someone else thought of it first, but I adapted it, so I'm probably still eligible to win an award if there's a category at the Superhero Awards. Hey, *are* there Superhero Awards?"

Ignoring the question, David asked, "Are you going somewhere else tonight? Some party or premiere or something?"

"I wish."

"It's just the way you're dressed. It's not very . . . I mean, it's nice, don't get me wrong, but it's not what I was expecting."

She sat down at his desk and picked up his She-Hulk action figure.

"I looked through all those comics you gave me. And all those costumes they wear would be great if I wanted to be both a superhero and a super-slutto. But I don't. All that cleavage bursting out of spandex? Not really me. I wanted something more classy. So I thought, what if Audrey Hepburn joined the X-Gang?"

Where David would once have corrected her with a dry, "Uh, I think you mean the X-*Men*," he now simply nodded and allowed her to continue.

"How would that look? So I went to the storage room . . ."

Alison's late mother had modeled for something like five minutes and acted for something like ten. She had accrued souvenirs of both professions and, Alison was pleased to discover, Carmen had neither ransacked nor tossed them out of the house.

That's where she found the short black wig she'd combed

into bangs, the little black dress, the white pearls, and the huge black vintage Chanel sunglasses that covered the entire upper half of her face. The calfskin motorcycle boots, the black fingerless cycling gloves, and the red leather jacket came from the depths of her own closet.

"And look," she said, wiggling her finger, drawing his attention to the hefty chunk of jewelry on display over her cycling-gloved right index finger.

"It's a ring. Very nice."

"It's a *mood* ring. It'll make an excellent visual aid. It'll turn black when I get mad."

"Like The Hulk. Except not green," said David, brightening.

His initial disappointment over her wardrobe choices was fading. She was as into her new identity as he was!

"One ring to rule them all!" he pronounced with a flourish. Alison gave him a blank look.

"You look awesome," he told her. She gave him an appreciative smile, then began hitting superhero poses in his bedroom mirror. David sat on the edge of his bed and stared at her, mouth hanging open. A few weeks ago, he'd never had a girl in his bedroom, now *this*.

Seeing his expression in the mirror, Alison said, "What? You look like you're in pain."

"I was thinking," he replied, trying to sound serious. "The name. We need a name."

"What about Audrey?"

"You can't be a superhero called Audrey."

"Audrey X?" she suggested.

"X is always good, but it still seems to have Audrey attached to it, so no. Something involving heat so that it gives people a clue about your powers."

David paced the room, picking up and discarding comic books and action figures in the hope they'd provide inspiration.

"Heat Seeker? Fire Starter? Flame Thrower? Fire Girl?"

Alison thought about the names that had defined her up to now: Best Friend. Girlfriend. Most Popular. Stepdaughter. None of them had worked out for her.

"How about Single Girl? She's on her own. Alone. Doesn't need anyone. Making her own way in the world."

"Something more mythological, maybe? Dragonette? Dragon Girl? Dragon X?"

"Like I wanna be called after a big, green, scaly beast with nasty breath. Single Girl's *good*."

"Dragons are good. Did you see *Dragon Wars*?"

"No."

"Did you see *Eragon*?"

"No."

"*Reign of Fire*?"

"Are you asking me this because you think the more dragon films you list, the more it's gonna make me want to go see a dragon movie? 'Cos it's not."

David stopped pacing. He looked at her. A big grin spread across his face.

"I don't want to hear another dragon movie, I mean it."

"I got an idea for a name. It's stupid, though. . . ."

Alison threw her hands in the air. "Say it."

He paused and then said, "Hottie." She didn't react.

"I know, I know," he said quickly. "It's lame. I just threw it out there."

Alison wasn't listening. She was mouthing the word *Hottie* to herself. Suddenly adopting the hostile growl of a bad guy, she said, "Who the hell are you?"

Then she jumped to her feet, put her hands on her hips, and proudly intoned, "I'm Hottie. And you're *fired!*"

With that, she hit her all-guns-blazing pose again. This time, David felt the surge of excitement he missed on her initial appearance. He hurried over to his computer.

"I totally know what your logo should look like. It should be like the anarchy symbol but with an *H*. And on fire. This isn't going to look great; I'm just banging it out on a graphic generator. But if you like it, maybe you could get it made into a gold chain or earrings or a brooch. . . ."

Where Alison would once have grimaced at the way David pronounced *brooch* like *pooch*, now she smiled affectionately at him as he pored through a font archive. *Maybe I am just his little dress-up superhero dolly, but so what?* she thought. *When everyone else abandoned me or shunned me, he understood me and he was there for me. He doesn't care what anyone else thinks about me; he treats me like I'm special.*

As she watched David, he bounced up from his seat and beckoned her over to look at his handiwork. Alison glanced at the Hottie-customized version of the anarchy logo and then, impulsively, hugged him.

"You know, you're pretty much my best friend now."

David felt her arms around him. He felt the warmth of her body pressed against his. He felt her breath on his neck. He felt her hair spill against his face.

"Hic!"

TWENTY-EIGHT

Carmen ruined everything!

Or rather Carmen's *publicist* had ruined everything—namely Alison's first official night as a crime fighter, her superhero debutante ball.

Apparently, at an earlier date, Alison had been made aware that the publicist had managed to beg or blackmail *Brentwood* magazine into running a profile of Carmen, her philanthropy, her impeccable taste, and her picture-perfect family. Alison had no memory of this whatsoever.

"I'm not going to be interviewed about how awesome Carmen is," insisted Alison to Roger.

"She *has* to be interviewed about how awesome I am," insisted Carmen to Roger. For an aspiring power wife like herself, a story in *Brentwood* was more important than being on the cover of *People*. Everyone who mattered in LA would see it and they'd think that *she* was someone who mattered. Carmen gave Roger a "fix this *now!*" look.

"Alison, we made a commitment. This family honors its commitments," insisted Roger.

"Please. This isn't a family. This is your mess. You married her. You have to do what she wants. *I* don't." Alison struck a defiant pose, almost daring her father to force the issue. Roger closed his eyes for a moment. This kind of drama was fine in the courtroom. But this was his home. He just wanted everyone to get along. Alison knew Roger wasn't going to make her do anything she didn't want to do.

Carmen glared at Alison. This wasn't just the usual expression of frustrated loathing. Carmen looked like she was trying to shoot laser beams straight through her stepdaughter's skull and out the other side. Her eyes were almost opaque. "You. Will. Do. What. You're. Told," commanded Carmen, low and deadly.

For a second, Alison wasn't sure if her stepmother's lips had even moved. It felt like she heard the words inside her head. And even though she wanted to zing Carmen with a rebellious response, her mind was suddenly blank.

With an effort, she looked away from Carmen and acknowledged that once again, she'd lost the brief power struggle. This was worse than when she'd come back from the clinic. *I'm strong,* she thought. *I'm a* superhero*! I ought to be able to stand up to her.* But standing up to her meant looking at those cold eyes again, and the idea of *that* made her tremble.

"I'll go change," she whispered.

★ ★ ★

"So your stepdaughter was happy to get involved in your charitable endeavors?" asked the *Brentwood* reporter as she sat in the Coles' opulent living room under the gold chandelier Carmen had installed specially for the occasion.

"That young lady was crying out for a direction in life," said Carmen, posing elegantly by the brocade windows she'd had treated, again, specially for the occasion. "I've tried to be a role model to her. I've attempted to be an inspiration to her in the way I live my life and the way I treat people. In everything I do, I strive to *shine down love on those who need love*. That's what my Christmas Ball, which I hope you'll be mentioning, is all about."

"Oh yes, the Christmas Ball. That's the one that's like Secret Santa?"

"Well, there's more to it than that. . . ."

Carmen was busy congratulating herself to the reporter. Roger was busy showing the photographer the improvements Carmen had made to the house. Neither of them noticed that Alison was silently easing her way down the stairs. Neither of them noticed her sneaking through the hallway. Neither of them heard the back door open and close behind her.

"Your pimp hand is strong, hombre," said an impressed Designated Dean to David as the girl in the big red jacket, little black dress, short black bangs, motorcycle boots, and huge gangsta gold chain with the flaming *H* logo clambered into the back of his filthy Honda. "This one looks like a mad freak. But you gotta give me that last honey's digits. She was beggin' me to tap that ass."

"I can hear you, Double D. Plus, it's still the last honey," said

Alison, smiling at Designated Dean in the rearview mirror.

The plan for Alison's first night as Hottie was for the pair to respond to any minor crimes or emergencies that were announced over Designated Dean's police scanner. ("I don't wants to know the details," interrupted Dean when David had attempted to construct a plausible lie about the events of the evening. "I just wants to get paid.")

If it seemed like something Alison could handle, they'd race to the scene of the crime and she'd mysteriously save the day before vanishing into the night.

"Who *was* that?" the stunned but grateful citizens would gasp. "Where did she come from?" they'd wonder. "How did she *do* that?" they'd ask. And that, David thought, bristling with excitement for the night ahead, was how legends were born.

TWENTY-NINE

Kellyn heard the booming bass. She ran to the window and saw the tricked-out Cadillac Escalade making its way up the winding road to her Hollywood Hills mansion. The Plus One Party was already a smash success; now it was on its way to becoming a phenomenon.

"Oh my God," she gasped. Her heart was pounding.

"You wanted snacks, I brought snacks." Marvelette grinned. She had instantly become Kellyn's BFF in the universe.

"It's *him*. It's *Nick*!" gasped Kellyn to Dorinda before instructing her, "*No one* bugs him, right? Everyone backs off, gives him his space. He's been through so much. And get *her* out of my sight."

Dorinda followed Kellyn's gaze. They found themselves staring at Ginger Becker, who was dancing by herself in a manner designed to (1) attract attention and (2) broadcast to Warren that she had quickly become as bored with him as he had with her.

Kellyn gave Dorinda a hard shove in Ginger Becker's direction and then ran off to grab Marvelette.

Dorinda watched her BFF in the universe laughing loudly and whispering secrets into the ear of another girl. She looked around the crowded living room and realized that everyone else at the party had a Plus One but her.

"'Sup, boo," slurred Nick Stygian to Marvelette as she met him at the door of Kellyn's home.

"How you doin', Nicky?" said Marvelette, allowing herself to be hugged and then quickly recoiling. Apparently, Nicky was a little too cool and street to shower.

Marvelette took Kellyn's arm and guided her toward Nick Stygian. "This is Miss K. She *is* the party."

When Nick enfolded Kellyn in his sweaty, unhygienic hug, she didn't feel the need to disentangle herself and run to take a long hot shower. She could have stayed in his embrace forever. Her cheek was hot against his chest. She touched the tattoos that ran up and down his arms. She could feel his heart beat. Then he pushed her away and she found herself looking at the four other guys who had made their way into her house.

They had the same number of tattoos as Nick. They had the same facial hair. They had the same long white tees and combat pants. On him, they looked cute. On those guys, they seemed intimidating. In fact, *they* seemed intimidating.

"It's cool I brought my boys, right?" grunted Nick to Kellyn.

"Oh God, yes," she breathed. "Chill. Have fun. Do whatev."

Nick's friends walked through the house, nudging each other and shooting admiring glances at the priceless artwork lining the walls.

"They're a'ight," Nick assured Kellyn, who nodded, unaware that Nick had brought them to ransack her house of all valuables and pay off his huge debt to S-Quid, the drug dealer whose patience had recently run out.

THIRTY

Designated Dean's nasty Honda roared through the LA night. Inside the car, David was still buzzing with excitement at the thought that he was going to be present at the birth of a superhero. This was the end of evil and injustice. The oppressed masses could sleep safely. David wasn't sure he heard Alison correctly when she suddenly spoke up. It seemed to him that she might have said something like "I changed my mind." But that couldn't have been right. Could it?

"What did you say?"

"I've changed my mind," she repeated.

"Huh?" replied David.

"She said she changed her mind," bawled Designated Dean.

As the Honda sped on, Alison found herself thinking not of

vanquishing evil and injustice but of how she had recently allowed herself to become a victim of it.

She had opened her locker some mornings earlier and a black envelope had fallen out. She'd picked it up and stared at it, a white +1 symbol on the front. Was this a peace gesture? It must have been. You can't be friends with someone as long as she'd been friends with Kellyn and Dorinda and simply walk away from all they'd been through together and all they'd meant to one another.

Even though they'd stabbed her in the back and the front, she wanted them back in her life. Maybe she'd even tell them about the superhero thing. Maybe they could go to Dr. Bracken and get superpowers of their own! Kellyn could crack complex computer codes with her brilliant strategist's brain and Dorinda could probably do something with baguettes. Alison felt excited, happy, and forgiving. She'd started to rip open the envelope when Kellyn snatched it out of her hands.

"Sorrrreeee." She smiled, radiating insincerity. "That's not for you. I don't know how that ended up there."

Kellyn turned to Dorinda. "How did that happen?" she said, handing her the envelope.

"I don't know," Dorinda replied in her thin, reedy Valley Girl voice. "I guess I'll have to reseal it."

"You *better*. We don't want anyone *important* thinking we forgot about them."

Then Kellyn saw Marvelette Bridgewater-Rivington walk out of a classroom and ran after her to get the latest update on Nick Stygian's Plus One Party status.

This left Dorinda standing awkwardly in front of Alison, the torn envelope in her hand.

"What happened to your voice?" asked Alison, who had never heard Dorinda's natural accent before.

"I assimilated," said Dorinda, hurrying away.

It had taken Alison the rest of the day to fully comprehend that in Kellyn's eyes, she hadn't suffered sufficiently for whatever it was she had done. Kellyn must have seen Alison laughing and texting and sharing meaningful looks with David, and she must have boiled over with frustration and decided to hurt her by holding out a little piece of false hope. And it had worked. She'd let them hurt her just like she'd let them shun her. But the more she thought about the Fake Invite Incident, the more she decided that they couldn't be permitted to hurt or shun her any further.

Which was why Alison had changed her mind and the dented Honda was now wheezing its way up Hollywood Hills.

What was the point of having a secret identity if you couldn't use it to crash the Plus One Party?

THIRTY-ONE

"So, uh, are you going back to *Signal Hill?"*

Kellyn's dream had come true. *Everyone* who mattered, *everyone* who could spread the message of her skyrocketing social status was in her house, watching her monopolize the attention of the hottest young messed-up actor currently taking a break from TV. She would be an icon on Monday morning. She would dictate the BHHS social agenda from here on in. Everything was perfect.

Except Nick Stygian. He was acting kind of weird. When Kellyn asked him about returning to his TV show, he'd just sneered and started *quacking*. She tried to play it off like she hadn't noticed. But every time she opened her mouth, he did his duck noises. As if talking to her was too much trouble for him. Like she was some *fan* bugging him for an autograph.

"Yeah, TV's lame." She nodded, showing him just how un-impressed she was with the trappings of fame. "You need to do movies."

He stopped quacking. "I'm reading for this indie thing. It's called *The Day After Yesterday.*"

Kellyn was excited. He was taking her seriously. He was shar-ing details of his life with her.

"Sounds awesome."

He gave her an appraising look, as if he was *really* seeing her for the first time. "You think I should do it? It's just a little art movie."

Kellyn nodded avidly. "I *love* little art movies. That's all I ever watch."

"Maybe I could get you a part."

Kellyn's eyes widened. This was going better than she'd ever imagined.

"Can you act? Course you can act. Every chick from LA thinks she can act."

"No, but I'm really good!"

"They haven't cast the leading lady yet. The girl who loses her memory and has to piece together her past from the way things smell."

"I could *totally* do that." The night had officially surpassed her wildest dreams!

"Her big scene is when she smells the French perfume she remembers her mother wearing when she was young."

"I'm tearing up just hearing you talk about it." Kellyn gulped.

"She sniffs the air, then she says, 'I smell Mayonfars.' That's the name of the perfume."

"I totally know it. By Chanel. It's my favorite."

Nick looked impressed. "You want to try the scene?"

Kellyn nodded and closed her eyes to really *get in the moment*. Then she took a breath and said, "I smell Mayonfars."

Nick shook his head. "I didn't believe it."

Kellyn tried again, louder, with more passion. "I smell Mayonfars."

A couple of Nick's friends heard her and laughed.

Nick shrugged. "I guess not every LA chick can act."

Kellyn did not take the prospect of rejection lightly. She screamed, *"I smell Mayonfars,"* at the top of her voice. Which was the *exact* moment Kellyn's DJ chose to fade the music. And the exact moment that everyone's attention was focused on their hostess.

Nick almost choked with laughter. His buddies joined in. Soon everyone was laughing. The kids scrunched up on the white leather sofa were laughing. The idiot riding his skateboard up and down Kellyn's mother's lovingly restored marble floor was laughing. The couple making out by the bay windows were laughing. For a moment, Kellyn laughed along with her guests. It didn't immediately dawn on her that she was the object of their amusement.

It didn't immediately dawn on her *what* they were laughing at. It took Nick Stygian high-fiving one of his boys and them both repeating, "She smells her own farts. Gross!!" that she realized what she'd been made to do.

She was going to say, "Duh!" and roll her eyes. She was going to turn it around on him like she knew what he was doing the whole time and was just indulging his childish whims like a good host. She was going to show him that she was a great sport who was totally able to laugh at herself.

She could have done any of these things, but instead she ran from the living room in tears.

Kellyn's world had come crashing down. She had just been humiliated by the guy she had loved since she was six, and *everyone* who mattered, *everyone* who could spread the message of her suddenly capsizing social status, was there to witness it. And now they'd all seen her run away like a baby.

She didn't care. All she wanted was to curl up in her bed and close her eyes and make it all go away. She walked past her parents' bedroom and, even in her heightened emotional state, was sure she heard activity from inside. Kellyn squeezed her fists together. She'd *had* it with Ginger Becker.

"Not in my house, little ho," she snarled, throwing open her parents' bedroom door.

"Oh, uh, are you looking for the bathroom?" was the first thing Kellyn thought to say when she saw two of Nick's friends in the bedroom. Then she saw that her mother's original Picasso had been yanked off the wall. And that it was lying on the ground next to a couple of her antique vases. And that her dresser drawers had been pulled open. The two guys had her mother's priceless jewelry in their hands. Kellyn was about to cry out. But then the intruders started to notice exactly how much effort Kellyn had put into impressing Nick. They noticed how her earrings shone. They saw that real diamonds sparkled around her neck. They began to move toward her.

THIRTY-TWO

David was beside himself. Reports of a situation in the Apple Store had crackled over Designated Dean's police scanner. There was a siege in the Genius Bar. This was the *perfect* venue and the perfect misdemeanor for Hottie's debut. But instead of hurtling toward the scene of the crime, what were they doing? Rolling up the Hollywood Hills so that Alison could ruin her stupid friend's stupid party.

"This is a waste. It's a wasted opportunity. It's an opportunity that's being wasted. By you." David tapped his fingers furiously on the dashboard. "Wasted," he said again.

Alison let David rant without replying. Her sensible self knew the trip to sabotage the Plus One Party wasn't her smartest move. What was she going to do? Set Kellyn's skating medallions and ballet trophies on fire? What would that achieve? But Alison's sensible side stood no chance against her shunned side, which just wanted to be as bad to her ex-best friends as they'd been to her.

Annoyed at her silence, David said, "I'm paying for Designated Dean's time. Double D, turn this thing around; we're going to the Apple Store."

Alison broke her silence. "Let me out here."

Designated Dean stopped the car.

She opened the door. "You want to go to the Apple Store, go. I've got other plans."

Alison slammed the door shut and began her three-hundred-yard walk up the hill toward Kellyn's house.

Designated Dean shook his head sadly. "You know nothing about women, Eels. You brought up money. You sounded like a little bee-hootch. Now you're gonna have to get down on your knees and beg if you wanna get her back."

David shrugged. "Let her go. I don't care. I'm not going to beg."

Three seconds later, David was scurrying after Alison. She could see he was gearing up to make some sort of emotional speech designed to make her feel that she wasn't living up to her superhero potential. He could see she was in no mood for the speech he was gearing up to deliver.

Both of them knew that the other person needed their space, but neither was prepared to back down. They were ready for a big, loud, messy, endless, wasteful argument.

Then they heard the screaming.

THIRTY-THREE

The Plus One Party turned ugly fast. Dorinda ran out of the living room, chasing after Kellyn. S-Quid took up guard in front of the door. No one else was getting in or out.

The slower Plus One Party guests who hadn't yet worked out that something was amiss got the point when another of Nick's friends started dancing with Ginger Becker. Except he wasn't really dancing. He grabbed her and pinned her arms to her sides. The more she tried to squirm away, the rougher he was with her. Panicking, she cried out, "Warren!"

Warren's heart sank. He did *not* want to get involved. But it was too late. Nick Stygian's buddies had followed Ginger's beseeching gaze. Nick, S-Quid, and the other thugs all started calling out, "Warren!" in shrill mocking voices. *Maybe there's another*

Warren here, he hoped.

But no, Ginger was staring straight at *him*. They hadn't officially broken up, and it would probably look bad if he took this particular moment to say, "You know, Ginger, things haven't really been working out between us, but you're great and I hope we can still be friends." So he walked over to the guy who had his elbow around her neck and he managed to get out the words, "Hey, man . . ." before the guy punched Warren in the face and he dropped to the ground.

Everyone screamed and grabbed for their phones. Nick Stygian, trained since he was a tot to calm manic crowds, stepped into the center of the room and raised his palms. "Guys, it's cool. We're just gonna have to ask you to hand over your phones. And your credit cards and any other valuables you might have on you. . . ."

"Wait a minute," said Marvelette, starting to grin. "Is *Punk'd* coming back? Are you in the new cast?"

Wow, thought Nick, who hadn't considered that he could rob people and still be popular.

He beamed and shrugged as if tipping off the guests that they had discovered his big secret. But then S-Quid jeered, "Nah, he's *a* punk."

S-Quid laughed coldly. So did his two friends. Nick tried to laugh along with them. They stopped laughing.

"Go get the goodies, Nicky," instructed S-Quid, as if he was talking to someone who worked for him.

Nick swallowed his remaining pride and began relieving the party guests of their phones and credit cards. He gave Marvelette an apologetic look as he approached her.

"My father represented you when no one else would touch you," she said, disgusted. "He said everyone deserves a chance."

"That right?" retorted Nick. "Think he'd give me a chance with you?" He leered at S-Quid and the rest of his boys. They laughed at that.

Then there was a knock on the door. Not a loud, insistent knock. Not a concerned-neighbor knock. Not a rowdy party-crasher knock. Just a brisk little knock. And then another one.

Ginger Becker started to scream, "Help!" but the guy with his elbow around her throat tightened his grip, causing her to faint. . . .

"Anyone else wanna try something stupid?" said Nick, who felt like he was starring in the kind of edgy action movie Marvelette's dad should have been scoring him. "That's what I thought," he sneered at the silent, scared Plus One Party guests.

S-Quid went to open the door. His hand gripped the door-knob, and then he yelped in surprised pain and pulled it away. He stared at his palm. It was bright red and it felt like it was on fire. He stuffed it under his armpit.

S-Quid's boys were taken aback. They'd never seen anything but swagger and skill from their leader. In the confusion, no one noticed the green eye peering through the peephole, observing the scene in the living room. They also failed to pick up on the thin jet of flame slicing through the door hinges.

On the other side of the door, Alison and David—whose superhero disguise consisted of a snakeskin cowboy hat from Designated Dean's crap-filled trunk pulled down low over his eyes—glanced at each other, mouthed, "One, two, three, four," nodded, and, in unison, kicked the door off its molten hinges.

The door fell forward, knocking S-Quid backward onto the floor and slamming into his face, cutting him off mid-yell.

Alison and David walked into the living room, stepping slowly and deliberately on top of the door. Trapped underneath, S-Quid grunted in pain.

"Say a cool entrance line about us standing on the door," whispered David.

"Like what?"

"Something like, 'This is adorable.'"

"Huh?"

"A-door-able. Get it?"

"Oh, that's *funny!*"

Alison was about to deliver the cool entrance gag when she saw Warren lying bruised and wheezing on the ground. He hadn't treated her well, but that didn't mean she wanted to see him hurt. Then she saw Ginger Becker, gasping for breath.

Her mood ring turned black.

From beneath the door, S-Quid struggled and yelled, "Get off of me."

Alison gripped onto David for balance.

Then she pointed the middle finger of her left hand down toward the keyhole of the door.

The unexpected appearance of the girl with the giant dark glasses and the huge burning *H* chain and the guy with the snake-skin cowboy hat was, in and of itself, a conversation stopper. But then something that looked like a burst of fire shot out of the girl's extended finger and straight through the keyhole.

S-Quid's reaction was approximately: "AAAAAAAAAA-OOOOOOOOOHHHHWWWWW!"

Alison made a sympathetic face. "That sounded nasty."

"Doesn't smell too good either," agreed David.

"I think I fried his waffles."

"Or you barbecued his sausage."

Alison found herself snorting with unexpected laughter. This was even more fun than hurling insults at Carmen!

The guy who had his elbow around Ginger Becker's throat made a sudden, furious rush at Alison, arms out, ready to tackle her and bring her down. She whipped two hands up toward his waist, shooting out flames that neatly severed his belt, causing his pants to fall around his ankles. The guy lost his footing and sprawled forward.

The assembled party guests let out gasps of shock and nervous laughter. The fallen guy started to struggle to his feet.

Alison couldn't help noticing the heart-shaped pattern on his boxer shorts. She nudged David. They both looked at the guy's boxer shorts and snickered.

This made him even madder. He started to run at Alison again. Reminding the guy that what happened to S-Quid could easily happen to him, she sent another shot of fire down through the keyhole:

"AAAAAAAAAAAOOOOOOOOOWWWWRRRRGGH-HHH!"

"And that's when she *can't* see what she's aiming at," explained David to the boxer shorts guy, who had stopped running. Now he was standing, pants at his feet, hands crossed over his crotch, trying not to tremble.

Alison and David hopped down off the door. From beneath, S-Quid emitted a sound of combined relief and agony.

They walked toward Boxer Shorts Guy, who backed clumsily and fearfully away.

Nick decided to take control of the situation. He stepped between the intruders and his accomplice.

He gave Alison an appraising glance and seemed unimpressed. "What are *you* supposed to be, some sort of genetically engineered superpowered vigilante action chick?"

"You're getting warm," said Alison, glancing back at David, who gave her an impressed thumbs-up.

"You're in way over your head, little girl."

"I was just about to say that to you." She grinned back.

"You're starting something you'll never be able to finish," growled Nick, seizing the chance to finally play the badass. "You don't know how deep this goes. Turn and walk away now. 'Cuz if you don't, you're gonna be running forever."

"This guy's good," said David to Alison.

"Of course he's good. Remember him on *Kickin' It with Tha Kidz?*"

David looked confused. "He used to kick kids?"

"What planet are you even from?" gasped Alison. "Saturday nights at seven? He was the bomb! He sang and danced and goofed around in sketches. Everyone in the world worshipped him."

Alison shook her head sadly at Nick. "I'm sorry about my friend. He lives in a bubble. . . ."

"Not literally," chimed in David. "Although that would be cool."

Alison rolled her eyes and smiled at Nick in a "*see* what I have to put up with!" kind of way. "If he could have seen how amazing you were on the show . . ."

Nick wasn't sure exactly what was happening, but he had a feeling he was losing control of the situation.

"That's history," he said, trying to maintain the thug edge in his voice. "This is right now, and right now you need to think about—"

"Why don't you show him?" said Alison, interrupting Nick. "Show him how good you were."

Nick didn't quite get what was about to happen. Boxer Shorts Guy did. "Oh no," he groaned to himself.

"My mom bought me tickets to the Kids Kickin' It Across America Tour. We sat through the whole show, but you never turned up," said Alison reproachfully. Her hands started to point at a spot inches away from Nick's feet.

"I was supposed to have my own hotel room," he said defensively. "They didn't tell me I'd be sharing with the Phat Twins."

"*Those* guys." Alison shuddered, brimming over with sympathy. "But you can make it up to me now. Let's see you dance."

Nick finally got it. He shook his head. Uh-uh. No way. He'd made mistakes. Bad choices. He'd done things he wasn't proud of. But he had his limits. He was Nick Stygian. He'd won Kid's Choice Awards. He was no smirking little super-brat's dancing monkey.

The first bursts of fire singed the toes of his *limited edition* Nike Vandal High Supremes!

Nick started dancing.

He was stiff and self-conscious at first, like a sullen adolescent boy dragged onto the dance floor by his over-affectionate mom. Alison didn't care. She whooped with pleasure and shouted,

"Go, Nicky!"

She turned to David, who had to admit he was impressed. "Dude's got moves."

"This? This is nothing. Wait till he really gets going. Show him, Nick! Show him how you do the Running Man!"

Boxer Shorts groaned.

Nick stopped dancing and folded his arms, defiant. *Enough.*

The laces of his *unbelievably rare* shoes caught fire. He threw himself into the Running Man.

"Now do the Electric Slide!"

Nick did the Electric Slide.

"The Sassy Chihuahua!"

Nick looked stricken. "The what?"

"Just do it," Alison snapped.

Improvising wildly, the angry young actor dropped to all fours and began crawling around like a dog.

"I just made that up!" Alison whispered, delighted, to David. She looked around the room. "Anyone got any requests?"

The collected guests were too astonished to speak up.

Alison pointed at Warren. "How about you, handsome guy? You got a dance for Nick?"

Warren had been immersed in his own world of pain since Nick's friends took over the party. The weird girl's words pulled him back into the present.

After a moment, he said, "The Worm."

"The public has spoken," said Alison. "Do the Worm."

As Nick undulated across the floor, Alison watched Warren. The light came back into his eyes. He pulled himself upright. He went over to Ginger Becker and held her in his arms. Alison got lost watching them for a moment.

He really has feelings for her, she thought sadly.

Then she heard the noise from above. Banging, muffled screaming, sharp, hurried bursts of movement.

She looked at David.

"Go. I'll handle this," he said.

Alison ran across the door, producing another moan of pain from S-Quid.

Nick stopped doing the Worm.

"Did someone request another dance? I don't think so. Keep doing the Worm till someone tells you different."

Nick tried to give David a defiant look.

"What, you think I'm just the sidekick? You think I don't have any powers of my own? Well, you might be right. Or I might gut you like a fish. Let's see which one of us is right."

David stared at Nick. Then he cracked his knuckles.

Nick went back to doing the Worm.

THIRTY-FOUR

Alison stood in Kellyn's cavernous walk-in closet and stared furiously at the vast and insulting amount of tops, dresses, shoes, and belts her former friend had borrowed from her and conveniently forgotten to return. The muffled moans of terror emanating from Kellyn's mother's bedroom snapped Alison back to attention.

She made her way to the back of the closet, where a sliding panel separated daughter from mother. Easing the panel open, Alison saw Kellyn and Dorinda sitting on the floor. Their hands had been tied behind their backs. Their mouths had been taped shut. Their eyes were wide with fear and streaked with tears. And the two guys who had done this to them were watching TV! They were totally immersed in a college basketball game.

Alison was enraged. Whatever her friends had done to her, however vicious and treacherous they'd been, they at the *very* least deserved the full attention of their home invaders. Instead, they were being disrespected and ignored. Even in the darkness of Kellyn's walk-in closet, Alison knew her mood ring was turning black.

The two bedroom burglars cheered like frat boys in a sports bar. Just as their favorite player took a free throw, a ball of fire blasted straight into the TV screen, blowing it to bits. The two guys shrieked in fright and turned around to see Alison standing by the sliding panel.

She gave Kellyn, Dorinda, and the two guys a moment to drink in her presence before shooting flames into the lights and plunging the room into darkness. Backlit beautifully by the lush LA sunset, Alison was suddenly a shadowy figure with glowing red fingers. Even in the darkness of Kellyn's mother's bedroom, Alison knew the two quaking bad guys weren't going to put up too much of a fight.

Downstairs in the living room, Nick was still dancing, accompanied by the human beat-boxing of Boxer Shorts Guy. Their performances were cut short when Alison herded the two bedroom invaders shame-faced into the room, their hands tied and their mouths taped. Kellyn and Dorinda, white-faced and shaken, walked in behind them.

"Did I tell you to stop dancing?" said David to Nick, who was forced to start doing his Soulja Boy steps again.

"Nice sidekicking." Alison smiled.

"Nice superheroing," said David. "Now leave 'em wanting

more!"

"Pick up your phones," commanded Alison to the party-goers, who immediately started filming Nick doing his dance.

"Call the police!" she said, exasperated. "But wait till I'm gone. Wait till I'm back in my . . . uh . . ."

She looked to David for help.

"Lair?" he suggested.

"It's nicer than a lair. It's a tastefully decorated hideaway with awesome views of the hills and the ocean. That's where I hang out when I'm not fighting crime."

David gestured toward the door. She nodded and turned to go.

"Who *are* you?" asked Kellyn.

Alison looked back around at the inquisitive, nodding, grateful faces of the partygoers, whose possessions, night, and, in some cases, lives she'd saved. She knew she had to make this good.

She held two clenched fists up by her face. Within seconds, both fists were engulfed in flames. The Plus One Party guests gasped as one. With a dramatic flourish, Alison opened her hands.

"They call me Hottie. But for those of you with short attention spans . . ."

Alison spun around and let the fire blast from her fingertips. She whirled her left hand in a circle and slashed her right hand in a triangle. Then she swept out of the house, leaving the partygoers slack-jawed and staring at the memento she'd left behind. A fiery representation of her *H* logo was burned into the wall. In fact, it wasn't just burned into the wall. It was also burned into the other Picasso that was still hanging there.

★ ★ ★

"You kids have fun at your fancy dress party?" asked Designated
Dean as he drove the Honda back into the heart of Los Angeles.

As oblivious to his question as he was to their hidden agenda,
Alison and David huddled in the backseat, ignoring the clutter
and month-old pizza, breathless with excitement.

"That was . . . I can't even think of words," she gasped. "I
need a new superpower that would describe how amazing that
was."

"Superlatives?" suggested David.

"When I'm Hottie, I'm awesome. When I'm her, everything I say is cool. Everyone was blown away by her. But it's
me! I thought nothing could ever be better than the first time
you wear an outfit you know no one else has, but this . . . it's
like you get to wear a whole new person. And she's fantastic! I
wish I could be her the whole time and not have to ever go back
to being Ordinary Alison. People are gonna be dreaming about
me tonight. . . ."

David felt momentarily deflated by her unchecked vanity.
But then she went on.

"And I really got it, David, for the first time, I really understood the whole superhero thing. Most of the people at that
party have been mean to me, but none of them deserved to get
robbed. I wanted to save them. I put their safety over my hurt
feelings. . . ."

David smiled and shook his head. She never stopped surpris-
ing him.

"So I get to feel great about myself and I don't have to feel bad about burning down half of Kellyn's house. I win! Sucks *not* to be me!"

Adrenaline was pumping through her veins like a Red Bull tidal wave. She felt alive and electric.

"Let's do more. Let's find more crime. Let's save more people. Let's do another mission. Let's . . . oh *no* . . ."

"What?" said David, worried by her sudden change of tone.

"We've got another mission. We've got to save my ass 'cos my dad and Carmen are gonna notice I bailed on her idiot interview."

Carmen was quivering with barely restrained fury when she made her way out to the pool to confront Alison. Her stepdaughter was sitting with her feet in the water, laughing loudly and inappropriately and in the company of a short, scrawny youth wearing a snakeskin cowboy hat and a grimy-looking ball of lard whose mere proximity to the water made Carmen make a mental note to have the pool drained.

"It's not enough that you treat me with so little respect. I'm used to it. But this was important. This was to highlight my charity work; it could have brought in donations, it could have changed lives, and for you to simply walk away is astonishing to me. . . ."

Alison glanced over Carmen's shoulder and saw her father and the *Brentwood* reporter approaching the pool. She let approximately one second tick by before letting herself tear up a little.

"But Carmen, you *inspired* me," she said tremulously. "I was so moved by everything that you stand for, I went out and made two homeless friends." Alison sighed. "But I guess I can't do anything right."

Carmen wasn't buying this for a second. But Roger and the *Brentwood* hack were now standing by her side.

Wiping her eyes, Alison said, "Daddy, these are my friends David and Dean. I thought it would be okay to bring them home, but apparently only Carmen is allowed to help people. . . ."

"That's not true at all," said an uneasy Carmen. "It's just that I don't know these boys. They didn't come to me through the appropriate channels."

"So they don't really count?" Alison looked at Designated Dean. "Tell everybody where you live, Dean."

"In the garage," mumbled Designated Dean.

"That's right." Alison nodded. "In a garage. With rats and roaches. He never takes a shower. He doesn't know where his next meal is coming from. He's probably got all sorts of diseases. No wonder he looks like that."

Alison stood up and took her father's hand.

"Daddy, that Bentley you were going to surprise me with on my sixteenth? It's sweet, but I don't need it. *Dean* does. And so do all the other Deans out there."

Roger started tearing up. So did the *Brentwood* hack. Carmen couldn't believe this. The little brat had stolen her spotlight.

Trying hard to produce tears of her own, Carmen walked over to Alison and attempted to show physical affection. Alison tried not to dissolve into giggles as Carmen's hand reached to stroke her hair, then pulled back, went to touch her face, and finally settled for a quick, nervous tap on the shoulder. "You make me so proud, Alison. To think that I've had this kind of influence on you. But I can't let you give up your birthday present. I know how important it is to your father. . . ."

Carmen turned to Designated Dean, trying not to fixate on the fungal substance that seemed to be oozing from between his toes into her previously pristine pool. "Let me help you, Dean. I've got three cars and there's only one of me. . . ."

"Oh my *God*, Carmen," screamed Alison. "You're giving him the *Mercedes!*"

Alison threw her arms around her stepmother. Carmen ground her porcelain veneers into dust and tried to act like she was happy. She'd been about to palm the Prius she'd bought to show she was environmentally aware (but that she secretly hated) off on the fat guy.

"That's right," she found herself saying through gritted teeth. "I know it's not much, but hopefully it'll help you make a fresh start."

"Know what else would help? Beer," mumbled Dean.

Carmen saw the *Brentwood* reporter scribbling furiously in her notepad. *Just smile,* she told herself. *Whatever you do, just smile. It's only a car. Everyone who matters in LA is going to read this!*

Roger looked from his daughter to his smiling wife. They were both amazing, kindhearted, and generous. He was the luckiest man in the world.

"Look at the time. It's, *wow*, almost ten o'clock. We should get back to the interview," said Carmen, desperate to direct all the attention back to her and her charitable ways.

Alison watched her father, her stepmother, and the reporter make their way back to the house, then she jumped into the pool, disappearing beneath the surface.

A moment later, she burst back up, breathless, soaked, and gasping with laughter. This was the *best* end to the *best* night ever. She'd made an awesome superhero debut and she'd manipulated Carmen into giving up her favorite car, which meant that she'd be riding to future Hottie missions in comfort.

As Alison laughed, she started to become aware that the water around her was bubbling and simmering. This made her even more ebullient. Splashing water at the two boys, she looked David in the eye and shot him her most dazzling smile. "Still wanna check out the Apple Store?"

He shook his head no.

"So come on in!"

Even though David was not a strong swimmer, he lowered himself into the Coles' pool. And as Alison swam up to him, laughing wildly, high on her whole night, David wondered if the chlorine in the pool might be having some sort of strange effect on him. The more he looked at Alison, the closer she got, she seemed to be moving in slow motion.

THIRTY-FIVE

Monday, Sept. 23

Time: 8:30 P.M.

Location: Laurel Canyon Dog Park

Crime: Attempted Shih Tzu Abduction

Method of Crime Prevention: Leash Set Alight as Miscreant Grabbed for It

Level of Firepower: Friendly Fire

Cool Catchphrase: "Hot Dog!"

Wednesday, Sept. 25

Time: 6:20 P.M.

Location: Little Tokyo Shopping Center, Roller Derby Arena
Crime: Attempted Assault on Star of Rolling Thunderettes by Bad Losers from Defeated Opponents
Method of Crime Prevention: Assailants' Skates Blasted by Flames
Level of Firepower: Five-Alarm Chili
Cool Catchphrase: "This Wheel's on Fire!"

Thursday, Sept. 26

Time: 5:15 P.M.

God, her eyes are amazing, thought David, his mind wandering, as it had all the way through his attempt to update *Hottie: Year One,* his archive of Alison's adventures and her ever-increasing prowess.

Lying down on his bed, he let his thoughts stray further. *Her laugh. She's got this one special laugh that comes out when she's at her most alive, when it really hits her how incredible she is, and I bet I'm the only one who's ever heard it,* he thought, his mind wandering as it had been ever since the previous Saturday night.

Then he went back to updating the archive. Then his mind wandered again to the way her breath felt on his neck when she'd hugged him and said he was her best friend. Then he picked up his phone and started to call her. Then he put the phone down and stared at the screen saver he'd made of the picture Alison had sent when she was choosing Hottie costumes, the one where she wore the pink hot pants. Then he picked up the phone again. Then he lay back down on his bed, stared up at the ceiling, and said, quietly and unhappily, "How did this happen?"

David was no stranger to crushes, infatuations, and brief, doomed obsessions. But up to this point, the objects of his desire had always been fictional. Up to this point, he always knew there was little chance that he'd ever have a real-life encounter with a Darqmoon, an Emma Frost, or a Huntress. And even if he did, he wasn't for a moment deluding himself that he'd forge any kind of connection with them. Like the one he had with Alison.

Toenail and the others had hooted with derision when, in a moment of weakness, he'd admitted out loud that he thought he and Alison had chemistry. But it had turned out to be true. Beyond their roles as superhero and sidekick—"Maybe more mentor than sidekick," he corrected himself—they'd developed a real friendship.

With Toenail and Odor Eater, Tiny Head and Phlegmy, the only way to express affection was through insult, and sometimes David wasn't entirely sure that they were even expressing affection. When he was with Alison, she was comfortable enough to show him sides of herself he was sure no one else had ever seen. And if she was that comfortable, if their friendship was that close, then it was only logical that the next step was . . .

That was where David got confused. Comic books were no help here. He and Alison didn't fit any existing superhero archetypes: they weren't Superman and Lois Lane, neither were they Batman and Catwoman or even Daredevil and Elektra. But maybe that was a good thing. Maybe the fact that he was a normal guy would keep her grounded, but his appreciation for her super side would always make her feel special.

He pulled a pillow over his face and moaned into it. He wasn't going to sleep tonight.

His mind had been throwing up and dismissing similar scenarios all week. Ever since the aftermath of the Plus One Party a week earlier, he'd been unable to concentrate; he'd feel close to tears one minute and almost exploding with happiness the next. He counted the minutes till he could see Alison again. At the same time he wished he could avoid her for fear of how he'd act around her.

Had she noticed the change in him? Hard to say. David remembered the dog park mission. The way she'd stroked the fur of the frightened shih tzu. The way she'd let it lick her nose. "That dogette was *so* cute," she'd gushed on the way home. "I wish I had a little pet. But I'd suck at looking after it. I can't even look after a *bag*. I'd forget to walk it. Or I wouldn't remember to feed it."

Without even thinking, David had replied, "I'd do it."

Alison had looked at him like she wasn't sure if he was messing with her. "You would?"

David had felt himself turning red. He'd started to say, "I'd do anything for . . ." Luckily, Designated Dean picked that moment to let loose a belch that could be heard several streets away and David was spared further embarrassment. He winced at the memory but continued to torture himself. Had he been staring at her too hard? Had he been overly tactile? He found himself touching her to emphasize important superhero points when they were together. But maybe she liked that. But what if she didn't?

This was ridiculous. He needed to get this out of his system. His phone rang. It was her! It wasn't her. The display showed a picture of a toenail. It had been so long since David had talked to Toenail, it took him a second to work out who was calling. He let it go to message. He hadn't talked to *any* of his friends in what felt like months. What did he have in common with them anymore? They spent their nights playing Dungeons & Dragons 3-D while he was out fighting injustice with a girl with eyes so green he felt like he could lose himself inside them. *"God,"* he groaned in frustration. He needed to express his feelings and then put an end to it, one way or another. David grabbed his phone, called Alison, let it ring twice, then hung up. What the hell was he thinking? He had nothing to say. He needed to write it all down. A prepared speech that articulated everything. He had all night to work on it. A second later, his phone rang. He stared at the burning *H* symbol. David knew he was in no state to talk to Alison. He decided not to answer.

"Hello," he said into the phone.

"Hey, did you just call me and hang up? You know I hate that. . . ."

"Did I? Are you sure it was me? I just got in. . . ."

"You're a freak; you know it was you. Listen. I was thinking about branding us, the whole team. You, me, the Hottiemobile, even Double D. I could make us all costumes with the logo. You wouldn't have to wear the wig or the dress. Unless you want to. You might be wearing them now for all I know. Oh my God, Double D might be wearing them now! Can you imagine? Ewww . . ."

David lay on his bed, the phone to his ear, listening to Alison talk, knowing that the sound of her voice would be echoing through his head for the rest of the night until he finally fell asleep. And then she'd be all over his dreams. . . .

THIRTY-SIX

Alison sat on the stairs leading up to the closed door of her parents' bedroom and listened to Carmen acting like she wasn't about to cry. She vividly recalled wishing that someone would have the guts to say to her stepmother, "What does that Shine Down Love stuff even mean? Who does it help? Where does the money go?" How unbelievable was it that her wish had actually come to pass? Not in words, not exactly, but through an ever-more-agonizing series of phone calls. Carmen had heard through her nutritionist who'd heard through her tennis coach who'd heard through her colorist who'd heard through her reflexologist that her *Brentwood* interview had been killed. *The one that everyone who mattered in LA was going to see!* There was no way to prove a conspiracy theory, but when Carmen learned that the pages meant for her stirring story were now to be devoted to some decrepit Tinseltown widow and her million-dollar dog shelter, it was obvious the old guard had closed ranks to slap down the new blood.

"You know what, I'm fine," trilled Carmen as sympathetic calls from her paid circle of sycophants poured in. "I don't have the death of another tree on my conscience. I don't need publicity. But we could have done so much more, we could have helped so many more people, that's the only thing that upsets me. But I'm *fine*. . . ."

Sitting on the stairs, a position she'd taken up some forty minutes ago when she'd heard the first howl of pain, Alison had settled in for a delicious morning's worth of cackling and vindication. She was about to text David with the hilarious news. But then, as Carmen attempted to convince yet another caller that she felt *fine*, Alison found herself experiencing something that seemed a lot like sympathy.

What if her shunned stepmom had a breakdown? What if Carmen drank herself unconscious or drove her Prius off Mulholland Drive? Forty minutes earlier, these would have been items she could have ticked off her wish list. Now she was shocked to feel slight pangs of concern. She'd won a decisive victory against her stepmother, but she wasn't a malicious girl. Besides, she reasoned, her dad had already lost one wife. For his sake, maybe she should take the morning off school and hang around the house just in case. . . .

David couldn't take another night like the previous one. He needed to consult an expert. "Hey, uh, Double D, you've been around girls, right?" he asked, trying and failing to sound casual and unconcerned.

"Around 'em. Under 'em. Over 'em; you know how I get down," said Designated Dean, who, in return for the unexpected gift of Carmen's Mercedes, was now Alison and David's unpaid but uncomplaining chauffeur.

There was no way David could discuss his emotional predicament with Toenail, Tiny Head, Phlegmy, or Odor Eater. He wasn't going to bring it up in therapy with Dr. Mee because of the deadly ukulele. Clearly, he couldn't talk to his mother. Which left Designated Dean. Alison had texted that she'd be late for school, so if he was going to ask Double D for advice in matters of the heart, now was the time. But he couldn't just come right out and ask him. Instead, he invited Dean to lunch at In-N-Out Burger. But the horror of watching Double D gnaw his way through a Double-Double stifled any questions about matters of the heart. Finally, on the fart-fueled drive back to BHHS, David brought up his *real* reason for seeking out the older boy.

"Say you were friends with someone, really close friends, but then you started to feel like you wanted to be more than friends with them, but you didn't know if they wanted to be more than friends with *you* . . ."

Designated Dean started flipping through the Mercedes' hundreds of Sirius satellite radio stations. David knew he was losing him.

"What do I do? Write her a letter, send her an email, burn her a CD, get her flowers—"

"You could compare the nice party dresses you both like to wear," interrupted Designated Dean, almost frothing over with derision. "C'mon, Eels, whatever species you're supposed to be, you're an embarrassment to it. This is how a man handles himself. You put it out there, you make your move. *You and me? Yes or no?*"

David was confused. "But what if she says no?"

"You get back on the horse. You move on to the next one. And there's always a next one."

"But what if . . ."

"Hey, I told you how a man handles himself. You got more questions, ask your friends at I'maprincessonalittlepinkpony. com."

THIRTY-SEVEN

Lego accessories were out. The flaming *H* logo was *in*! As Alison made her midday appearance at BHHS, she saw style monkeys with *H* earrings. She saw students with her *H* temporary-tattooed on their ankles and necks. She saw the *H* on armbands and backpacks. And yet no one was looking at *her* with admiration and awe. No one wanted her picture on their phones. No one made the connection between *H* and *Hottie* and *her*.

When Alison had shown up at school the previous Monday, the mysterious appearance of the weird flamethrower chick at Kellyn's Plus One Party was the talk of the hallway.

"Who *was* that girl?"

"How did she *do* that?"

"You're so gullible. It was all a stunt. That Kellyn girl arranged the whole thing!"

"Shut up, you idiot, I did not!"

Alison had let the conversations swirl around her, loving that everyone in school was talking about her without actually *knowing* that they were talking about her. She had walked through the school, listening to all the theories and the exaggerated accounts of what had happened last Saturday night. ("Dude, she shot electricity out of her *eyeballs!*")

They were obsessed with her and they didn't even know it. This was the perfect revenge on all those who had shunned her. "Should I tell them?" she asked herself. "Or should I let them keep on talking about me?"

The answer didn't matter. Ten seconds later, Alison had been dethroned as the school's premier topic of conversation. In the middle of a discussion about whether the flamethrower chick could more accurately be classified as a freak or a mutant, someone screamed, "Bianca White's back!"

Unlike Alison, Bianca White wasn't able to make an anonymous entrance. Rumors had been rife online that the BHHS eighth grader who played Treasure Spinney's bff on *Signal Hill* was not hitting it off with the actress in real life. The show's message boards were abuzz with speculation that Treasure had accused Bianca of *stealing* her favorite imported peanut butter and replacing it with identical jars filled with an inferior supermarket brand. And now Bianca was *back* in school. Was she fired? Did she quit? What was going on? That was all anyone wanted to talk about.

Alison remembered feeling deflated as the school immediately forgot about her. But as she looked around the hallway, it was clear they hadn't forgotten her fashion sense. Then it hit her. It wasn't *her* fashion sense. It was David's *H.* The most fashion-conscious school in America was currently having its dress code dictated by the least fashion-conscious dork in America. Alison laughed out loud. No one reacted to her amusement. No one even seemed to notice she was there. Well, almost no one . . .

"I just want you to know I didn't approve of how that whole thing went down," said T, falling into step with her as she wandered into the hallway. . . .

The freshman presidency was buried so far in her past she had no clue what he was talking about. Alison then started to remember the remedial way she'd acted around him the last couple of times they'd been together. *Not this time,* she assured herself. Then she remembered the way his hand felt holding hers. She remembered the way he looked in his fire uniform. She remembered the way just thinking about him sent her firepower shooting out of control. *She'd roasted pigeons!* But things were different now. She had a superpower and secret identity. Thinking of words and forming them into sentences in front of T was *nothing.*

"If it means anything, I seriously thought about stepping down as a gesture of solidarity."

"Wow," replied Alison.

"But would that have served the greater good?"

"Uh . . . no?" ("You can be *funny,*" mourned Inner Alison. "You have things to say that are interesting and smart. Why can't you say them around T?")

"But that doesn't mean you can't have a voice in the decisions that affect you. If there's something you particularly wanted to address as president, you know you've got my ear."

"Nice ear," said Alison. ("You don't say anything forever. Then you say *that?*" raged Inner Alison.)

But T didn't puke. He laughed. He was charmed.

"Seriously, anything you want to discuss. We could talk over lunch. If you don't have a date."

"I'd love a date." ("Whatever," sulked Inner Alison.)

Bianca White was *furious*. She'd remained tight-lipped about the reason for her abrupt departure from *Signal Hill* for a whole week. As a result, she was the constant center of attention and speculation. But today, she'd arrived at the cafeteria, anticipating the usual outbreak of whispers and pointed fingers. No one was looking at her! Every table—the style monkeys, the lacrosse team, the Madrigal Singers, the Mental Dental Collective—was focused on the junior president and his lunch companion.

"You get the feeling we're being watched?" asked T.

"You mean by the new surveillance cameras?" she said.

"No." He laughed, seemingly delighted by her every utterance. "I mean the beady eyes of your friends."

Alison followed his gaze. Kellyn, Dorinda, and the new member of their pre-va circle, Marvelette, did the whole look-but-pretend-you're-not-looking maneuver.

Alison didn't care. If the subject wasn't T's eyes or his mouth, she had no interest.

"They're not really my friends," she said.

"I get that. You're not like them."

Alison stared at T. Could he tell just by looking at her?

"You've got a mind of your own. They don't. Look at the way everybody wants to look like everyone else."

Alison saw him looking at Ginger Becker, whose sailor suit had been altered to include a flaming *H* on the sleeves.

But what if tomorrow she comes to school wearing fluorescent water wings and it totally catches on and everyone forgets about the H? thought Alison. "It's just fashion to them, but it's not to me. I can't just move on to the next thing." The more she thought about this, the more she worried. *I'm not like the other girls. I'm really not.* In David's case that had turned out to be a point in her favor, but what would T think?

Alison fumbled her way toward a question that was suddenly of vital importance. "Would you, if you liked someone, accept everything about them, even if they turned out to be really different from the way you first thought they were? But not different in a bad way. Just different in a . . ." ("Please don't end this by saying 'different in a different way.' *Please*," commanded Inner Alison) ". . . different way," said Alison.

T wasn't entirely sure what she was asking him. But he was aware that his answer was important to her. And he hadn't become junior class president by not knowing how to tell people what they thought they wanted to hear. Speaking slowly and with maximum sincerity, he said, "I think we allow ourselves to be so concerned with outward appearances and with what other people think that we miss the chance to develop really special relationships with people who might not fit into our social circle. I think, at the end of the day, nobody's perfect. I'm as flawed as anyone else, so who am I to not accept someone else's flaws?"

T still wasn't entirely sure what he was saying. But the way

Alison's eyes were shining when he finished talking convinced him that he'd never made more sense.

"Good answer," she said quietly.

The flickering eyes and rapid head-turns had reached epidemic proportions. Cameras were clicking, fingers were texting, whispers were getting louder. The shunned girl and the junior president. The freshmen looked nervous: Could Alison's star be rising again? The juniors looked disapproving: Would Alison drag T down to her level?

"I guess we're done having lunch," said T, visibly irritated by the attention.

"Oh." Alison was crestfallen.

She'd happily have sat there all day fixating on his—brown? Maybe burnt sienna?— eyes, even if the other students had begun bombarding them with bread rolls.

"Next time, we'll find somewhere more private. Where it's just you and me. Maybe Saturday night. If you're free."

"Oh, I'm free. I'm *so* free."

With that, T got up and walked out of the cafeteria, leaving Alison sitting alone and thinking to herself, *Tingly jingly.*

THIRTY-EIGHT

"Hi, I'm Kayla," chirped the bright orange bleach blonde sitting in the front passenger seat of the Mercedes.

Alison, who was climbing into the car, got an eyeful of the unexpected extra passenger's generous allocation of fake boobage. She shot a questioning look at David, who merely shrugged in reply.

"Love your outfit. That chain's crazy, I need to get one," gushed Kayla to Alison. "Are you a dancer too?"

"Uh, I dance. I have danced. I like to dance," babbled Alison, freaked out by the addition to her superhero crew.

"I'll call you if I get another night like tonight. Three bachelor parties one after another. Help! What would I do without Dean to drop me off and pick me up? He's the *man*! But don't worry, we'll still get you kidlets to your fancy dress party in time."

If Kayla hadn't been in the car, Alison might have told David about Carmen being evaporated from the pages of *Brentwood* and about T Hull asking her out on Saturday night. David might have acted on Designated Dean's advice and confronted her with a blunt "You and me? Yes or no?"

But Kayla was in the car, and they both felt inhibited and uncomfortable. Kayla was anything but. She reapplied fistfuls of makeup while simultaneously sending text messages and squealing, "That's my jam!" whenever she came across a familiar song on the radio.

Alison let herself get lost thinking about Saturday night. What should she wear? What was she going to say? T seemed like the sort of guy who had opinions and convictions. That would take up a slice of the evening. She believed there would, at some point, be kissing. That took care of the end part of the date, but there was still some unaccounted-for time where she would have to speak in actual sentences that made sense. She could ask him about his . . . mongoose? . . . marmoset? . . . *meerkat!* They could compare toothbrush loyalties (did he, like her, owe his startling smile in part to the Oral B CrossAction Revitalizer?).

Maybe David could come over before the date and they could work on it together. He'd come up with *Hottie*. He'd come up with *a-door-able*. He could help her with a few conversational bullet points.

David couldn't stop looking at Alison's mood ring. It had been brown—anxious, nervous—when she got into the car and Kayla said hi. Now it was blue—relaxed, calm. Because of him?

Because of their close proximity? Because of their unspoken bond? Because of their mutual desire to embark on a relationship where they'd be more than friends?

Alison leaned in close to David, ready to ask him about bullet points. David leaned in close, ready to say, "You and me? Yes or no?" when the street was suddenly filled with honking horns and screeching tires.

Classic automobile enthusiasts would have been able to identify the vehicle that was tearing through the Miracle Mile traffic as a 1955 Bandini-Maserati A6 1500.

To Alison and David, it was an old red car being driven by a maniac who cut right in front of the Mercedes, causing Designated Dean to slam on the brakes. The honking didn't stop. Another old red car—this one a 1948 Fiat Stanguellini—had a similarly reckless driver who, in turn, showed equal disregard for the safety of fellow motorists.

Alison and David swapped glances, their previous romantic fogs forgotten.

"You get a bad guy vibe?" she asked.

He nodded. "Floor it, Double D. And crank the police scanner."

"Hey, man, Kayla's got a party to get to," complained Designated Dean, who, by this time, was *sort of* aware that Alison and David were doing more than attending fancy dress parties.

"Yeah," agreed Kayla. "And if no one minds, I like to listen to music to get me in the mood before I go to work."

"No one cares," yelled Alison. "Car goes fast. Police scanner goes on. Fat guy shuts up."

Furious, Kayla turned around. "Listen, little rich girl, some of us have to work for a living; some of us . . ."

Quick as a flash, Alison darted out a glowing finger and touched the tip of Kayla's tongue.

"You bih!" screamed the orange-colored dancer. *"You buh ma tuh! Fuh!"*

Designated Dean hit the gas and switched on the police scanner, which, after a few moments, revealed that several priceless vehicles had been stolen from a private exhibition at the Petersen Automotive Museum.

If Kayla had been able to make herself understood, she'd have called for help. She'd have begged someone to save her from the demonic teenagers who had abducted her and made her an unwilling participant in their sinister ritual. She'd have attempted to describe how the little hateball rocking the bug-eye glasses and the big gold chain had squeezed herself up through the sunroof, how she'd shouted out something like, "Burn rubber!" and how, seconds later, two fireballs flew through the air and smashed into the back tires of the Fiat. She'd have given a blow-by-blow account of the way the Fiat driver lost control of the vehicle, hopped the curb, and ended up driving straight into the fountain outside LA Fitness, the gym where *she* did cardio-boxing! But Kayla's throbbing tongue meant she couldn't speak, so she remained curled up and sneaking scared sips from her water bottle as Designated Dean gained on the Bandini-Maserati.

Designated Dean kept on the Bandini-Maserati's tail, following the car as it sped toward Miracle Mile's famous rock club, the El Rey. The art deco nightspot was crowded with hipsters lined up for that night's Lozenge show. They barely noticed the high-speed chase happening right in front of them. After all, this *was* LA. A night without a frantic getaway was a rarity.

"This is sort of like prom night," said Alison as she started to push her way up through the Mercedes sunroof in preparation for her fire attack on the second stolen vehicle. "You know, all dressed up, being chauffeured around in a fancy car, looking out through the sunroof, the man of my dreams waiting below."

David's stomach lurched. This was it. If there was ever a time for a "You and me? Yes or no?" it was now. Then the Italian car went into reverse.

Designated Dean slowed down as the red car came closer.

Alison pulled herself up and crouched on the roof of the car, ready to ignite at the first sign of trouble.

The Bandini-Maserati stopped a few feet in front of the Mercedes.

The front passenger door opened. A woman dressed in black leather, face hidden inside a black hood, emerged. She stood in front of the red car, hands on hips.

Alison was on the roof of the Mercedes, also placing her hands on her hips, the night breeze causing her jacket to billow out behind her like a cape.

I hope someone films this and puts it on YouTube, she thought. *'Cos there's no way I'm not looking fan-frickin'-tastic right now.*

Neither of them moved.

"It's a standoff," said David, who had poked his head out of the sunroof.

"How long do they usually last?" Alison asked.

"Until someone makes the first move."

The woman in black extended a hand and made the beckoning gesture familiar from a million martial arts movies. Except the beckoning hand didn't usually have such professionally manicured nails.

"She made it," said David.

"And I'm gonna end it. Watch me freak her out."

Alison extended her hand and made the same gesture. Then she relaxed all her fingers except the middle one, which remained extended. And which now had a flame pushing out of its tip.

The woman in black didn't move, didn't react in any way.

"Ooh, tough cookie," mocked Alison. "But I'm tougher and cookier and I bet I can make you pee your panties."

Still no reaction from her black-clad adversary. But from within the hood that obscured her features, two tiny points of white light pierced the darkness.

Alison raised her fingers, started to summon up the emotion necessary to singe the woman's hood, and . . . nothing.

Nothing happened.

Or that's how it seemed. She wasn't standing on top of the Mercedes anymore, about to blast a black-clad, beautifully manicured carjacker. Alison was lost. She felt weightless, floating in space, nothing supporting her. Just endless blackness. She couldn't feel her body; she couldn't utter sounds, much less form words. There were thoughts in her head, but she wasn't thinking them. But they were soothing thoughts. They felt warm and comforting. They were like the tinkly-tonkly sounds old music boxes made. There was a melody swimming around in her head. She'd never heard it before, but it was so familiar. And there was a voice just beneath the music saying her name over and over again.

"*Alison*," it kept repeating. "*Alison*."

"Alison! Alison!" yelled David. He didn't know whether to shake her or slap her across the face or administer CPR. There was nothing about this in the sidekick's manual. In fact, there *was* no sidekick's manual, but David felt he'd ingested enough comic book procedure that he should have been prepared for any emergency. But he hadn't foreseen Alison falling into a trance.

She had suddenly shut down, swaying on top of the Mercedes roof, half humming, half singing a weird, wordless ghostly melody. And that's when the jaded crowd of Lozenge lovers started laughing. They had barely reacted when she'd climbed up on the roof. Bizarrely dressed young girls get up to more outrageous high jinks outside clubs on a nightly basis. They didn't even comment when she faced off against the woman in black. Drivers were always getting into fights. No biggie. But now the woman in the hood had driven off, and it seemed like the girl with the gold chain was paying the price for her wild night. All the El Rey patrons thought that was *hilarious*.

With their laughter ringing in their ears, David and Designated Dean helped Alison down from the roof. They positioned her against the trunk of the car. David removed her glasses and searched her face for signs of recognition. "Get her some water," he told Designated Dean.

"*Tha bih's no geh ma wa,*" said Kayla.

"Can you hear me? Do you know me? Do you know where we are?"

David was starting to panic, both at Alison's catatonic state and the prospect of CPR when he'd never kissed anything other than the back of his hand and he knew his breath wasn't as fresh as it might have been.

He started to go in for the kiss when Alison woke up. David took a few stumbling steps backward, surprised and embarrassed.

"What happened to you?" he said.

"What happened to *you*?" she replied, noting his red-faced discomfort.

"Do you remember anything?"

Alison felt scattered, disoriented. "You need to be more specific," she mumbled, aware she wasn't making total sense. "I remember lots of things. I remember telling people that Nadia Turner was totally gonna win *American Idol*. She just picked the wrong song."

David stared at her. "Do you remember being on the roof? The standoff with the woman in black?"

"Sure do. I made her pee her panties."

"And then?"

"Then what? Superhero duty done for the night."

"There was no superhero duty done. There was no action. You froze up. Or you shut down. There was an unexpected occurrence. . . ."

Alison stared at David.

"Something occurred that was unexpected," he repeated as if to a small child.

Alison felt her memories fall back into place. "I remember getting ready to blast the woman in black. . . ."

"Then that's the last thing you remember. 'Cuz you didn't.

You just stood there. And you sang. And she drove away in her stolen car."

Alison took a second to process this information.

"I sang? In public? I've conquered my biggest fear! Was I good?"

"I've heard better." Designated Dean shrugged. "It was all kinda woooooo-wooooo," he mewled, imitating her ethereal lullaby.

"Yeah, you suh. You cah si fo shi!" taunted Kayla.

As Designated Dean continued to imitate Alison's spectral song, David appeared deep in thought. He mouthed soundless words to himself. He counted on his fingers. He stroked his chin. He shook his head.

Finally, David slapped a palm off his forehead.

"Of course! How could I have been so dumb? Why didn't I see this coming?"

"What?"

"Supervillain!"

•

THIRTY-NINE

As the Mercedes drove back down Fairfax Avenue toward his condo, David became more animated and more excited. "What's the opposite of fire?" he asked. Not waiting for an answer, he continued, "Water? Maybe she's Waterwoman? Or Wettie! Maybe Wettie's come up with some kind of . . . I don't know, I'm just guessing here . . . invisible liquid kryptonite that renders you powerless. . . ."

"It was her eyes. Something in her eyes. Her eyes. Okay? Eyes," said Alison, trying to explain that the woman in black had put her in a trancelike state, surrounding her with a warm, soothing feeling that, she surmised, was how it felt to be back in the womb.

But David couldn't get comfortable with Mesmer Eyes or Dr.

Womb or The Soother. Not when Wettie was so perfect. "Polar opposites pitted against each other. It's *classic!*"

David knew he was talking too much and too fast. He knew Alison wasn't really listening, but he couldn't help himself. He *loved* this stuff. He yammered a mile a minute about the relationship between superheroes and supervillains and how they existed to destroy each other but how neither could function without the other.

Designated Dean parked the Mercedes outside David's condo. He was still talking.

"I'll tell you what she's doing right this minute: quivering with fear. She knows that she gave up the advantage. She's lost the element of surprise. I've read enough comics to know that Wettie knows next time you meet, you're giving it back to her a hundred times harder than she gave it to you. Your clashes are going to be *epic*." David paused for breath, then started up again. "I'll start researching all her possible flaws. She'll never put you in a trance again, I'll tell you that. You just do what Darqmoon did in Volume 5: *The Revenge of Shin Sun*. You find the one thing that really matters to you and you hold on to that. And you use it to push your consciousness through. We'll work on it this weekend. . . ."

Alison, who had barely said a word during the entire journey, suddenly spoke up. "Can't Saturday. Got a date."

David didn't immediately reply. The thudding of his heart made him think he was about to drop dead. He stared straight ahead and tried to concentrate on breathing.

Alison beamed.

"With T Hull. The Junior President of Cuteness? Who I've

nursed a mild crushette on for about a million years but, obviously, could never admit to till now. And who, it turns out, likes me back." She nodded happily at David and held up a palm, expecting to be high-fived.

David said nothing and left her hanging. She touched his arm. Once again, his heart pounded.

"But listen, I really need your help. We need to come up with a list of things that I can talk about so it seems like I'm a brilliant conservationist."

David, who had never before corrected her, mumbled, "Conversationalist." And he didn't say it with a smile.

"See, right there." She laughed. "That's why I need you."

"You don't need me," said David.

He had to get out of the car. He was either going to sulk in silence or he was going to yell at her or he was going to blurt, "You and me? Yes or no?" at the exact wrong moment.

He opened the door. Alison reached out to hug him. He evaded her arms and climbed out of the car, aware she was staring at him, perplexed.

"So I'll call you, okay? About the conserv . . . the conversationalism . . . ? And the supervillain."

"Whatever," muttered David as he walked away from the car, embarrassed he'd made such a graceless exit.

"What was *that* about?" asked Alison, watching David unlock the gate to his Mediterranean-style condo as the Mercedes drove away.

Designated Dean said nothing. His mind was on the last thing Kayla said to him when he dropped her off at her bachelor party before driving David and Alison back their respective homes.

"*Do bo co ba to pi me uh.*"

Did that mean, "Don't bother coming back to pick me up," or "Do bother to pick me up"?

Alison repeated her question. "Double D, what's going on with David?"

"Who?"

"*Eels.*" She sighed. "Did he seem like he was in a weird mood? Is there something going on with him? Does he ever talk to you about stuff?"

"Ah, the kid's fine. He's just hung up on some chick. Doesn't know how to get out of the best friend ghetto and make the move to Ass Town, Population: Ass. Thinks she'll laugh in his face if he tells her how he feels. Which she will. He'll be fine, though. I gave him some good advice. I told him to . . ."

Alison didn't hear Designated Dean's advice. She didn't hear it at first because she thought it was adorable that David had got himself a little crush and resolved to be there for him the way he'd been for her.

Then she thought about all the time she and David had spent together and the way that he looked at her sometimes. And all the times he phoned her and then hung up without leaving a message. *We're* friends, she told herself. But there was something about the way he acted around her that reminded her of the way she acted around T.

"We're *friends*," Alison said out loud.

"Yeah, sure, you and me're friends." Designated Dean yawned. "But me and that chick Kayla? *That's* a whole different situation. We're gonna do some damage, I'll tell you that. . . ."

Designated Dean continued muttering to himself. After a moment, he glanced in the rearview mirror. Alison was wiping her eyes.

"Hey, you okay back there?" he asked.

"I'm fine," she managed to whisper.

"First Eels turns weird, now you. You kids must've caught something off each other."

FORTY

Alison spent Saturday wrestling with how to deal with The Whole Eels Thing. She even thought about canceling her big night with T. But after a morning of calling David and neglecting to leave messages and an afternoon spent composing and deleting emails, she couldn't wait for T to show up for what turned out to be the Best Date Ever. He arrived on time, insisting on meeting and impressing her father. Then he drove her to their surprise date: a laser show at the Hollywood Bowl!

Cheeseball? Absolutely. That's why he chose it. He wasn't just some deadly earnest, cause-oriented snooze button: *he had a sense of humor.* He was considerate enough to cover potential conversation gaps by giving them both the laser show and the opportunity to laugh at the type of audience member who sincerely thought the laser show was awesome. Also, he'd brought a picnic basket from Joan's on Third, the Hollywood gourmet café that counted Reese Witherspoon, Jake Gyllenhaal, and Kirsten Dunst among its regular clientele.

They had entertainment, they had Joan's famous pumpkin cupcakes, and, as it turned out, they were not troubled by conversation gaps. They compared stepmothers: he sympathized with Alison's situation and noted that he'd gotten very lucky when Birgit the beautiful Swede moved into the Hull family home. They spoke about their hopes and dreams: he was passionate both about bringing irritation—irrigation?—to drought-stricken African villages and taking his father's high-end speaker business to the next level; she told him about AlDoKe and how, even though she was currently being shunned by her friends, she still hoped one day that the spa would become a reality.

Again, T was sympathetic. "Friendships are fragile things," he said. "You never know what's going to break them apart. You never know what's going on in someone else's head. Something small and insignificant to you could be the biggest thing ever to someone else."

Which brought Alison back to the issue she'd been strenuously avoiding all day. The Best Date Ever was not the appropriate arena to bring up The Whole Eels Thing. T would probably know exactly how she should deal with The Whole Eels Thing but if she brought it up it would ruin the mood; she'd get sad and start feeling guilty, like she had all last night even though, rationally, she knew she had nothing to feel guilty about.

She sighed heavily, feeling like she'd just ruined the Best

Date Ever. But T, proving his point that you never know what's going on in someone else's head, took her melancholy silence as a nonverbal go-ahead to kiss her. Which he did. Just once, soft and sweet enough to ensure that she'd never forget the laser show.

T drove his Chevy Impala through the darkened streets of Brentwood. Apparently, Alison's senses had been malfunctioning during the previous part of her life because they had *never* worked as great as they were right now. The lights of LA had never seemed so bright. The smell of his . . . *cologne? Natural musk?* . . . Whatever it was, it swam around her head. The taste of his lips stayed on hers. She never wanted to eat anything or drink anything or do anything that might remove it. Although this would make brushing her teeth difficult.

Her hearing seemed to have improved as well, because she found herself listening to the *greatest and most moving piece of music she had ever heard.*

"What's that song?" she asked. The information on the satellite LED identified the tune as "With Every Heartbeat," by someone called Robyn. Neither the title nor the artist meant anything to her. But she knew one thing: this pulsing, melancholic declaration of heartache and devotion would always remind her of tonight. They let the song play on, neither of them breaking its spell.

"Pull over here," she said as Robyn faded away and the Best Date Ever drew to its end.

"It's okay. I know you don't live in a hut by the railroad tracks. I don't mind dropping you at your door."

"Where someone might be watching. So pull over here."

T stopped the car. A kiss at the laser show was a perfect romantic memory, but she wanted more.

Alison pulled him close, her hand stroking the back of his neck as their mouths met. Suddenly, he gasped in pain, jerked away from her, and banged his head against the driver's side window.

"OW!" he yelled. "Jesus!"

"What? *What is it?*" said Alison, shocked. *Oh God, did I bite him? Please, tell me I didn't bite him. I'm a good kisser. Warren always thought I was a good kisser. But maybe he wasn't a good kisser, so he wouldn't know. . . .*

But even as she argued with herself, she could smell the burning. She saw T touch a hand to the back of his head and wince with pain.

That didn't happen, Alison told herself. *That* can't *happen.*

He looked at her, unsure of what was happening, taken aback by her reaction and the expression of fear spreading across her face.

"So many unknown factors can start a fire," she murmured. "Leaking gas lines, head gaskets, cracked radiators . . ."

T felt the night was lurching toward a bad end. It had all gone so well, and now she was acting weird. He tried to laugh off the tension that suddenly filled the Chevy.

"Hey, I got an electric shock or maybe we have better chemistry than I thought. Don't worry about it."

He reached for her again. Alison snatched her hand away before he could touch her and struggled to open the door.

"We don't have to do anything. Stay in the car. I'll drop you at your door. It's fine."

"It's not fine. I can't be close to you. I can't touch you." *I can't touch you!*

She knew how she sounded. The scared little schoolgirl suddenly realizing she was way out of her depth. And that made T sound like the mature, experienced guy trying to allay her fears. "Alison, we don't have to rush things. We can go as slow as you like. I understand, okay? You're scared of getting hurt."

Walking the two blocks back to her house, Alison laughed bitterly as she replayed the end of the Best Date Ever and especially T's final sentence. So caring, so empathetic.

Except there's no way in the world he would ever understand if he knew what she really was. *Fortunately*, she just had the perfect night with the perfect guy. *Unfortunately*, if she got excited around him, she would set him on fire. And not in a good way.

She had spent the minutes before the Best Date Ever constructing cute couple names for herself and T. But there wasn't going to be a Tomlison or an Alimmy or a T&A. A kiss at the laser show was all she would ever have. And why? Because of her emotions. Her stupid emotions.

She laughed again, a long, hard, bitter laugh that died in her throat the moment she saw David trying to act like he wasn't watching her from inside the Mercedes parked near her house.

FORTY-ONE

The rational part of David (aka, the part of him that had not been completely overruled by his rampaging hormones and doomed infatuation) was painfully aware that he should not have spent his Saturday night staking out Alison's house.

Even the hormonal part had to admit there was no plan. When she came home, what was he going to do? Confront her? Accuse her? Finally bust out the "You and me? Yes or no?" All he knew was he couldn't stay home, obsessing over what she was doing on her big date.

Which is why he was crouching down in the back of the Mercedes while Designated Dean snored in the front. Ironically, having spent two and a half hours waiting for her to return, David almost jumped out of his skin when Alison banged on the window.

Leaving Designated Dean slumbering in the Mercedes, they walked in awkward silence for a few moments. This was what she got for avoiding The Whole Eels Thing. It was ten forty-five on a Saturday night and she was walking down an empty, chilly Brentwood block with her best friend. The best friend who had suddenly developed feelings for her that neither of them could ignore but neither wanted to acknowledge.

David knew it was up to him to say something first. He'd been caught stalking her. But he could be cool about it, not sarcastic or wounded or needy or defensive. He could break the oppressive silence by quipping, "If one of us doesn't say something soon, we'll be having breakfast in Santa Monica."

And she would have laughed and the tension would have been broken and they could have talked like the friends they were.

Instead, he said, "So did you have fun on your *date?*" and he sounded sarcastic, wounded, needy, and defensive.

Alison's heart sank. She'd hoped he would say something funny and break the oppressive silence and they could have talked like friends. He was the only person who could understand what had happened at the end of the Best Date Ever. But now? If she told him she couldn't touch the boy she adored without burning him alive, he would laugh.

"What do you want me to say, David? I see that you're hurting and I'm sorry, even though it's not my fault. I wish things could be the way you want, but they're not the way I want either."

Sticking with the sarcastic, wounded, needy, and defensive

tactic that had served him so well, he sneered, "Oh, right, when has anything not been the way you want *ever?*"

She gaped at him. "Have we even met? Do you even know me?" Since she'd been shunned by Kellyn and Dorinda, she'd come to rely on David. He never made her feel stupid. He was genuinely interested in her. But for him to say something like *that* . . .

Everything was going wrong. He wasn't saying what he wanted to say. He was showing her he really *was* the tragic loser she'd met the day of the election.

Alison could see he hated how he was acting.

"I'm flattered, David. I'm *so* flattered. You're so smart and funny. There're so many girls out there who would be lucky to . . ."

This wasn't working. Alison made a mental note to excise the word *flattered* from sentences designed to let guys down gently because it tended to make them look as if they were about to vomit.

"You're my best friend. We've been through stuff no one else will ever understand. Why does that have to change? Why can't things stay the way they are? You, me, Double D, the Hottiemobile, the after-school superhero stuff, the cool catchphrases?"

"And I just forget how I feel? Keep it to myself? Don't make you uncomfortable? Pretend that everything's the same?"

She nodded. He'd summed it up perfectly. That's what she wanted.

"Why would I do that?"

"Because I'm pretty?" She smiled hopefully.

If he laughed, if he remembered how much they shared, they'd be okay.

Instead, he just nodded. "Yes, you are. That's the problem."

Fortunately, he was her best friend. *Unfortunately*, he was in love with her and that was killing their friendship.

Upset and frustrated, she said, "You helped me control my emotions—why can't you control yours?"

David had a million replies to that question, but he knew they would all make him look even worse. So he turned and hurried back to the car, secure in the knowledge that Designated Dean would never notice he was close to tears.

FORTY-TWO

On the worst night of her life, the night she discovered she could never be close to anyone she desired, the night she lost her best friend, Alison walked into the house and straight into Carmen. She looked meaningfully and disapprovingly at her watch. Alison ran upstairs and slammed the door behind her.

Audrey Hepburn gazing down from the wall. The stars glittering down from the ceiling. The closet full of shoes and bags and hats and tops. None of it mattered. None of it made her feel better. *What a teenage cliché I am,* she thought as she hurled herself down on her bed and buried her face in the pillows. There was a knock on the door.

Daddy, she thought. *Thank God. Someone who cares. Someone who won't judge, who just loves me.*

"Go away!" she screamed, knowing that would make him more concerned and more comforting.

Another knock. Then the door opened.

"Are you okay?" asked Carmen.

Carmen? Where was the comfort? Where was the love? Was she sitting down? On Alison's bed?

"I'm just guessing. Is it a boy?"

There was something a little off in the tone of her voice. She sounded . . . gentle. Compassionate, even.

Alison turned around to see if her visitor was really Kelly Ripa, the epitome of gentleness and compassion. God, if only her dad had married Kelly Ripa!

But Kelly Ripa wasn't sitting on her bed looking gentle and compassionate. Carmen was.

"Boys with an *s*," said Alison.

"Uh-oh," said New Carmen.

"One I like too much. One likes *me* too much."

"I'm sorry."

"And now I can't see either one of them ever again."

"I'm sure it's not that bad."

"It is. Terrible things happen when I'm around either one of them."

"Did one of them take out a restraining order keeping you from getting within twenty miles of them?"

"Uh, no. Not yet."

"Did one of them hire a hit man to run you over?"

"No."

"Anyone stuck pins in voodoo dolls with locks of your hair attached?"

"I don't think so," Alison replied, surprised that Carmen was taking the time to have an actual conversation with her. And seemed actually *concerned* about her. Any other time, Alison would have had her guard up, ready for the inevitable put-down, but tonight, for some reason, she didn't think that was going to happen.

"Then you know nothing about terrible things."

Carmen suddenly winced and clutched her arm like she'd been stabbed.

"What is it?" yelped Alison.

Then Carmen grinned. She'd been making a joke about the voodoo doll. She was funny! Or at least she was taking a shot at it, and that was enough to make Alison laugh.

Carmen extended a hand and said, "Hi, I'm Carmen."

"I know. We met at the wedding," replied Alison before she realized what was happening. "Oh. You're saying that because you think we should start over."

Carmen nodded. "Don't you?"

She leaned forward, pulled a pillow from the bed, and made herself comfortable. *She looks so young,* thought Alison. *Not evil at all.*

"I don't know what I'm doing, Alison. Not as far as being a mother goes, anyway. The more I try, the more you act out, and I don't blame you. So I'm done trying. This is a big house. We can ignore each other till you move out, if that's what you want. Or we could be friends. Which is something I don't have a lot of right now. And after tonight, it sounds like you could use one too."

Carmen reached for Alison's hand. If she'd attempted this

even a matter of hours earlier, Alison would have been horrified. Now she allowed her hand to be held. It felt so soft and comforting. "You're a sweet, lovely girl," said Carmen in what Alison now noted was a lilting, almost musical voice. "And hard though it may sometimes be to believe, so am I. You can always come to me. You can always talk to me."

How can we trust our emotions? Alison wondered to herself. *They change so fast and they're so unreliable. David thinks he loves me, but when he walked away tonight, he looked like he hated me. I thought I hated Carmen, and here she is, lying on my bed being nothing but nice to me.*

Alison wished she could tell Carmen exactly why she couldn't be around either David or T again. Instead, she delivered a truthful but heavily censored version, which was enough to elicit nods and smiles of recognition.

And the way Carmen sighed when she got to the part about the kiss at the laser show made Alison realize that while she might have lost a lot that night, she'd also gained an unexpected friend.

FORTY-THREE

The day after the Best Date / Worst Night Ever, Carmen had burst into the bedroom, muted Alison's chosen self-pity party sound track—"With Every Heartbeat" already downloaded and on repeat—thrown open the curtains, and declared she was taking her new BFF to The Ivy for lunch. That was a surprise in itself. But Alison was stunned at the fuss the staff made over Carmen.

She hadn't even bothered making a reservation, but the maitre d' hustled them past the minor celebrities pretending they didn't want their pictures taken and deposited them at a fantastic table.

"They love you here," Alison said, impressed, watching the lines of hopeful diners waiting for their names to be called.

"It's sad that you say that with so much surprise."

Over lunch, Carmen revealed that the maitre d' and some of the ridiculously good-looking waitstaff had been grateful clients of Carmen's successful life-coaching business.

Alison had thought Carmen's so-called career was a fake: a nonjob she'd invented so she didn't seem like a sponge soaking up Roger's hard-earned cash. It wasn't like she needed any qualifications: any con artist could call herself a life coach and spout babble to the mentally impaired.

But Carmen was, apparently, *the real deal.*

"This woman showed me what my life could be," intoned the waiter, who looked like a Greek god come to life. "She took someone who was unfulfilled, directionless, just floating through life, and helped me focus and define my goals. She taught me that fears are just clutter in my mind. Anything Carmen tells me to do, I'll do. That's how good she is."

"You hear that?" Carmen smiled, enjoying Alison's amazement.

Alison couldn't believe how wrong she'd been about Carmen. She was sweet, she was fun, she was spontaneous, she was silly, and—despite all that mean stuff Alison had said about her plastic surgery—she was lovely. *I could look at her all day. She makes me feel warm and safe,* thought Alison.

Carmen smiled back and began to speak when a guy approached the table and dipped down to hug her. She took it in her stride, hugging the guy back, then pulling away, which allowed Alison to see that although he was clean-shaven and smartly dressed, the visitor was Nick Stygian.

"I took your advice, Carmen. I turned my life around. My

lawyer got me a suspended sentence and something like four hundred years' worth of community service, and honestly, it's way fairer than I deserve."

Alison stared down at her crab cakes. She knew he wouldn't recognize her, but what if she did or said something that gave her away?

"I wish you nothing but luck on the journey. Oh, Nicky, this is my stepdaughter, Alison."

Nick extended a hand.

Alison started to reach out and realized she was still wearing her mood ring. The mood ring Nick had previously seen around the finger that aimed flames at him and made him crawl on all fours like a sassy Chihuahua.

Thinking quickly, she clasped her hands together, grinned like a moron, and stared awkwardly down at her food.

"I think someone's got a little crush," said Carmen, correctly interpreting Alison's hasty improvisation.

Nick exuded self-satisfaction. He still had the magic touch. Turning back to Carmen, he said, "So the excitement over the Christmas Ball is reaching fever pitch."

Carmen nodded. "It is, however, a mammoth task. I've even had to draft poor Alison to help me."

Poor Alison looked surprised at this piece of information.

"I feel so bad, she should be out having fun and I've got her working on the guest list, deciding who gets invitations. It's a lot of power for someone so young, but I've got a feeling she won't abuse her position."

Nick nodded and smiled at Alison. "You're lucky to have Carmen in your life. She's a wonderful woman."

"I am, you know," said Carmen to Alison, seconds after Nick left the table.

Feigning outrage, Alison said, "Thank you *so* much for letting me know I'm working on your Secret Santa event."

"You're quite welcome. I had planned to ask you, but I thought it might be more amusing bringing it up in front of a cute guy who had you all flustered."

"You're so funny for *such* an old woman." Alison smiled. This was the sort of thing she would once have thrown at Carmen with malice. Now it was playful, and they both knew it. Alison turned serious. "Guest list, though, Carmen? I don't know anything about . . ."

Carmen raised a hand, held it mere inches from Alison's lips. "Don't finish what you were about to say. You'll make the sentence real and it isn't. It's just more fears, and what are fears?"

"Fears are just clutter in your mind," recited Alison, dutifully repeating Carmen's favorite life-coaching rule.

"And you know what we do to clutter?"

"The maid gets it?"

"You *know* what we do to clutter," repeated Carmen, pursing her lips in mock severity.

"We clear it away."

"*Exactly.* You're young and cute and hip. Between us, we can attract the perfect mixture of old and new Hollywood. Cutting-edge designers, extreme sports icons, hip-hop tycoons. If they've got money or their sponsors have money and I've never heard of them, *I want them.* And if you don't know how to get them, you'll know someone who does."

Alison understood what it had been like for her father. It was impossible to say no to Carmen. What a waste of energy hating her had turned out to be! Since she'd allowed an adult female influence into her life, she'd found herself newly motivated. She was a good person and good things were happening to her. Everything was going back to the way it was supposed to be.

As if she could follow the workings of Alison's mind, Carmen said, "And I'd be grateful if you'd stop referring to it as my Secret Santa event. It's the Christmas Ball, and if you're going to be helping me organize it, you should probably know that it will take place on December fifteenth at the Los Angeles Pacific Museum of Art & Culture."

"LAPMAC!" repeated Alison, blushing as soon as she realized she'd said it loud enough to turn heads.

Carmen raised her glass of water and repeated, "LAPMAC!" at the same volume.

Alison clinked her Diet Coke off Carmen's drink. Carmen raised her glass to the observers.

"LAPMAC!" she said.

"LAPMAC!" they found themselves repeating.

Carmen winked at her stepdaughter.

Alison inhaled with delight. Carmen had saved her from embarrassment and involved the whole of The Ivy in their little private joke. She was awesome!

FORTY-FOUR

"*The good news* is, we've got her sedated and locked up in her special room. The bad news is, she's liable to escape again. Apparently, she's learned to pick locks with her teeth. . . ."

T stared at Alison, speechless and confused. After a week of avoiding him and failing to return any of his texts, he was shocked to find her waiting for him on the school steps, looking characteristically sunny and full of conversation. But what was she talking about?

"My emotionally unhinged identical twin sister, TraumAlison? I don't like to talk about her. She's put my family through so much heartache. Just last week, she wriggled out of her constraints and went to the laser show with some poor guy. It's such a tragedy. She *almost* passes as normal, then she shows her true colors and cue the freakish meltdown and the craziness. It's so pathetically obvious that she needs to be back under lock and key."

"Not you." T grinned. "Her."

"That's right. Her. Not me," said Alison, smiling back at him, grateful that he accepted her explanation for her previous flakery and even more grateful to Carmen for rehearsing her in the exact way to approach him.

"Listen," he said, moving closer to her, his face turning serious. "I meant what I said. I never want you to feel uncomfortable. I never want you to feel like you can't trust me."

She considered what he had said and then replied, "I haven't met every guy in the world; it's like an ongoing project of mine, might take a little time to complete. But until I do, I'm gonna go out on a limb and say that you might be the nicest, sweetest guy in the world."

She then stuffed her hands into her pockets, arched up on her toes, and kissed him quickly, one time, on the lips. And just like that, any lingering doubts that T might have been harboring about whether Alison was really as amazing as she seemed were wiped away.

Passing junior girls rolled their eyes and clicked their tongues in disgust at the public display of affection. *Go ahead and hate me,* thought Alison as she watched the junior girls shoot hostile backward glances at her. But suddenly, their attention was diverted elsewhere. The junior girls were staring up toward the school roof. Alison followed their gaze. Her mouth fell open. Standing on a classroom window ledge was David in his homemade superhero costume.

FORTY-FIVE

"*Go about your* business. I see all. I hear all. Evil will not triumph today!" intoned David through a plastic bullhorn as he stood on the ledge outside the second-floor classroom window. Every eye was on him. Cameras were clicking. Maybe this wasn't such a bad idea! Then a Fiji bottle boinked off his head ("That kid has a great arm!" David later reflected) and two janitors pulled him back inside.

Alison and T were waiting outside the principal's office when David was finally dismissed.

"Are you okay?" she asked, curling a hand around his arm, her eyes wide with concern.

"I know how things can get to you," said T, patting David's

shoulder. "Anytime you need to talk it out, you got an ear right here."

And just for a second David considered attempting to explain to T exactly what he was doing out on that ledge. But what could he say? "Well, *T*. It all started after you hooked up with Alison. . . ."

And then David would go on to tell T that he hadn't expected to be greeted with open arms when he'd shown up the previous night at Toenail's house for the weekly D&D 3-D-a-thon. That wasn't how guys acted. David had planned to simply make his way down to Toenail's murky basement, grab a bag of Doritos and a Cherry Vanilla Dr. Pepper, and then spend the night outwitting Odor Eater's slow-witted Dungeon Master. But Odor Eater hadn't been in character. Tiny Head wasn't wearing his tiny elf hat. Tiny Head was sitting behind a drum kit, tightening his ride cymbal. Phlegmy was snorting, "One, two . . . one, two . . ." into a microphone. Toenail was tuning a guitar. And some long-haired kid David had never even seen before was playing bass. "What's going on?" he'd asked. No reaction. "Should I have brought my accordion?" Nothing. David got it. "Look, I know I haven't been around much . . ." Tiny Head had counted the band in. They'd started playing, a little shambolic, a little out of time, but *loud*. And repetitive. They played the same lumbering riff over and over. None of them acknowledging David's presence.

He'd tell T that his ears were still ringing when he left Toenail's house and began the long walk home. Then his phone rang. He grinned. He'd been punished enough. The big silence was over. *"That was excruciating,"* he'd Simon Cowelled into the phone. *"It was rather like the sound you hear when a baby goose is ripped to pieces by an angry rottweiler."*

"Huh?" Alison had said at the other end of the phone.

David hadn't been expecting to hear from her. He'd thought about her every second and he'd imagined what he'd say if she called. Now that she was calling, he was mute.

"David? You still there? We were thinking of driving to Swingers, you know, that diner on Melrose? Maybe get a burger and one of their yummy Creamsicles? What do you think? Should we pick you up?" David had bitten into the skin inside his lower lip. *Should* we *pick you up?*

Then he'd heard a male voice—*your voice, T*—in the background. "Where's his place?" He'd heard Alison say, "It's just off Fairfax."

Alison's voice was in his ear again. "We can be there in like twenty. You down?"

David had shut his phone off.

Later that night, he'd lain on top of his bed and stared at the ceiling. *Nice work, Eels,* he'd thought. *You alienated all your old friends and you can't be anywhere near your new friend because she's a million miles out of your reach.* As the night wore on, David had remembered what life was like B.A. (Before Alison. Or should that have been B.H.? Before Hottie?) He'd recalled how much he wanted to be noticed as something other than just another faceless member of a geek gang. Last time he'd donned his home-made superhero suit, he had met Alison. It had been *fate.* Maybe if he wore it again, something life-changing would happen.

As he climbed out of the classroom window the following morning, he had the feeling that what was a brilliant idea at three in the A.M. might not be so smart in the cold light of day.

"And *that* brings us up pretty much up to speed," is what David might have told T.

Instead, David looked at the two of them, united in their sympathy. Then he walked quickly away, grateful that he'd been sent home for a couple of days. T started to follow, but Alison said, "Let him go. He wants to be on his own. He's got some stuff he needs to work out."

For David, working things out meant a day in his bedroom convincing himself he'd be better off if he never saw or thought about Alison again. He stared at his phone. His display was the picture of Alison's early Hottie costume choice. The one where she was clad in pink leather hot pants, high-heel boots with flames running up the sides, bikini top, and cutoff silk bomber jacket. "I need to get rid of that," he told himself. Day 2 was a little more complicated. Did he feel so wounded because she'd fallen for someone else rather than the perfect guy who was dangling right under her nose? Or was it the fact that she hadn't thought for a second before choosing conformity and a bland boyfriend? *That* was it. He *knew* her. She was *alive* when she was Hottie. How could she deny that side of herself?

From now on, he was going to devote himself to guiding Alison back to the Hottie path. He was going to be a good friend who was there to remind her of the potential that was burning inside her. David started to smile. The numbness of the last few weeks was starting to drain away. He had a mission again. . . .

FORTY-SIX

"*The Jomac 625* Flame-Retardant Glove is capable of withstanding temperatures up to seven hundred degrees Fahrenheit. It comes in yellow and brown. It has a reversible Kevlar outer shell and it is 5.5 inches thick."

Fortunately, T was officially Alison's boyfriend. They'd been an official couple for three weeks. He took her to school in the mornings, they ate lunch together, they hung out after he volunteered with the fire department, and she spent all her minutes talking and texting with him.

Unfortunately, the no-touching, limited-kissing thing was still a problem. T was the very essence of understanding. Never wanted to make her uncomfortable. Never wanted her to do anything she didn't want to do. But touching and kissing were things that she *very much* wanted to do.

Which was why she searched Amazon until she found the reasonably priced Jomac 625 Flame-Retardant Glove.

Next time they hung out at her house, there would be no awkward, embarrassed pecks on the cheek at the end of the night. Next time she could touch him. Next time would be *special*.

Had David known that flame-retardant gloves were so important to Alison, he wouldn't have made the trek to the ivy-covered bungalow that houses Fred Segal, the famously expensive Los Angeles fashion emporium. But the first step in David's plan to assume the identity of a good, caring friend was to surprise Alison with a present of a shoe or a bag or something shiny that she'd covet. Now that he was in the store, however, he began to think he'd been over-ambitious. The shoes cost millions of dollars. The bags cost billions of dollars. The shiny little trinkets cost gazillions of dollars. "Maybe I'll get her a stuffed puppy," he considered, remembering how much she liked the *idea* of a pet.

One of the seven-foot-tall salesgirls shot a bored look his way. "We're about to close. So if you want to make a purchase . . ." She let the sentence dangle. David checked his watch. It was almost seven. Maybe he'd try the Beverly Center.

As David was about to leave the store, a group of shoppers swept past him. The salesgirl suddenly turned on a bright welcoming smile. And she didn't say anything to *them* about closing for the night! *But then,* they *look like they spend millions of dollars on bags and shoes,* he thought as he took note of their all-black ensembles. Then he remembered the last time he'd seen someone in an all-black leather jacket with their features obscured by a black hood. David whirled around. The leader of the group was a woman with her hood up. *Wettie?*

★ ★ ★

While David was encountering a supervillain, Alison and T were spending another night watching the film that had become Their Movie. *License to Wed* could not be described by anyone in their right mind as either good or well made. But every time T came over to help Alison study, they ended up sitting on her bed, talking and laughing. Then they'd stop talking and laughing and she'd sprawl against his chest and flip cable channels. And night after night, *that* was the film they wound up watching all the way through. Unlike almost everyone who had ever endured it, Alison was sad when *License to Wed* ended because that meant they were headed toward the end-of-night awkward nonkiss with all the embarrassment that came immediately before and after it.

But not tonight. Once the movie limped to its un-heart-warming conclusion, Alison shivered.

"Brrr. It's subzero in here. It's freezing. Are you cold? I'm cold."

T looked concerned. Her room wasn't in any way cold. "Are you coming down with something?"

Alison jumped off her bed, ran into her closet, and, moments later, emerged wearing her huge, thick, yellow flame-retardant gloves.

"Mmm. Toasty warm and snuggly." She sighed, climbing back on the bed and reaching for her boyfriend.

Their lips almost touched before her phone rang.

"Itswettieitswettieitswettie," whisper-babbled David into the phone

from inside the Fred Segal changing room. He knew he was prone to overfantasizing. But not this time. He'd followed the black-clad group back into the boutique. He'd watched in horror as the sales assistants and the shoppers had all fallen into the same swaying trance as Alison. He'd listened in disbelief as the exact same ethereal melody escaped from their open mouths. *"Itswettiewettieitswettie,"* he continued to gasp into the phone.

"David? What are you saying? Where are you?"

T nodded resignedly. *Of course* the weird kid would pick this moment to call. *Perfect* timing.

"Don't do *anything*," Alison was saying. "Just stay where you are."

Alison clicked the phone off. She looked over at T, then looked down at her gloves. *Of course* David would pick that moment to call. *Perfect* timing. But what could she do? He hadn't talked to her in weeks. Now he was finally reaching out.

"What's up?" asked T. "Anything I can do?"

There wasn't. Except that he was right there. And he had a car.

"Let's go shopping!" she said brightly.

This was *unbelievable*! Wettie and her cohorts were walking around the store, removing all the million-dollar shoes and billion-dollar bags. They were yanking purses and credit cards straight out of the frozen shoppers' hands. No one was stopping them. Everyone was trapped, swaying and singing, in their own private little worlds. Everyone but him. Suddenly, David realized the danger of his situation. He was *alone* with a supervillain. If he said *one* word. If he so much as *breathed*. If he even . . .

"Hic!"

FORTY-SEVEN

"*Can you go* faster? Go faster. You must be able to go faster. Why aren't you going faster?"

With Alison yelling in his ear, T drove his Chevy toward Melrose Avenue and wondered if he *really* knew his girlfriend. It had been a perfect evening. They'd lolled on the bed, they'd laughed, they'd recited *License to Wed*'s terrible dialogue along with the actors. Then she'd donned the big rubber gloves, which was weird but seemed to make her more affectionate than usual. But after the phone rang, she'd become a different person. One word from Eels and she was a woman possessed, desperate to hit Fred Segal and barking in his ear to put his foot down. *Is there something wrong with her? Like, really wrong? Bipolar-disorder-level wrongness. Could I handle that? Would I be supportive?* he fretted.

"*T!*" screamed Alison. T had been lost in his thoughts. He snapped back just in time to see David run wildly out of Fred Segal, pursued by a pair of black-clad figures. T slammed on the brakes. David froze in the middle of the street. The Chevy screeched to a halt. But it didn't stop quickly enough. David bounced off the hood and went teetering backward.

"*David!*" screamed Alison. She and T rushed out of the car and ran toward David, who was lying stunned on his back in the middle of the street. As they stared down at him, they barely heard the roar of the engine as the Bandini-Maserati flew out of Fred Segal's parking garage and disappeared down Melrose Avenue.

FORTY-EIGHT

An angel gazed down on David. An angel with ash blond hair, ice green eyes, and a warm, caring smile. The angelic face dropped low until it was next to David. Until he could feel its warmth next to his cheek. The angel leaned close to his ear. The angel said, "You *idiot!*"

David scrambled back to consciousness. He was lying on his side in a bed in Midway Hospital. The old guy in the next bed was watching *Jeopardy* and eating mashed potatoes. Get Well Soon balloons were attached to his bed. *How did I get here?* David wondered. *And where are my balloons?* And why was Alison hovering over him with her perfect features locked in a struggle between concern and rage?

"What the eff were you thinking? I *told* you not to do anything.

I *told* you to stay where you were," she was hissing. Why was she so mad?

Fragments of memory started to fizz their way to the surface. Wettie! The phone call. The *hic*-ing. The cold, dead expressions on the faces of Wettie's operatives as they closed in on the changing room. The mad rush from Fred Segal. The accident. *The accident!* He'd been hit by a car! He couldn't feel his legs!

He started to roll onto his back. Alison grabbed his arm and held him steady.

"You can't lie on your back. You've got a bruised coccyx."

David reached behind him. Sure enough, his butt was encased in bandages. He winced. Not the coolest kind of injury.

"I'm *so* sorry, man. Totally my bad," said T, walking up to the bed. "A few weeks of R&R, you'll be back in the game."

"What's he doing here?" sulked David.

"Helping," replied Alison sharply. "He dragged your broken butt out of the gutter and brought you here."

"Didn't he break my butt in the first place?"

Alison squirmed in discomfort, unsure whose side to take.

David peered up at T. "Did she tell you what I was doing out there? Did she say why I called her?"

Alison quickly slapped a hot hand on David's bandaged behind. He yelped in pain.

"Can you run and get a nurse?" Alison asked T. "I think his coccyx is relapsing."

"Hang in there, champ," said T as he headed out of the room.

"What a guy," sneered David.

Alison scorched David's butt a second time.

"That *hurts!*" squealed David.

"Does it? Does it hurt like you ignoring me and never calling except when you're in trouble?"

"Wettie's *back*, Alison. I *saw* her."

"What do you want me to do about it?"

"Fight her. Beat her. She's evil. You're good."

Alison shook her head. "I'm not good."

David opened his mouth to disagree. She talked over him. "You're here because of me. My relationship is filled with lies because of me. I can't live two lives. I can't be a superhero and a regular girl."

"So don't be both. Be one. Be the superhero."

"I think I want to be the other one," said Alison.

"What about Wettie?" demanded David. "She's out there."

"She's nothing to do with me," said Alison.

David stared at her. Alison sat down on the bed beside him. She knew they needed this moment. Once they'd cleared the clutter from their lives, they could go back to being best friends. She could see from the look in his eyes that he knew she was right.

David swallowed hard. Alison waited for him to speak.

"You *suck*," he spat.

T stood outside the hospital room and watched Alison and David shout at each other. He was an intuitive, empathetic person who understood that Alison's request to find a nurse was really a diversion to give her space to deal with some issues between herself and David.

Watching them yell, he could guess the dynamic. She'd

been sweet to David the way she generally was with people. He'd misinterpreted her warm and generous nature and developed a crush. It had turned ugly and uncomfortable when he couldn't accept that he was only ever going to be her friend. T was a pretty good judge of people, but he hadn't managed to completely encapsulate the conflict between Alison and David.

T didn't know Alison was saying, "You are sick and demented. You can't tell the difference between fantasy and reality."

T didn't know David was saying, "Don't you talk to me about fantasies. What kind of bippy dream world are you living in? You can date the Junior President of Cuteness, you can play Secret Santa with your stepmom, but you can't deny who you really are."

T didn't know Alison was replying, "I know who I really am. I'm *normal.* I'm a normal girl who wants to live a normal life. I'm the bip you always knew I was. So you don't ever have to talk to me again. I'll have the Hottie costume UPS'd to you so it's ready and waiting for the next freak. I'm done. Unsubscribe me!"

With that, she stomped out of the room.

T was waiting in the hospital corridor for her.

"I knew you'd find a way to let him down gently," he said.

FORTY-NINE

Kellyn didn't want to be the one who said it first.

Dorinda didn't want to be the one who said it first.

Neither of them wanted to say it. But deep down, they both knew.

Marvelette was *awful*.

Of course, before she was *awful*, she was *wonderful*. A kind, caring, and completely cool friend with whom they had become inseparable during the aftermath of the Plus One catastrophe.

At first they enjoyed the constant barrage of Twitter tweets; she micromessaged them to let them know that she was awake, that she was heading for the shower, that she had returned, that she was torn between cereal and a smoothie. It was as if she had opened up every aspect of her life for their approval.

But as it turned out, this was the exact *opposite* of what she was doing. Marvelette continued inoculating Kellyn and Dorinda with the minutiae of her personal life so that they would become obedient little soldiers who understood what their leader expected of them.

"What are you guys wearing tomorrow?" she would ask. Not because she was thrilled by their individual senses of style. But so she could coordinate their outfits. ("We're going to look *so* cute in our glittery crocheted berets!") "What are you guys listening to right now?" she would demand. Not because she was impressed by their tastes. But so she could create personalized playlists based on her impeccable choice of songs. ("We're the only ones in the *entire school* who listen to Croatian hip-hop! How cool are we?") She also insisted on programming their DVRs so they could all watch and discuss the same shows. ("*Ghost Whisperer* is *so* spiritual!")

In short, she was a scary, needy control freak who filled their iPods with audiobook extracts from her ongoing memoir, *Everything Happens to Me*, and issued arbitrary fashion commands ("It's Marc Jacobs Monday!").

But if Kellyn and Dorinda acknowledged that Marvelette was *awful*, they'd also have to fess up to the colossal blunder they'd made in ridding themselves of Alison.

Everyone wanted to be Alison's friend again. The Christmas Ball was a hot-ticket event. Alison had prevailed on T to get his father, the high-end speaker guy, to get his clients interested in the ball. T-Dad's customers were super-rich guys who knew other super-rich guys. At the same time, Alison provided Carmen with a list of names young and hip enough to confer A-list status on any event. And Carmen had worked her magic. Everyone RSVP'd. Everyone wanted to go to the Christmas Ball. Which meant, for the students of BHHS, that everyone had to be extra-super nice to Alison because she had access to tickets. If Kellyn and Dorinda approached her, they knew she would probably arrange for them to go. She was non-grudgy like that.

But she'd be doing it out of pity or, at least, that's how it would seem to them. And that would be worse than awful. So they dressed the way Marvelette instructed them to dress and listened to the songs she told them to listen to and neither of them said anything.

FIFTY

"LAPMAC!" squealed Alison in stunned delight. She had seen the museum's West Central Suite. It was vast and majestic. She was sure it would make a fine location for the event. But until she saw what Carmen and her team of designers had done to the space, she had *no* idea just how perfect the night was going to be.

Carmen had basically transformed the West Central Suite into a giant snow globe. The guests who walked through the palm-tree-arched doorway to the museum found themselves guided inside a glass dome. And once inside, they were in a different world. They walked through a picturesque little village filled with snowcapped cottages and a choir of apple-cheeked children. The five-thousand-dollar-a-head tables were arranged around an ice rink. An orchestra played in a band shell on a stage raised slightly over the ice. Snowflakes fell from the ceiling, but due to a clever air-conditioning arrangement under the floors, constant puffs of oxygen kept the snow dancing in the air just above the heads of the guests.

If the eye-popping over-the-topness of the Christmas Ball wasn't enough to melt the cold, hard, cynical hearts of the various luminaries in attendance, Carmen had many more tricks up her sleeve.

Eight-year-old Ashley Marie from Inglewood was one of those tricks. As the orchestra played "White Christmas," the brave little angel from the hood appeared on the giant video monitor displaying the bright green scarf she'd knitted for the head of the Four Seasons hotel group. She hadn't even finished wishing the guests a merry Christmas before the billionaires gathered under the glass dome began dabbing at their eyes.

Equally impressive was the poise and charm displayed by Alison as she mingled with the monied attendees, collecting their checks and making sure they were aware that the problems of the underprivileged would not be solved with this one donation, wonderfully generous as it was.

"All I'm doing is saying, 'Hello, Mr. Money, have you met Mr. More Money?'" complained Alison.

"You're doing a lot more than that," purred Carmen's voice over Alison's Bluetooth earpiece. "You're making an amazing impression on very influential people who could well have a say in your future."

Arguing with Carmen was futile. Besides, she was right on several counts:

1.   Alison looked amazing. She wasn't sure she could carry off a pristine white Dolce & Gabbana evening dress. But there were no complaints.

2.   She was amazed to find herself feeling at ease among the guests. She didn't say anything goofy. She conversed with them like an equal rather than a precocious kid playing cutesy among the grown-ups. This she put down solely to Carmen instilling confidence in her.

3.   Many of her old friends, the ones who had once shunned her, were there to witness her wowing the wealthy. And even though Alison had come to accept that Warren and Ginger Becker had unexpectedly evolved into a cute and caring couple, she was also sure that to-night was one of the nights when Warren found himself wrestling with the question, *Did I make the wrong choice?* Adding fuel to this conviction was the fact that Ginger Becker rolled her eyes at him every time she so much as suspected he was staring at how amazing Alison looked in the pristine white Dolce & Gabbana evening dress.

But if Alison really was radiant, it was chiefly because she felt Carmen's voice in her ear and her father's proud eyes on her all night. She felt safe and secure and part of a strong, loving family, which was something she'd missed more than she'd ever really admitted to herself. This led her to thinking about David. *He should be here,* she thought sadly. But then she told herself, *He'd hate this. He'd think it was the bippiest thing in the world.* Which made her smile. Which then made her sad. Which was the *last* thing she wanted to be tonight.

Instead, she concentrated on thoughts of T, who had texted to say he was running late. If he said he'd be there, he'd be there. He was an excellent, reliable boyfriend. They made the cutest couple imaginable. Tonight was going to be the highlight of what had been a turbulent-but-ultimately-awesome year. Alison smiled her brightest smile and passed by the table where Warren and Ginger Becker sat so that they could see how fabulous she was. She kind of knew she was rubbing Warren's idiot decision in his face. She resolved that this was the last time she'd allow herself to descend to such petty levels. She walked toward Warren and Ginger, positively *glowing* with gorgeousness. This gave them a clear and uninterrupted view of Alison colliding with the waiter and the subsequent deluge of red wine that soaked her pristine white D&G evening dress.

FIFTY-ONE

"*I'm on the* list. Eels. E-e-l-s. David Eels. Of Eels Industries, Inc. I'm invited. I'm an invited guest. Alison Cole invited me. I'm right there on your clipboard; I can read upside down. How come you let that guy in? I've been here all night. Hello?"

The big, unsmiling guy behind the LAPMAC velvet rope refused to acknowledge David's presence. The bigger the fuss David made, the more the guy behind the velvet rope gazed through him and fawned over other invitees.

David pulled off his backpack and brandished it in front of the guy. "I've got a very important present for a poor person in here. It's a heart. That's right. A human heart. Without this heart, a child could die."

David didn't know what was more humiliating:

1. Being treated like a nonperson by the power-mad guy behind the velvet rope.

2. The failure of his brilliant improvisational skills to see him into the party.

3. That he was only here because of a gnawing fear that something might go wrong. Which made him think that maybe deep down, he *wanted* something to go wrong.

4. Being rescued by the Junior President of Cuteness.

"What's up, man?" breezed a tuxedo-clad T as he approached the guardian of the velvet rope. "Tommy Hull." The unsmiling guy was suddenly grinning and friendly.

Without so much as changing his tone, T smiled over at David. "Hey, dude, hope you haven't been waiting long. I had some stuff to take care of."

"Stuff, right," responded David, confused.

Nodding at the velvet rope guy, T said, "This is my plus one." The guy was still smiling, still friendly.

And just like that, the forbidden rope lifted, allowing David access to the Christmas Ball.

As he followed in T's footsteps, David peered at the junior president. *People* like *him,* he thought. *They* believe *him. How do you get* those *powers?*

FIFTY-TWO

Carmen's voice sounded worried over the earpiece. "Alison! Where *are* you? I'm about to make a big emotional speech thanking all our guests for their contributions, and I want you by my side. I couldn't have done this without you. Where *are* you?"

Alison pulled out the Bluetooth and dropped it down the toilet. She should have told Carmen what happened the moment it happened. "I had an accident. I'm covered in wine," she should have whispered into her earpiece, and Carmen would have instantly known how to handle the matter. But as soon as the first splotches of Napa Valley cabernet sauvignon turned pristine white Dolce & Gabbana to purple and Ginger Becker's shrieks of delight cut through the chatter of the guests, Alison turned and fled. Now she couldn't leave the bathroom. This was the *last* thing she'd wanted to happen. (Getting splattered in front of Warren and Ginger was the second-worst thing.) But this: hiding in the bathroom, feeling stupid, feeling like a baby. And after Carmen had been *so* great.

Alison reflected on the past couple of months. Carmen had included her in *everything*. She'd made her feel strong and smart and grown-up. *But if I was* really *strong and smart and grown-up, I wouldn't still be cowering in the bathroom. I wouldn't be dying of embarrassment,* she thought miserably.

Under the flurry of gently dancing snowflakes, Carmen greeted enraptured guests and, at the same time, glanced at a pair of waiters and mouthed the words, "Where *is* she?" When Carmen failed to get a satisfactory answer, she gestured to them to conduct thorough searches of the museum.

Aware she had a capacity crowd of busy VIPs who had neither the time nor the inclination to cool their heels waiting for a fourteen-year-old girl, Carmen stepped up to the dais, clutching a colorfully wrapped Christmas gift, and addressed her guests. "Thank you all for coming. Thank you a million times."

The crowd applauded. Several of the guests looked over at Roger Cole and nodded their approval. It hadn't happened overnight, but Carmen had finally been accepted by Hollywood.

"I know I've asked a lot of you tonight, but I'm going to prevail on your goodwill one more time. I'm going to ask you to make a gesture that shows your solidarity with the people we're trying to help. When you came here tonight, we gave you a symbolic Christmas tree. We ask you now to wear it with pride. . . ."

A slight murmur of distaste rippled through the crowd. *This* was where her emotional speech was going? She was trying to make them wear those tacky silver Christmas trees that you'd find at the bottom of a cereal box?

But then Carmen looked up at the big screen. Eight-year-old Ashley Marie, the same little girl who had touched the collected hard hearts of Hollywood with her bright green scarf, proudly pinned her silver Christmas tree to her shirt exactly over her heart. "Merry Christmas everyone, from my heart," she said sweetly.

The same cynics who, only seconds earlier, had sneered at Carmen's cheap silver trees were now desperate to display them.

Carmen smiled at her guests. "I thank you and Ashley Marie and all the other Ashley Maries who, because of your generosity, are going to have the best Christmas ever, thank you. Now I ask you to join with her and touch your trees."

On the big screen, Ashley Marie touched her hand to the silver Christmas tree pinned over her heart.

Every guest at the Christmas Ball made the same gesture, each one pressing their fingers on the cheap silver Christmas trees. At that exact moment, Carmen opened her Christmas gift, pulled out a Gucci gas mask, and slipped it over her face.

Many of the guests were confused—and some envious—about why Carmen and the waitstaff had suddenly donned designer masks, but they didn't have time to raise any objections. The moment they had touched their silver Christmas trees, the tacky trinkets immediately disgorged streams of gas that almost instantly rendered their wearers unconscious.

Up on the big screen, Ashley Marie laughed. "Can I take this off now?" Carmen knew none of her guests would be conscious by this point, so she hadn't bothered to edit the footage of the brave little angel ripping the cheap silver tree off her shirt and tossing it away. On the screen, Ashley Marie continued to giggle, relieved of the burden of having to act sweet and grateful, happy to let the real girl show.

Beneath the screen, Carmen looked out at her unconscious guests. She, too, started laughing for exactly the same reasons as Ashley Marie.

FIFTY-THREE

Yay! thought Alison as she heard the
footsteps draw closer to the bathroom door. Finally, someone
was going to rescue her from her lonely exile. The door opened.
Two men walked in. Clad in head-to-toe black. Unsmiling. Staring straight at her.

"Your stepmother's looking for you," said one.

"Get out of here!" Alison yelled.

Then she looked closer. There was something familiar about
these unexpected intruders. One of them was the waiter from
The Ivy, the one who looked like a Greek god. The other was
the effusive maitre d'. They weren't intruders, they were the
answers to every red-wine-stained girl's prayers. They salvaged
similar situations every night of every week!

"You guys probably have code names for stuff like this," said Alison, gesturing to the blemished dress. "You probably say things like, 'We got a Britney,' or, 'There's a Lohan goin' down in the ladies' room.' I'm in your hands. Work your magic. Rescue me."

"No problem whatsoever. Come with us," said the maitre d'.

"You kidding? I'm not leaving here looking like this. Go get me a change of clothes. We got a Britney!"

"Do you know where you are?" asked the maitre d'. "You're in LAPMAC! The Costume and Textile Department is the envy of the world. You want to dress like Marie Antoinette, Scarlett O'Hara, or a Chinese courtesan, the clothes are all there waiting."

"Waiting to be borrowed and then returned, hopefully without wine stains," cautioned the Greek god.

"You guys are like American heroes," breathed an impressed Alison. "Let's do it!"

Excited by her sneaky trip to steal classic couture, Alison allowed her new BFFs from The Ivy to escort her out of the ladies' room.

"You smell something?" David asked T as they approached the West Central Suite. The junior president gave David a withering look, suspecting an inappropriate fart joke was on the horizon. David sniffed. The lingering aroma was *a lot* like nitrous oxide. T hurried toward the West Central Suite. Then he froze. David caught up with him. He saw the confused look on T's face and followed his gaze. Something was happening in there and it wasn't . . . *Christmassy!*

* ★ *

Alison had completely forgotten the trauma of her wine-stained dress. Having the two guys from The Ivy by her side was like being granted an audience with the pope, if the pope knew a bunch of dirt on D-list celebs.

"So who's the worst tipper? Who brings the biggest entourage and expects to be seated even if they haven't booked in advance? Who calls the paparazzi to let them know she's coming and then acts all outraged when she shows up and they're waiting for her? Who's gone to the bathroom the most in the shortest period of time? Who looks the most plastic close-up? Hey, you guys, we're having such a fascinating conversation that we're totally headed the wrong way! We're going back to the Christmas Ball. Which is not where I wanna be."

Alison turned around only to find that her two confidants from The Ivy had grabbed her arms and seemed intent on dragging her back to the West Central Suite.

"Hey! Take it easy! I don't need to be manhandled. It's not *really* a Britney!"

"Are we allowed to hurt her?" asked the Greek god.

"If it's justified," confirmed the maitre d'.

Alison didn't know what they were talking about, but she *did* know that they were not the fun, friendly, loose-lipped observers of celebrity misbehavior she thought they were.

"You don't have to be so rough with me," she said, suddenly looking fragile and vulnerable.

At first, David didn't see anything wrong with the scene in the Christmas Ball. The decadent, bone-idle rich lying slumped at their tables, too spoiled to move so much as a muscle. The black-clad waiters in Gucci gas masks going through their pockets, removing their watches, their jewelry, their Blackberries, and their wallets. That, as far as David knew, was what happened at every charity event patronized by the obscenely wealthy. But the more he looked, the more he knew that this was no ordinary Christmas Ball: the orchestra were asleep. The children's choir lay motionless on a bank of fake snow.

With rising shock, David recognized Alison's dad lying unconscious, facedown on his table. And not too far away were Warren and his lollipop-sucking girlfriend. All of them were being relieved of their valuables by the black-clad waiters. "Oh my God!" exclaimed a freaked-out T.

"Told you I smelled something," muttered David.

Satisfied that Alison was aware who was in charge, the maitre d' and the Greek god relaxed their grips on her.

"Can't you see how upset I am? My big night ruined. Everyone laughing at me."

The two Ivy staffers glanced at each other. Reducing a young girl to tears didn't make them feel particularly good. They weren't monsters.

"No one wants to hurt you, Alison," said the maitre d'.

"We're your friends," said the Greek god.

"Really?" asked Alison, who held out her hands for them to take.

Both men smiled at her. Both men felt protective. Both men took her hands. Both men screamed in pain and snatched their hands away, gasping in pain, staring at their red, raw, peeling palms and fingers.

"She's armed," whimpered the maitre d'.

"Handed. To be accurate," said Alison, wiggling her glowing, sparking digits.

The Greek god, in common with the vast majority of Los Angeles' population of waiters who really wanted to act, spent most of his free time at the gym. He'd taken enough kickboxing, tae bo, and krav maga classes to be able to handle a little girl in a wine-stained dress. No matter that one hand was incapacitated, he had elbows, he had knees, he had feet, he was a human weapon. He advanced on Alison ready to show her what he could do.

From his hiding place behind a huge palm tree, David continued to stare in amazement as the beautiful, picture-perfect Christmas mugging continued. With quiet, calm efficiency, the black-clad waiters continued to visit the tables of paralyzed guests and relieve them of their valuables.

Behind him, T whispered into his phone, "Police. Hi. We're at LAPMAC. Something's happening. I think there's a robbery in progress. It looks like there's . . . *damn!* Low bat!"

David spun around and put his finger to his lips, gesturing for T to stay quiet so as not to jeopardize their excellent hiding place behind the huge palm tree. "Gimme your phone," ordered T. "Mine's dead."

David tossed his phone to T and, *at the exact second he did so*, remembered that he'd neglected to delete the picture of Alison from his display. The moment T flicked open the phone, he'd see a picture of his girlfriend wearing pink leather hot pants.

Despite the fact that a heinous and surreal crime scene was

taking place a few feet away from him, David's only thought was to save himself from an awkward, embarrassing moment. "I'll do it," he squeaked. "I wanna call the cops!" David hurled himself straight at T, reaching out to grab the phone. T stared in complete confusion. "You're stressed out! Calm down!" Too late. David collided with T. They both grabbed at the phone. Their grasping hands knocked it skittering across the ground.

T went scampering after the phone. David, who had never been anywhere near a non-Xbox fight in his life but who had built up a hefty amount of hostility toward T, charged after the Junior President of Cuteness.

"Don't touch that phone. That's *my* phone!"

"What's going on here?" asked an unfamiliar voice.

T, who was a good head taller than David, was holding the phone out of his reach. David, undaunted, was leaping in the air trying to grab at it. Both of them stopped and turned in the direction of the voice. It was one of the black-clad waiters. Blank face. Dead eyes. Intimidating manner. Both boys started to back away.

"Come join the fun," said the waiter, making it sound like a command.

"No, thanks," said David. "I'm kind of a party pooper. That's not just a figure of speech. It's an actual medical condition."

T gave David a sidelong glance of despair.

Two more black-clad waiters emerged from the Christmas Ball. All three started moving toward David and T.

"Run!" yelled T.

"You think?" snarked David.

Alison looked disappointed as the Greek god advanced on her. "I don't even know what to think anymore. You lie to me, you drag me somewhere I don't want to go, you're rough. How am I supposed to believe anything you say?"

As she spoke, Alison tucked her index fingers under her thumbs and began flicking shards of flame at the Greek god.

"Who ordered everything on the menu and then walked out without paying?" she asked, flicking flames that caused the Greek god to fall out of his human weapon stance and start slapping frantically at the small fires that had begun breaking out all over his clothes.

"Who has the brattiest kids?"

Alison widened her flame-flicking, sending shards hurtling toward the maitre d'. Within moments, both Ivy employees were putting out tiny fires and shrieking over each other:

"Zac Efron!"

"Teri Hatcher!"

"The blonde on *Gossip Girl*!"

"Tyra!"

"That was fun," said Alison. "What do you wanna do *now*?"

The maitre d' looked at the Greek god. The two guys decided that what they wanted to do was run as far away from Alison as they could get.

"I can't *believe* you wouldn't let me use your phone," panted T as he and David ran through a hall filled with ancient Celtic mud paintings. "What are you, five?"

Emotionally, thought David. But he was too breathless to summon up a reply.

"And *Alison*'s here. She's caught up in all this. You get that she's in danger?"

David couldn't stop the smile of excitement spreading across his face. If Alison was in danger, then Hottie was out of retirement and back in action.

T stared at David. "And that makes you *smile?*" he said, shocked.

"No," said David, gasping for air. "It's not that. It's just . . ." But he couldn't complete the sentence. Partly because he could barely speak. Partly because he couldn't explain to T exactly why he was smiling.

"Come back, guys," called Alison after the maitre d' and the Greek god. "We were having fun." Which was sort of true. She'd forgotten how *powerful* she could be. But then she remembered she was lost in the museum in a wine-stained dress and immediately felt unpowerful again. It was a matter of urgent importance that she find the Costumes and Textiles Department. She turned around and attempted to retrace her steps. "Which way did I come?" she wondered. It's not like there weren't signs everywhere.

She hurried through a floor filled with rare paintings and sculptures. Then she trotted down the long, curved glass staircase, trying not to trip over her dress as she sped past the Architecture and Design exhibits on the floor below. Hurrying down two more floors led her to the lobby. Alison burst through the lobby doors and found herself in an unexpected oasis of calm.

She was in LAPMAC's famed Sculpture Garden. Palm trees lined the walls. Concrete lovers stared into each other's eyes. A bronze baseball player swung at an invisible ball. A floral arrangement made of stone hands rose up from the marble ground. Alison stared, fascinated, at the pieces surrounding her. She made a mental note to return to LAPMAC as a guest one day. Then she heard the running and the shouting. The sense of calm and quiet was gone. She felt her fingers start to tingle.

My friends from The Ivy coming back with the dessert menu, she thought.

But it wasn't her friends from The Ivy. It was T! Looking foxy in a tux! And running toward her! Like in the big romantic scene at the end of the movie.

And I'm a tragic purple disaster! she thought bitterly. So *not fair.*

Then she noticed T wasn't alone. Who was that red-faced skinny kid trying to keep up with him?

"Hey, hot pockets," wheezed David, trying to sound all casual and nonchalant.

Eels! With T?

"I'm so not talking to you," she said to David, though, surprisingly, deep down, she found herself pleased to see him. . . .

Alison noticed that the two boys looked scared to death.

"What did you do?" said Alison instantly to David.

"Me?" he responded, breathless but outraged.

That's when Alison realized that David and T were being hotly pursued by a small group of big, angry men wearing gas masks with the Gucci logo.

FIFTY-FOUR

"Alison, run!" shouted T as the black-clad waiters stomped toward LAPMAC's Sculpture Garden.

But Alison didn't run. She didn't do *anything*. And David knew why. What was one of the things he'd told her she would need to qualify for the superhero club? "A never-ending conflict between your two diametrically opposed identities." Right in front of him was that conflict made flesh.

Alison did nothing as the pursuers gained ground on David and T because she knew that if she summoned up her powers, she'd expose her true self to her boyfriend. Superhero vs. Bip.

Alison shot David a pained glance. Despite everything that had happened between them, she knew he understood her conflict better than anyone. David gave her a quick nod, let himself fall back behind T, and then hurled himself forward, grabbing T's legs and bringing him crashing down to the ground.

Alison gaped at David and T wrestling on the ground. Her fingers started to spark.

The waiters pulled off their Gucci gas masks and shot Alison cold stares designed to terrify her into instant submission. She took a few steps toward them.

"You don't scare me," she said. "But you know what does?"

Before either waiter could answer, Alison held up her index finger and shot a burst of fire into the nearest palm tree. As the palms fried, a cacophony of high-pitched squealing filled the air.

The community of squirrels that had been nesting in the tree leapt from their burning home. At least a dozen residents fell from the air and directly onto the heads and shoulders of the two waiters.

Alison hugged herself and shut her eyes tight. This was her worst nightmare come to life. She cracked open an eye. Just as she feared, the squirrels dug their claws into the waiters' heads and wouldn't let go. Even worse, a couple of them had burning tails, which they tried to put out by repeatedly slapping them against the waiters' faces. The men howled in pain and ran screaming back into the museum. *"Ewwww."* She shuddered, failing to notice that David was still trying to push T's face into the ground so he couldn't see her firepower.

"Get *off* me, Eels!" barked T. David knew this was going to be bad. The thing with the phone. The smiling reaction to the possibility of Alison being in danger. And now he was shoving the junior president's unblemished face down onto the cold marble floor to stop him from seeing Alison in full fire action.

Sure enough, T whirled and shoved David off him. Jumping to his feet, T grabbed David by his shirt, jerked him halfway to his feet, and drew back a fist.

"Hic!"

"NO!" screamed Alison, running toward them and grabbing T's arm. He tried to shake her off and then found himself gasping in pain. There was a hand-shaped scorch mark on his tuxedo sleeve. Smoke was rising from it.

T's mouth opened and closed. He looked at his arm. He looked at the burning palm tree. He looked at Alison and David. He had *no* idea what was going on.

"What?" he spluttered. "I mean, I don't . . . it's like there's something I haven't been . . . *What?"*

T looked like he was about to lose his mind. Alison looked to David for help.

"Uh . . . electrical fault?" was the best he could manage.

"They're robbing the place," shouted T. "We're in the middle of a crime scene."

Again Alison looked to David. He nodded.

"It's true. There's a whole gang of them, and they know what they're doing. They used knockout gas. All the billionaires in Beverly Hills are lying facedown in their linguine while the waiters steal their wallets."

"Your dad's in there!" cried T. "Warren. Ginger Becker, all of them. Unconscious. We could have called the police if *someone* wasn't so weird about their phone. . . ."

"Wanna hit me?" challenged David. "That make you feel better?"

"SHUT UP!!!" yelled Alison. Her fingers started to glow.

David's eyes widened in panic. What if T saw? Luckily T was focused on her face. Her horror-stricken face.

"You're telling me my *father* is unconscious? That someone is stealing from him? And what about Carmen? Is she okay?"

T scratched his head. "I didn't really see her."

Alison breathed hard. "This was her special night. It meant *everything* to her." To both of them. They had worked *so* hard on the Christmas Ball. And they had done it together. Carmen had made her feel so important, so needed. "Just when I thought I was part of a real family again," she said to herself. Alison felt the tears coming but willed them back. This wasn't the time to cry. This was the time to *burn*.

Her mood ring turned black.

She started to walk toward the West Central Suite.

"Alison," said T, "where are you going?"

He hurried after her. "I know you're upset, but the best thing you can do for your father and Carmen is stay with me. They wouldn't want you to get hurt. We need to get out of here and get help."

She turned around. T took a step back. He had never seen this particular expression on her face. She was a study in contained fury.

"Help's on the way," she said, making it sound like a threat.

T reached for her hand. As soon as he made contact, he gasped in pain. He looked at his fingers. They were red and tender.

David rushed to put himself between Alison and the quickly unraveling T. "I know you want to be a hero," he told T. "But the position's filled."

Alison nodded at David and resumed her walk to the West

Central Suite.

"Alison," David called after her.

"What?" she said, glancing behind her.

David took off his backpack and held it out to her.

"You might want to change your clothes."

T stared at David. This guy just got weirder and more incomprehensible.

Alison took the backpack. It was half open. She could see the glint of the gold *H* symbol. Even looking at it made her feel powerful again.

"Thank you," she said.

"Thank UPS," he replied.

A secret, rueful smile passed between them.

T stared at Alison, then back at David.

"What's going on with you two? For real? I thought he was just your weird stalker, but it's like you encourage him."

Alison felt guilty about lying to T. She also felt hurt that he wasn't being a little more supportive. But there was no time for any of that . . . Instead, she just said, "I've got to change. Wait here."

"Yeah, wait here," repeated David as he followed Alison toward LAPMAC's gift store.

"You too," she said, gesturing to David to keep an eye on T. Then she walked into the darkened store to change into her secret identity.

Alison's mind was whirring as she changed out of the wine-stained white dress and into her Hottie uniform.

I can't believe how mean and suspicious T was. I can't believe my dad is unconscious. I can't believe that David brought the Hottie costume with him. I wonder if he had it dry-cleaned? Wig or no wig? I don't have time to pin my hair up. But I sort of feel naked without it.

Alison's mind was still racing. So much so that she didn't realize she was no longer alone in the gift store.

FIFTY-FIVE

Tiny pinpoints of white light pierced the darkness, and then Alison was lost. She felt weightless, floating in space, nothing supporting her. Just endless black. She couldn't feel her body; she couldn't utter sounds, much less form words. There were thoughts in her head, but she wasn't thinking them. But they were soothing thoughts. They felt warm and comforting. They were like music. There was a melody swimming around in her head.

But there was also a memory. What had David said? "She'll never put you in a trance again, I'll tell you that. You just do what Darqmoon did in Volume 5: *The Revenge of Shin Sun*. You find the one thing that matters most to you and you hold on to it. You use it to push your consciousness through."

Alison tried to focus. What mattered to her? What meant the most to her? She saw a brief flicker of her mother's face. The image faded to be replaced by brief flashes: her father, Carmen, David, T, even Kellyn and Dorinda. And then the burning golden *H* logo. *This* was what mattered most to her? Even in her barely conscious state, she realized at the moment what mattered the most to her was her ability to help those she loved. She couldn't save her mother. But she had the power to rescue her father and all her friends. She could do it. In Alison's mind the golden *H* burned brighter. She felt it push through the black. And she felt herself come back.

"This is what happened to me before."

She wasn't lost anymore.

"It's not happening again, Wettie!"

Alison blasted a jagged burst of fire at the woman in black standing a few feet away from her. The woman scrambled backward, lost her footing, and fell to the ground.

Alison's sparking, glowing fingers lit up the darkened store, revealing the unhooded face of her adversary.

"Wettie?" said Carmen. "What's that about?"

"Carmen?" gasped Alison, pulling off her huge Chanel glasses.

Since they'd become friends, Alison had changed her opinion that Carmen's face was only capable of a limited number of expressions. Her repertoire, it turned out, extended beyond haughty disapproval and included affection, mischief, and sincerity. But Alison had never before seen her stepmother perform so many consecutive facial reactions.

When Carmen realized the identity of the flame-throwing freak behind the dark glasses, she was disbelieving, shocked, enraged, despairing, and, finally, bleakly amused.

"The irony is that I'm not a mind reader." She chuckled.

"Huh?"

"Huh?" said Carmen, nastily echoing Alison. "I'm a mind *controller.*"

"Huh?" repeated Alison.

"You know the hardest part of these past few months? Treating your stupidity as if it's cute."

There it was. The haughty disapproval Alison had come to know so well and hoped she'd never see again.

Pulling herself to her feet, never taking her eyes from Alison's stunned face, Carmen addressed her stepdaughter in a cold, condescending manner.

"I love LA," she said. "Everyone's so desperate to be better-looking and richer and more successful. And everyone believes that there's someone out there who can make all those things happen for them."

"Like Tyra?" said Alison, trying to use snark as a shield to hide how freaked out she was.

"Like me," said Carmen, scowling. "I have a gift. I can open other people's minds like they're notebooks. I can erase what's there and rewrite their lives."

"Cool gift. Was it from the Apple Store?" *Bring it on, Botox. 'Cos I could do this all day.*

Carmen put a finger to her lips.

"Listen," she said softly.

The gift store was silent. From outside, Alison heard the faint sound of two voices humming a familiar nursery rhyme melody.

"Thank me for taking care of your boy problems." Carmen smirked.

"Thanks," said Alison, who actually *was* grateful that she didn't have to worry about what David might say to T and if T might kick David in the coccyx.

"I didn't grow up like you. I didn't have everything," said Carmen bitterly.

"Snore," responded Alison.

Scowling with displeasure at Alison's continued insolence, Carmen got louder and more melodramatic, like she was performing in front of a packed theater.

"I could have. I should have had everything you took for granted and more. My father should have been a billionaire. Everyone should have known his name. His inventions should have changed the way we live. If he'd been taken seriously, if he'd been given the financing, we'd be traveling in time and living for hundreds of years. But he was as paranoid as he was brilliant. So he stayed down in his basement so that no one could steal his ideas. Well, almost no one. I got sick of waiting for him to show the world what he could do. So *I* showed the world. . . ."

Carmen waited to see Alison's stunned reaction.

"Bet you wish your girlfriend was hot like me," sang Alison, aware how much her bored, short-attention-span voice would irritate her psychotic stepmom.

Carmen picked up speed. "I used one of his inventions to paralyze your daddy and all his rich friends. And I used another to put you in a trance. Remember how it felt?"

Carmen gazed into Alison's eyes with unsettling intensity. Suddenly, Alison felt herself transported back to the night of Carmen's big *Brentwood* magazine profile. The night her stepmother's eyes turned opaque. The night Alison couldn't look away. The night she thought she heard voices in her head. The closer she looked, the closer she saw: tiny pinpoints of light getting brighter. She felt herself slipping away. Alison fought to summon back the burning *H*. It was harder this time. Carmen's face. Her smug, self-satisfied *evil* excuse for a face kept appearing in her mind.

Then the lights dimmed and Alison shook herself back to full consciousness.

Carmen touched two fingers to her eyes. A second later, she had a pair of absolutely average-looking contact lenses sitting on her fingertips.

"Imagine being thirteen and having access to a device that allows you to instantly strip away other people's identities and implant your thoughts and suggestions into them with just one glance."

Alison smirked. "I've got that device. It's called being cool. You've probably never heard of it."

Carmen couldn't believe that Alison was still capable of getting under her skin. With her voice rising slightly, she continued, "I made teachers give me straight A's. I made men buy me cars. I got whatever I wanted. But as I got older, I got . . . I hesitate to call it a conscience. But I started to doubt myself and what I was doing. That made it harder to manipulate minds. So I came to LA."

"*Stellar* story, Carm, not even remotely boring," said Alison in a jaded monotone.

"I haven't finished. I came here to reinvent myself. I actually thought I could use my father's invention to help people forget their fears and overcome their problems. Amassing a clientele to legitimize my life-coaching business was so easy, I knew I could transform myself into a philanthropic wife. I mean, if I could breathe confidence into a bunch of insecure actors and interior designers, how hard could it be to recruit a wealthy husband . . . ?"

Alison inhaled sharply. "You used your trick contact lenses on my dad?"

"A grieving widower scared to let go of the past but even more nervous about moving on? A dedicated dad trying to be a good father but afraid he's in way over his head? Please. *So* easy. But then there was you."

"I like this part."

Carmen curled a lip. "Not just a spoiled brat but, as it turns out, one of nature's little jokes."

"At least I'm funny." Alison shrugged.

"As much as I wanted to wipe your tiny mind clean, I couldn't do it. You hated me too much, and that made you too strong for me."

Alison nodded proudly.

"As if I cared. I had your father. I could make him do anything I wanted. *Anything.*"

"You made him clumsy," said Alison accusingly.

"Just my little way of getting back at you. It was quite therapeutic. But then you screwed me out of my Mercedes and my *Brentwood* spread and that's when I knew I was fooling myself. I didn't want to help anyone. I wanted to run this town, and I wanted you out of my way and out of my life. I ought to thank you for bringing me back to my senses."

So saying, Carmen slipped her hypnotic contact lenses back onto her pupils.

"You're welcome," breathed Alison, remembering something T had said during the good part of the Best Date Ever.

"You never know what's going on in someone else's head," he'd said. *"Something small and insignificant to you could be the biggest thing ever to someone else."*

Robbing Carmen of her flashy car and her magazine story had caused her to revert back to her supervillainous ways! *Wettie was petty!*

"But you crossed me. Which does *not* happen without repercussions."

Alison didn't react. She wasn't sure what *repercussions* meant but she suspected it was something she wouldn't like.

Carmen was annoyed that Alison's attention seemed to have wandered again. "So I waited till you were vulnerable and then I made you love me."

Alison's oh-so-bored pose slid right off her face. Hurt and dismay took over. Betrayal—even when it's at the hands of the person you hate most in the world—still stings.

"No way," said a shocked Alison. "You liked me. We hung out, we had fun, we were close."

"I feel like you're not quite grasping the mind control concept. The affection you felt, I manufactured."

Why did this hurt so much? "You didn't like me a little bit?"

"Fake Carmen adored you. After spending so much time around you, Real Carmen despises you even more than she ever thought possible."

Alison was confused. "Wait, so there's two of you?"

Rolling her eyes, Carmen continued, "But painful as it was, I had to get you to trust me enough to agree to play a part in the Christmas Ball. Which, your friends might have told you, is currently being robbed. By me."

"That's brilliant, Carm, stealing stuff worth thousands from people who make billions. That's the kind of plan that—"

Carmen seized her big moment: "An out-of-control fourteen-year-old might come up with," she preened victoriously. "An out-of-control fourteen-year-old who told her therapist she thought she could shoot flames from her fingertips."

"Which I can testify to," said Dr. Mee, walking into the room.

Carmen went on, "An out-of-control fourteen-year-old with a dangerously delusional crush on her favorite actor."

"Which *I* can testify to," said Nick Stygian, walking into the room.

Alison opened her mouth. No sounds emerged. *Betrayed again!!*

"Who's the sassy Chihuahua now?" sneered Nick.

"You are," Alison spat back.

"If by me, you mean you," retorted Nick.

"If by you, you mean poo," said Alison.

"Freak show."

"Uberdouche."

"Enough!" snapped Carmen.

Alison shook her head in bemusement. "So, wait, let me see if I got this right. You're setting me up for the big Christmas Ball robbery?"

Carmen nodded. "Your reputation will be shattered. No one

will ever believe you again. No one will ever trust you. Your father will have you institutionalized."

Alison started counting on her fingers. "(1) There's no such word. (2) How's this gonna happen? You already got your butt scorched. This is your backup plan? A bunch of waiters, a dud therapist—no offense, Kimmy—and a wack TV actor who I made crawl on the floor like a dog. And (3) and (4)."

"What are 3 and 4?" asked Carmen.

"More excellent reasons why your plan is retarded. And if anyone's going to end up intuitionizable, it's gonna be you."

Carmen turned to Dr. Mee and Nick Stygian.

"Eagle claw stance!" she barked.

The therapist and the TV actor fell into martial arts stances and advanced on Alison, who cackled with laughter.

"Kimmy, Sassy. I know this isn't you. I know Carmen's Botoxed your brains. So I'm gonna do you a favor. . . ."

Alison slashed bars of fire in front of Dr. Mee and Nick Stygian, halting their progress. Then she sent horizontal jets of flame across the vertical bars, effectively trapping them in a cage of flames.

Alison smiled at her handiwork, then glanced upward as the intense heat in the enclosed space set off the sprinkler system, instantly soaking her. Just like it had that time at Barneys. And, like that time at Barneys, Alison looked down at her hands and saw wisps of smoke float from her fingertips.

Carmen began walking toward her. "I made an educated guess as to why you called me Wettie."

The sprinklers extinguished the cage of flame. Dr. Mee and Nick Stygian advanced on her.

Alison pointed her left hand at Carmen and jabbed the right at the doctor and the actor. Nothing happened.

"You got an idea in your size-zero brain that I was your nemesis, the water to your fire."

Alison began to panic. How could this have happened? Why didn't David warn her that water could put out her fire? Why did he have to name her Wettie? Why did it *never* rain in LA?

Carmen enjoyed Alison's distress. "It's called being smart. You've probably never heard of it."

The more Alison panicked, the more her fingers refused to ignite. The closer Carmen, Dr. Mee, and Nick Stygian got, the more her mind was filled with fear. Then she was lost, weightless, floating in space. . . .

FIFTY-SIX

"We're having such a better time than Alison," said Kellyn.

"*So* much better," agreed Dorinda.

"I wouldn't go to her party if she paid me a million dollars."

"*Two* million."

"Try ten."

"And got down on her knees and pleaded."

"*Pleasepleaseplease come,*" squeaked Kellyn, cracking up at her impression of her former friend. "Imagine how boring her party is!"

"*So* boring." Dorinda yawned.

"Fake. Tacky. Stupid. Everything I'm anti."

"I can't even stand it."

"She'll be *sick* when she hears about our night," said Kellyn.

"She might cry. Boo hoo."

"She'd hate it because she wouldn't be in control of it. And Alison can't live without everyone doing what she says."

"Shush now, girls," called out Marvelette.

Kellyn and Dorinda looked over their shoulders at their friend. As soon as Marvelette had heard about the Christmas Ball, she had put her foot down. Her father would happily have bought tickets, but Marvelette was *not* about to be the supporting player in someone else's movie. If there was going to be a big, glittering Christmas party, she was going to be its shiny centerpiece. That's why all the guests at her Even More Special Christmas Ball were gathered in her father's back garden. "Merry Christmas, everybody," sang out Marvelette, looking cute in her matching fur-trimmed Santa hat and miniskirt as she sat atop her neon-lit sleigh and tugged at the reins of her two loyal reindeer.

And even though the reins bit into their necks and the reindeer costumes itched and they wondered when they were going to get to change back into their party dresses and mix with the rest of the guests, Kellyn and Dorinda both agreed they were having *such* a better time than Alison.

FIFTY-SEVEN

David almost didn't want to wake up. Being under Carmen's mind control was a lot like being behind the dark curtain at the gym just before he invaded the stage and interrupted Alison's presidential acceptance speech. Nice and warm and dark and comforting. But he knew he couldn't stay there. He had to emerge from the trance. David concentrated on the thing that meant the most to him. Alison's face shone through the darkness. He held on to the memory of her and pushed his way back to consciousness.

The first thing he heard was the nursery rhyme melody being mumbled by the still-comatose T. The first thing he saw was the water on the ground. He followed the trail of water to the gift store. He saw the burn marks on the ceiling and on the floor.

"She's okay," he told himself. "There's nothing she can't handle." If he kept repeating it, he'd start believing it. . . .

Carmen felt fantastic. She felt like a blockbuster movie director with a billion-dollar budget and the obedient awe of a loyal crew at her disposal. She took her time arranging the incriminating scene that the LAPD were going to find when they answered her call about the disturbance at LAPMAC. Carmen placed the tranced-out Alison in the middle of numerous manufactured scenarios among the paralyzed VIPs in the West Central Suite.

Should she be captured in the act of snatching a diamond necklace from its owner? Stuffing her pockets with six-figure checks while running for the exit? Apprehended while drugging and attempting to abduct her obsession, Nick Stygian? Every option appealed. It might take her a few more minutes before she was ready to make that call.

"Later, dude," muttered David to the still-frozen T, and began to make his way to the West Central Suite.

But then he stopped. "What am I doing?" he asked himself. "I can't just leave T in limbo. Alison may be in trouble, and the only two people who can help her are . . ." He paused and savored the moment. "The only two people who can help her are . . . *adversaries brought together by their shared feelings for her*! This is classic!"

David couldn't help it. He understood this was a bad situation. Alison in jeopardy. T floating in nothingness. But he was getting to live out his comic book fantasies! He turned back to the nursery-rhyming T.

"Push through it," he commanded. "You can do it. You're the junior president. You've got principles and beliefs. On a personal level, I'm not a fan. But who would I rather have on my side in a crisis? Toenail? Phlegmy? Tiny Head? No. You. So push through it. Think of the one thing that really matters to you. The one thing. Come on, man. We both know what it is. It's the same as mine. Just think about her!"

Nothing.

David waited for signs of life. A flicker? A blink? *Anything?*

Nothing.

Growing agitated, he drew back his fist. "I'm sorry about this, dude . . . actually, I'm not sorry. You hit me with a car. My coccyx still twinges."

David punched T full in the face.

Nothing.

He drew back his fist to punch T again.

This time T woke up, saw the punch headed straight for him, moved out of the way, hooked his leg around David's ankle, shoved him to the ground, and drew back his own fist.

"Great," squealed David. "You're back! Alison's in trouble. We gotta save her."

T paused in mid-punch. Fragments of memory returned. Something about her going to change clothes? A big gold chain with the letter *H*? A burning palm tree?

David pulled himself to his feet and began running toward the West Central Suite.

"You coming?" he called back to T.

FIFTY-EIGHT

"*Police. Hello? Oh,* thank God. I'm at LAPMAC. A teenager's gone crazy. She's drugged and robbed the guests. I think she's trying to abduct an actor who didn't return her crazy deluded obsessions. For God's sake, send help!"

Carmen clicked off her phone and smiled at the scenario in front of her. She'd contact-lens-mind-controlled Alison into scrawling a tragic confessional note, full of if-I-can't-have-Nick-no-one-will melodrama.

When the cops arrived, they'd be in time to catch her dragging the handcuffed actor down the museum steps, thousands of dollars' worth of jewelry spilling from her pockets.

Perfect.

★ ★ ★

David knew he risked blowing T's not entirely open mind if he told him *everything* about Alison. So he skirted around the truth. He told T Alison had a chemical imbalance. He told him she was off her meds. He told him the only way to reverse her slide into complete catatonia was to make her mad. And because T was a helper and a fixer and a carer, his heart went out to Alison and the medical problem she'd been foolish enough to hide from him, thinking he wouldn't understand.

Watching T kick open a locked door, David couldn't help thinking, *He's got the muscle. I've got the brains. Alison's got the firepower. We just need a semi-trustworthy mutant who's a reluctant team player and we're a super-*gang*!*

Inside the locked door was the PA system playing Christmas music. David faded "We Three Kings" and went to press the Talk button. As he breathed in, he felt the *hic!* coming. *Oh no,* he thought. This was too much pressure. Too much responsibility. His finger remained hovering over the button.

"David?" said a worried T.

David knew the next few moments would affect the rest of Alison's life. There was nothing more important to him than her life. He swallowed the *hic!* And pressed the button.

"Wake up, *bip!*" boomed the voice that echoed around the giant snow globe. "No one likes you. Because you're pretty. Everyone hates you. Because you're pretty. Everyone talks about you behind your back, everybody looks down on you, everybody thinks the world would be a better place without you in it. . . ."

Once again, Carmen's face was forced to register surprise

and anger.

Glaring at the nearest pair of minions, she said, "Find that voice and shut it up."

The PA system tirade continued: "Wouldn't we all be better off without you? Doesn't everyone you know end up getting hurt? And it's always because of you. Because the world revolves around you, because you always get everything you want, because you're pretty. . . ."

Mouth pressed close to the microphone, David kept talking. "Why don't you stay in that trance? If you're out of the way, no one's going to get confused about their feelings. No one's going to dread going to school in case they see you. No one's going to pick up the phone to call you a hundred times a day. No one's going to miss you the way I do."

T tapped David on the shoulder. "Is this really helping?"

David looked startled. For a moment, he'd completely forgotten the actual reason he was berating Alison. Embarrassed, he continued. "Also, you've got untrustworthy eyes. Everyone thinks so, not just me. And you eat too fast. . . ."

The broadcast room door flew open. Carmen's henchmen stormed in.

The sounds of glass breaking and howls of pain came over the PA system. Carmen nodded, satisfied another problem was taken care of. She turned her attention back to Alison, making sure she was positioned perfectly for her showdown with the LAPD. Carmen stepped back to admire her handiwork. The handcuffs. The jewelry. The note. The concerned therapist standing close by, attempting to talk sense into her sociopathic patient. Perfect.

Making the moment shine just a little bit brighter, Carmen turned to see her minions drag the bruised, bleeding, struggling David and T into the West Central Suite.

"The accomplices!" she sang out cheerfully.

"The bad guy," retorted David.

Carmen smiled at David. "Oh, you're the one that likes her too much. The one who wanted to be *more than friends*. I could do that for you, you know. Easiest thing in the world. I could make her fall completely in love with you. Would you like that?"

David would never have named Carmen Wettie if he'd known how scary and charismatic and hypnotic she was. He'd have gone with something like Deathglare.

She went on, "Or I could wipe her from your memory. You'd never have to lie awake and cry over her anymore. Would you like that better?"

Carmen turned her attention to T, who was visibly shaken by the situation in the West Central Suite.

Assuming an almost motherly tone, she moved closer to T. "Or maybe *you'd* like that better. You've seen who she really is and you don't like it, do you? You're not the sort of boy who has room in his life for a freak. And that's what Alison is."

With her attention devoted to David and T, Carmen failed to see the obsessive love letter in Alison's hand start to smoke and then catch fire.

Nick Stygian saw it. But he never managed to say anything about it because the handcuffs connecting him to Alison were suddenly red-hot.

"Hey, Kimmy," said Alison to Dr. Mee, who was standing

close by, immersed in her role as concerned therapist.

The doctor's eyes flickered in fear.

"Ask me how I'm feeling."

Dr. Mee couldn't speak.

"Just ask me."

"How . . ." The doctor's voice emerged in a squeak. "How are you feeling?"

"Flammable," she said, staring straight into Dr. Mee's terrified eyes.

Without looking away, Alison stretched an arm out behind her and pointed two fingers at Carmen, who was still toying with David and T. The anxiety evident in the two boys' eyes made Carmen smile with pleasure. Her smile faded when she realized her earrings were on fire. Screeching in pain, she ripped them out.

The guys who had beaten up David and T suddenly relaxed their grips on the two boys. "What are we doing here?" said the nutritionist to his black-clad colleague, the personal trainer.

In her freak-out over her scorched earrings, Carmen had released her grip on the minds of her LA underlings. They were innocent victims whose yearning for personal advancement had made them easy prey for Carmen's fake life coaching. They could not be blamed for their actions.

Of course, that didn't stop T from kicking the personal trainer in the nuts and David from picking up a silver drinks tray and slamming it in the face of the nutritionist.

From outside LAPMAC, the sound of sirens got closer. Carmen tried to collect herself. She could still salvage this.

"I hate you too much and that makes me too strong for you.

That's what you said, right, Carm?"

Alison walked slowly, steadily toward her stepmother, dragging the whimpering Nick Stygian, who was still attached to the burning handcuffs, like a dog behind her.

Carmen discovered a brand-new sensation. Fear.

The handcuffs snapped. Nick Stygian slumped to the ground, cradling his burned wrist.

Alison kept walking toward Carmen.

Carmen fought her fear and looked Alison calmly in the eye.

"What are you going to do, Alison? Are you going to burn me alive? I don't think so. You don't have that in you. You don't want to hurt people, even if they've hurt you."

Alison came to a halt a few feet away from Carmen.

"You might be right. Or you might be wrong. I've never done it before. I might love it. Like sushi. And look at how much you get off on being worshipped. If I barbecue you, it could be the best thing that ever happened. You could be the new Noah of Arc."

Carmen smiled.

"I thought you hated having to act like my stupidity was cute," said Alison coldly.

"I was wrong. I didn't know who you were. But now I do, and that changes everything. We don't have to be enemies, Alison, not when we've got so much in common. It can get lonely when you're the only one. But we're not alone anymore. We're both special."

Alison went slack-jawed with disgust. "Stay out of my head, Carmen."

But Carmen wasn't in Alison's head. As she fed Alison a fantasy she knew her stepdaughter would mock, Carmen regrouped her powers and shot a quick, opaque commanding glance in Nick Stygian's direction.

"She treated you like a dog," Carmen's voice taunted the fallen actor. *"Make her pay."*

David saw Nick drag himself to his feet and start to run toward Alison.

"Alison, behind you!" he shouted.

Alison didn't take her eyes off Carmen. Instead, she raised a hand to her neck, gave her string of pearls a hard yank, and then stepped aside as Nick tripped on the pearls and went flying across the ground, slamming into a table and bringing an ice bucket crashing down on his head.

Alison arched a victorious eyebrow at Carmen. That was it? That was all she had left?

It wasn't. Unlike the motionless, ice-spattered Nick Stygian, Dr. Mee hadn't been fooling when she locked into her tiger claw stance.

The therapist hurled herself across the floor of the suite, swept Alison's legs out from under her, spun her around, and lifted her by the throat, her feet dangling a few inches from the ground.

David stared, horrified, while also subconsciously making a place for Dr. Mee in his late-night ass-kicking superbabe fantasies.

"You should have come back to therapy, Alison," Dr. Mee said in the same low, calm voice she used during sessions. "We could have worked through this."

"Change of plan." Carmen sighed. "The cops will find her unconscious, which isn't anywhere near as satisfying as the crime scene I had planned, but what can you do? Put her to sleep, Dr. Mee."

Dr. Mee applied further pressure to Alison's throat. As she began to black out, she heard the doctor murmur, "And AlDoKe is a *stupid* name for a spa."

That was all Alison needed. She rallied against the pressure of the doctor's fingers clutching her windpipe. She squeezed her fists together, let out a harsh gasp, and two blasts of flame shot out of her hands, propelling both her and the shrieking therapist into the air.

"She can fly. Unexpected," noted David.

"She can fly!" gasped T.

"I can freakin' fly!" screamed Alison, whose trajectory was halted when she grabbed onto the huge chandelier at the top of the glass dome for support.

Dr. Mee clung onto Alison's hand and started to pull herself up. Then she inhaled sharply. The hand she clutched was burning hotter and hotter.

"Alison, help," moaned the therapist.

"Ask me what you're doing right now," replied Alison.

"Alison, please. I can't hold on much longer."

"Just ask me."

"What am I doing?" asked the doctor.

"I think you're crying out for help," replied Alison, sending a wave of heat through her fingers. The doctor tried to cling on. She dug her nails into Alison's palm. She tried to swing herself up toward the chandelier. But finally, the doctor lost her grip and crashed onto the ice rink directly below.

"Get her! Stop her! Kill her! Do something!" Carmen's voice was shrill and panicked and completely out of control.

Still hanging on to the chandelier, Alison saw the remnants of Carmen's army spill onto the ice. She saw them reach for weapons. She saw crossbows. She saw gas canisters. Lashing out an arm, she unleashed a fireball that smashed into the ice below, causing it to splinter and crack. Carmen's squad started to grab each other for support. Their weapons fell from their hands and dropped through the rapidly melting ice. Alison shot another burst of flame into the rink. The orchestra stand began to capsize.

"Bet she says something about breaking the ice," muttered David to a frazzled T.

"That broke the ice!" called out Alison as she watched the Christmas Ball sinking into the water beneath her.

FIFTY-NINE

Waking up inside a snow globe proved a weird experience for the guests of the Christmas Ball. As they came out of their trances, the assembled billionaires and corporate heads saw dancing snowflakes. They saw a picture-perfect little village, an ice rink, an orchestra, and a choir of children. Some of them started weeping. Some of them started freaking out. Some of them started calling their lawyers. When the LAPD arrived, they had a million questions. Who melted the ice rink? Why did every billionaire in LA fall asleep at the same time? Why were all the waiters and personal trainers muttering about clearing up clutter? Why did no one remember what had happened?

Amid the growing chaos, Alison had something she needed

to say. If she didn't get to deliver this particular sentence, she thought she might explode. But how could she say, "I told you so!" if she couldn't find her father?

She needed to tell Roger and to see him hang his head. She needed him to admit that he'd been woefully misguided. She needed to hear him say that he would never again make a decision that affected their futures without consulting her. But she couldn't see him. Or Carmen. Alison started to feel queasy.

David rushed up to her. "Did you know you could fly? How did it *feel?* Are you completely freaked out? It was beyond awesome. . . ."

"Have you seen my dad?" she asked, looking around the West Central Suite.

She saw Warren and Ginger Becker clinging to each other, looking dazed. She saw Nick Stygian being questioned by a cop and responding with a display of injured innocence pathetic and whiny enough to win him another Kids' Choice Award. She saw T standing by one of the fake houses in the little village. He didn't move, and he certainly wasn't making the slightest attempt to meet her eyes.

This would have had a greater impact on her if Alison hadn't been filled with a gnawing certainty that something bad had happened to her father.

The moment she allowed uncertainty to grow into fear, she heard Carmen's voice in her head. *"Come to the roof. Alone."*

Earlier in the evening, when she had the Bluetooth in her ear, having Carmen so close was comforting. Now it made Alison's blood run cold.

The voice returned. Mocking. Vindictive. Terrifying. *"Hurry, now. Don't keep Mommy waiting."*

SIXTY

Alison didn't know what was worse: the first sickening sight of her father perched on the very edge of the museum roof, swaying precariously in the night wind, inches away from falling to his death. Or the knowledge that his life was now entirely in Carmen's hands. Seeing Carmen standing serenely, a few feet away from her father, caused Alison to crumble. *I can't keep fighting her,* she thought, her eyes welling up.

"Don't cry, Alison," said Carmen sympathetically. "I'm not going to let him fall. I'm not going to hurt him in any way. As long as you do what I say."

"Please, Carmen, please don't hurt him," Alison sobbed. "I'll do anything you want."

"I'm so glad you said that," Carmen replied. "Because there

is something I want. I want us to be close again the way we were when we were both pretending to be people we weren't."

Alison tried to stop crying. "Okay. Sure. Just let him go."

Carmen was pleased. "That's great. I'm so relieved. I couldn't bear for us to be at each other's throats when we're really so alike. I just know we'll make an amazing team."

"Me too. Totally." Alison sniffed, wondering if Carmen wanted them to try out for *The Amazing Race*, which, when she thought about it, wasn't a bad idea, because a stepmother-stepdaughter supervillain-superhero combination had probably never applied for the show before and would fly through the audition process.

Carmen went on, "Obviously, LA's not going to work for me anymore. But where else will I find so many suggestible people with so much money? Manhattan? Maybe. Washington? Possibly. It's a risk, though. Or at least it was, before we combined my mind control with your firepower. Who's going to say no to us? Who's going to stop us?"

"Huh?" replied Alison.

"*Huh?*" imitated Carmen. "We really have to work on that if we're going to be partners."

"Partners?" repeated Alison.

"Why not? We've got *so* much in common."

"We're nothing alike," said an increasingly wary Alison.

"Of course we are. We destroy everything we touch. You just haven't learned to accept it yet. You're as responsible as I am for your father's fate."

Alison glanced at Roger, who began half singing, half humming the familiar nursery rhyme melody.

"He's happy," said Carmen. "He's with your mother. I put

that in his head. I'm not the monster you think I am."

"How do you know? You're not a mind reader," snapped Alison.

Carmen turned her gaze toward Roger. The wind hadn't picked up, but he seemed to be swaying, as if he was in danger of losing his balance.

"Don't!" screamed Alison. Her fingers caught fire.

"There's my little match girl," murmured Carmen, looking enraptured by Alison's abilities.

Alison pointed her fingers at Carmen. "You told me I didn't have it in me to hurt someone. *Really* hurt them."

"That was just tough love. I believe you do have it in you. It's just like anything; you have to work at it."

Both of Alison's hands were engulfed in flames.

"I'm giving you the chance to walk away. Leave my father alone. Leave me alone. *Go.*"

"And if I don't?"

"You're ashes."

Carmen grinned. "My supervillain retort to that threat is . . . kiss my ash."

Alison wasn't smiling. Her fists were fireballs.

"I'm holding back, Carmen."

"Don't. Hit me with your best shot. Maybe you can burn me down before I wipe out your frightened little mind. And if you do, then your daddy doesn't die. That's a pretty good incentive."

Alison clenched and unclenched her fists. Sparks flew across the roof every time she did so.

"Of course, if you don't, then he's dead and you're all mine."

Alison shot both hands out, aiming them straight at Carmen.

Before the fireballs burst from her hands, both arms jerked upward as if she was being pulled by unseen strings.

Fireballs streaked up into the night sky, disappearing into the blackness. Her arms slumped limply by her sides. The light in her eyes seemed to go out.

"You're all mine," said Carmen softly.

She walked toward Alison and tenderly ran a hand through her hair. "The one thing I never had that I always wanted was a child, a daughter. When you wake up, you're going to think of me as your mother. And if I grow tired of you, which I will, getting rid of you won't hurt as much."

Inside her trance, Alison writhed and groaned like she was trying to say something.

"You're a fighter," said Carmen, nodding admiringly. "One last word before the old you goes to sleep."

Alison's eyes flickered open. She said, "Ten-oh-six."

Carmen furrowed her brow. She had always been able to rely on Alison for a terse put-down, but that one wasn't very memorable.

Shrugging, she took a few steps back and allowed herself a self-congratulatory moment as she surveyed what remained of the Cole family of Brentwood. *Perfect.*

As Carmen herself had previously admitted, she was *not* a mind reader. Had she been, she would have picked up that in the middle of Alison's fury, she still remembered that the 10:06 British Airways flight from Heathrow Airport was scheduled to pass overhead.

She would have also picked up on Alison's recollection of the last person she told about her ability to memorize the flight schedule.

She would also have picked up on David Eels's response to Alison's emotional revelation.

If she had picked up on any of those thoughts, Carmen might have wondered why Alison was spending her last conscious seconds thinking about some dork talking about faulty airline waste disposal systems.

That might have guided her toward the idea that Alison had jerked her flaming hands up into the air a matter of moments before Carmen took total control of her mind.

She might have suspected that Alison was shooting fireballs through the waste tank of the plane flying overhead.

If Carmen had been a mind reader, she might have moved out of the way before a giant ball of frozen poo fell out of the bottom of flight 10:06, dropped through the night sky, and crushed her like a bug. But, as Carmen had said, she was not a mind reader.

"What the hell am I doing up here?" shouted Roger Cole, coming out of his trance to find himself at the edge of the museum roof. He scrambled to keep his balance.

"Dad!" screamed Alison, snapping back to full consciousness and hurling herself toward the edge of the roof in time to grab her father around the waist and pull him back.

"How did we get here?" he asked, though he didn't dwell on his confusion because his daughter was hugging him tightly and sobbing her heart out.

★ ★ ★

The impact of the object hitting the roof sent the cops scurrying up to discover the source of the latest in a night full of inexplicable incidents.

"What's that?" said a cop, staring at the huge brown frozen ball with the two motionless Christian Louboutin—clad feet sticking out at the bottom.

"That's just some shit I had to take care of," replied Alison, keeping her arms tight around her father.

SIXTY-ONE

Alison walked her shell-shocked father to the Mercedes that Carmen obviously wasn't going to be needing anymore and glared at Designated Dean, silently warning him not to freak Roger out. She watched him climb inside and wondered what she could say that would ease the pain of the sudden demise of his second wife. Nothing came to mind.

David walked up to her. "*That* was clas—"

Before he could finish, she threw her arms around him. "Your lack of social skills saved my life. Mine and my dad's, you dork."

As she hugged David, she saw, over his shoulder, T hanging back by the museum steps. She let go of David and took a few steps toward her boyfriend. His ambivalence was glaringly evident. He wanted to get as far away from Alison and the events of the evening as he could. But he also wanted to do the right thing.

"I didn't lie," she said, anticipating accusation.

"You didn't tell the truth either," he replied.

"I thought you'd be freaked out."

"If you'd trusted me. If you'd started me off slowly by, I don't know, toasting a marshmallow or something. Instead, I got to see you fly. . . ."

"That was cool, though. I didn't even know I could do it."

"Imagine what else you can do."

Alison felt like T wasn't saying that like it was a good thing.

"I work with the fire department," he said, staring at the ground.

"I work with fire too. I love that we've got so much in common," she yammered. Then, seeing the somber look on his face, she said, "I won't do it when we're together. We don't ever have to talk about it."

"So what would we talk about? Who hooked up with who? Who dumped who?"

"Seriously, can you believe Warren and Ginger Becker are still together?"

T pulled a velvet box from his jacket pocket. "I got this for you. For our two-month anniversary."

He opened it to reveal a necklace with a small diamond *A* at the center.

"I love it," she gasped.

Alison went to hold up her hair so T could attach it around her neck. Instead, he found himself holding the slender, delicate *A* against the big, burning *H*. He couldn't reconcile himself to the differences between the two letters and, by extension, the differ-ences between her two lives. T dropped the diamond necklace into Alison's palm and walked away.

"Nobody's perfect. That's what you said," she called.

She watched him go, fighting back the desire to run after him.

"But I bought gloves," she said to herself sadly.

Fortunately, good had triumphed over evil. *Unfortunately*, good was a boyfriend-repelling freak.

David walked up to her and put a consoling arm around her shoulders.

"Another thing you need to be a really successful superhero? A messed-up love life."

SIXTY-TWO

For Alison, Christmas this year meant twelve straight days of lies. She lied to her father, feeding him a heavily censored version of the story regarding Carmen and her absence from the Cole household. Rather than vilify the mind-controlling monster, Alison selflessly denied herself the pleasure of a well-deserved "I told you so" and improvised a fairy story about Carmen being a dedicated wife and mother who sacrificed herself to save her family from frozen poo.

As for New Year's Eve, her carefully considered plan was to spend that night and the rest of her life barricaded in her room, away from the rest of the world so that there was no chance she could hurt anyone else or ruin any more lives. She didn't know whether to laugh or cry when David texted her: "EMRGNCY.

HOTTIE NEEDED. PICK U UP N 20."

Surely he couldn't be expecting a response? But then, she thought, why not? It was the last night of the year. Why not put on the Hottie costume one last time? Go out on one last adventure and then end it for good. She liked it. It was symbolic.

"Happy New Year's, Double D!" said Alison as she climbed into the Mercedes in full Hottie garb. "Made any resolutions for next year?"

"Lose twenty pounds. Gain thirty-five."

"I believe your goal is attainable."

She smiled cautiously at David. The last time they had both been in the back of the Mercedes had not ended well.

"How about you, my young friend?"

"Keep on fighting crime," he said, deadly serious. "Keep the city safe."

Alison wanted to climb out of the car and barricade herself back in her room, but then she remembered: This was the last time. This was symbolic.

"Okay, what's on tonight's menu? Heist? Home invasion? Kidnapping?"

"Something far more heinous," replied David, once again deadly serious.

"I don't get it," said Alison as the Mercedes came to a halt outside the Hollywood Bowl.

"You will," said David, opening the door.

Alison followed him out. She saw T waiting at the entrance to the Bowl. He carried a basket of cupcakes from Joan's on

Third. Alison looked back at David.

"Hurry up," he said. "They're using fireworks and an orchestra. It's going to be a slaughterhouse if you don't get in there."

Alison stared at him. "Did you do this?"

David shrugged, calm, casual, unemotional. "I'm a sucker for a happy ending."

Alison swallowed hard. She hadn't been expecting this. "I don't know what to say."

David checked his watch, still acting like this was no big deal. "Uh-oh. Gotta run. I stay out here much longer and Double D turns back into a pumpkin."

He turned and walked back toward the car.

"David," she called after him. "Thank you."

Without looking back, he raised his hand and gave her a quick thumbs-up gesture.

Alison walked up to T. As she did, she was fully aware that the other New Year's Eve revelers were staring at her costume. She didn't care. She only wanted to see T's reaction.

"Are you going to heat up my cupcakes?" He smiled.

"Not on a first date," she replied.

"This isn't a first date," he said before realizing this was his first actual encounter with Hottie. "Oh, wait, it is."

"You know what I can do. You're not afraid of what might happen?"

"I'm fully prepared for spontaneous combustion."

The doubt in his eyes was gone. She knew he meant it.

David wasn't quite sure how he was going to feel after having delivered the girl he thought he loved into the waiting arms of the boy *she* thought she loved. Should he feel:

1. Good?
2. Decent?
3. Noble?
4. Vomitous?
5. All of the above?

Among the sensations swimming around his head and stomach were nausea and emptiness. For the first time, he was glad to know he had Designated Dean waiting for him.

Demonstrating that he empathized with what the younger boy was going through, Double D rolled down his window so that David could hear Pink, singing "It's just u and ur hand tonight."

SIXTY-THREE

"*This is so much* better than last New Year's," said Kellyn.

"*So* much better," agreed Dorinda.

What had they done this time last year? Hung out in Alison's bedroom, watching a marathon of eighties high school movies, played "Guitar Hero," gorged themselves sick on popcorn and pizza?

That had been fun, kind of. But it was immature. Juvenile. Like when Alison prank-called the local Domino's. "Let me spell my name out for you just so I know you've got it right," she'd giggled into the phone. "It's I-a-v-a-b-i-g-b-u-t. Can you read that back to me?" Sure, it had been mildly amusing when the guy said, "Iavabigbutt," and Alison had tried to reply, "Oh, you have a big butt? Well, get on the StairMaster!" And it was funny that she couldn't get the words out because she was laughing so hard Coke squirted out of her nose.

But that was last year. They weren't little kids anymore. They were grown women. Why else would Marvelette have invited them to spend New Year's with her mother? And why else would her mother have shown them the highlights of her amazing walk-in wardrobe and invited them to try on her beautiful dresses? As the night wore on, Kellyn and Dorinda felt like they were valued confidants of Marvellete's mother. Each dress she brought out of the wardrobe had a story that was somehow connected with the downfall of her marriage. Kellyn and Dorinda were thrilled at the way they were being treated as equals. But then Marvelette's mom emerged from the wardrobe wearing her wedding dress. "And it still fits me!" she howled. She thrust bridesmaids' dresses at her daughter, Kellyn, and Dorinda.

"Put 'em on!" she roared. "We're going to your father's house. Let him see exactly what he threw away!"

"Mom, no!" wailed Marvelette.

And moments later, Kellyn and Dorinda were alone in the dress-strewn bedroom, with the sound of Marvelette pleading with her mother to unlock the door echoing out in the hallway.

"Iavabigbutt," murmured Dorinda wistfully.

SIXTY-FOUR

Only an idiot could have failed to comprehend that New Year's Eve at the Hollywood Bowl with an orchestra swelling to an emotional crescendo and fireworks exploding in the sky was the perfect moment for a kiss. T was not an idiot. He leaned close to Alison, pushed her glasses up onto her forehead, and pulled a crumpled brown paper bag from his jacket pocket.

"I got you something," he said.

She looked suspiciously at the package.

"You might consider opening it," he suggested.

Alison eased a cautious hand into the bag and pulled out a pair of bright yellow flame-retardant gloves.

"Jomac!" she said as if greeting an old friend.

She slipped on the gloves and closed her eyes. Seconds later, his lips met hers.

Alison surprised both herself and T when she heard the words, "I need to find David," flying out of her mouth.

"What?" said T.

"What?" repeated Alison. Had she really just said that? Out loud? Why would she say something like that? In the middle of a moment like *that*?

"Alison, what are you doing? David's gone."

"I know," she said helplessly. "I'm sorry. I just need to see him." *She was saying it again!*

Then she was up out of her seat, squeezing past the New Year's Eve revelers, hurrying downstairs and out of the Bowl with T rushing after her. Even as she ran downstairs, she knew she was being stupid and irrational.

She'd blown the most perfect and romantic kiss opportunity she'd probably ever have, and for what? She didn't know.

As she left the Hollywood Bowl, Alison felt a little of what David felt. She was sick and empty with a side order of stupid thrown in.

She'd messed up something potentially better than the Best Date Ever and David was probably a million miles away by now.

Except he wasn't. He was standing twenty feet away, watching Designated Dean being yelled at by Treasure Spinney, whose limo he had backed into a half hour earlier.

SIXTY-FIVE

The bench at the bus stop outside the Hollywood Bowl wasn't the most romantic location to see in the new year. Neither David nor T looked particularly comfortable sitting there together. Alison didn't care. She knew what she had to say.

"I'm sorry, T. You were perfect tonight. You were everything I could ever have dreamed of. And so were you, David. You did maybe the sweetest thing that anyone's ever done for me, and I couldn't not be with you. I've lost so much this year. But you guys, both of you, have been there for me time and time again. You've shown me you believe in me, you trust me, and you've got faith in me, and I can't even tell you what that means to me . . ."

"Hold on, wasn't that your class president acceptance speech?" said David.

"It applies. Look, what I'm trying to say is, Carmen said something to me just before I smooshed her. She said we were alike; she said we destroyed everything we touched."

David interrupted, "That's standard supervillain psychology designed to mess with your head."

"But it might be true. I might hurt the people I care about. And *you're* the people I care about. I don't know if I'm ready for a relationship. Just like I don't know if I'm really ready to be a superhero. I'm going to have to figure both these things out, and I'm gonna have to do them by myself."

David and T swapped glances. Were they both being dumped here?

Alison sat on the bench and held both boys' hands.

"That's why I'm glad I've got friends who understand me better than anyone. Friends who know that I need time to find out who I am."

The crowd in the Bowl took up the countdown to the new year.

"Ten . . . nine . . . eight . . ."

"Seven . . . six . . . five . . ." said Alison.

Then they all joined in.

"Three . . . two . . . one. Happy New Year!"

They went to hug, and as they did, an SUV filled with jacked-up young punks, laughing and throwing the contents of the car out of its windows, screeched past.

"HELP! HELP!!"

A distraught heavyset man ran toward the bus stop. He

gasped for air, then, after a few attempts at speaking, moaned: "My car! They stole my car!!"

"But you get to keep your fat pants." One of the jacked-up young punks who had taken the man's SUV for a New Year's joyride was laughing and cheerfully hurling his clothes out of the window.

Alison watched fat pants, fat pj's, and fat T-shirts stream out of the window.

She saw the look of pain on the heavyset man's face.

No one deserved to have their fat pants laughed at. Not on New Year's Day. Not on any day.

"So much for my one last symbolic mission." Alison stood up, shook off her Jomacs, slipped her dark glasses back over her eyes, stretched out her hands, and blasted two fireballs of flame into the back tires of the SUV.

The car spun around wildly.

The punks scrambled out.

Alison walked toward them.

"She's going to exchange insurance information," David told the freaked-out heavyset man.

"You could have killed us!" yelled one of the punks.

"*But I didn't.* Happy New Year," said Alison, letting the flames play around her balled-up fists and watching the punks' bravado dribble away.

The punk who had enjoyed himself throwing the fat pants out of the SUV took a step toward Alison.

"We're gonna remember you, little girl. We're gonna come looking for you."

"Make sure you ask for me by name," replied Alison. Then,

without warning, she spun and slashed her hands, burning her logo into the road. The punks stared at the flaming *H* for half a second before turning tail and running into the night.

"It's Hottie," she called after them. "Starts with an *H*. Ends in flames."

There was her logo, burned into North Highland Avenue. Keira Knightley might drive over that *H* one day and wonder what it meant. "It's Hottie, Keira," she imagined herself telling the angular Brit. "I don't have your cheekbones. I don't have your accent. I don't have your pout. I didn't even get to do *one* TV show. But in my own way, I make the world a safer place." And then she realized that she'd just figured out who she was.

Fat pants had shown her where her destiny lay. Like it or not, she had two identities and she was going to have to learn to live with both of them.

"But of course, she eez a super 'ero. She 'az everyzing else, why not geev her powers also?"

"And she chooses to call herself 'Hottie.' 'Cuz she's *so* humble and modest."

Alison looked up from her logo.

Standing on the other side of the flames, a few feet away from their limo service, Kellyn and Dorinda stared at her, shock, fear, resentment, and bitterness evident in their expressions and posture.

Alison wanted to run up to them and grab them and say, "It's a new year. Can't we just forget everything and be friends again?"

But she wasn't going to be the one to make the first move.

T and David, sensing further conflict, took up protective

stances by her side.

Both groups glared at each other.

Then Kellyn spoke.

"Dorinda's got something she wants to say."

Dorinda's mouth dropped open. *Me?* She stared furiously at Kellyn, then turned back to face Alison.

"Ah am not from Fwahnce. Ah 'ave nevair been furzer zan Zanta Barbaira. . . ."

Dorinda paused, gulped audibly, and concentrated on enunciating in her rarely used normal tone of voice.

"But the first time I met you, I was so scared of you and how beautiful you were. I thought no one would ever notice me again. I thought I'd go through high school life invisible. So I did something stupid. I pretended to be someone I wasn't. And I got too scared to stop."

"Secret identity. Cool." David nodded understandingly. Dorinda glanced in his direction, seeing him for the first time.

Alison stared at her. "But I never knew you felt like that. You never said anything."

"What could we say?" Kellyn sighed. "That we were dumb, stupid, jealous—"

"Bips," said David.

"*What* did you call me, dork?" snarled Kellyn.

Alison shot David a "shut *up*" look.

Kellyn collected herself and went on. "That we were so obsessed about being eclipsed by you that we never recognized how lucky we were to have the sweetest, nicest, most fun girl in the world as our friend? We should have said it."

"But instead we undermined you and talked behind your

back," mumbled Dorinda. "And we made you think you needed an operation you totally didn't need because you were *so* symmetrical already. And then we treated you like a nonperson, like you didn't even exist."

Dorinda's eyes filled with tears.

Alison lifted her dark glasses and wiped her own eyes.

And then Kellyn, caught up in the rising emotion, said, "And Marvelette and her scary mom just *abandoned* us. We didn't even get *pretzels.* . . ."

"But we're sorry," said Dorinda quickly.

"We're *really* sorry," confirmed Kellyn. "If we could, we'd add an extra month to the calendar just to keep saying sorry. We'd call it Apologember."

Dorinda continued, "And we'll totally keep your superhero secret even if you don't want to be friends with us again."

"But we'd really like to be friends again," said Kellyn.

Alison chewed her lip and said nothing. She gave David and T a searching look.

"Don't look at *them*," yelled an exasperated Kellyn. "A dork and a do-gooder. We're your *real* friends."

"Nobody's perfect," T reminded Alison.

"Oh, that's *brilliant*," sulked Kellyn.

Alison remained silent.

David surveyed the quintet gathered around the flaming *H* logo. Then he grinned.

"So let's see what we've got here."

He pointed to Kellyn. "The bitch." Kellyn slitted her eyes at him.

David pointed to himself. "The brains."

He pointed to T. "The muscle."

He pointed to Dorinda. "The mystery." She gave him a surprised, grateful smile.

Then he pointed to Alison. "And our fearless leader. We've got the makings of something here. That moving little speech about not being ready to be a superhero, you wanna remix it?"

"Maybe you should," agreed T.

Alison looked at her two old friends and her two new ones. She thought about what she wanted when she was a pimply loser and what she wanted when she was fabulously popular. She was the same person in both incarnations, just as she was the same person when she was Hottie.

And all of them wanted the same thing: a small tight circle of friends who cared about her.

"I used to have a superpower," Alison said slowly, haltingly. "It was called popularity. And then I got a real power and it put an end to everything that I thought mattered to me. I thought I hated being Hottie. I tried to deny that part of me. I just wanted everything to go back to the way it was. But I can't go back, and now I know I don't want to. Being Hottie is what makes me special, it's what makes me *me.* . . ."

Dorinda started crying.

Kellyn tried to act like she was rolling her eyes but couldn't hide the fact that she was getting choked up.

David and T both gestured to Alison to continue.

"I can't honestly say that there's no 'unfortunately' about this," said Alison, reprising her class president acceptance speech one last time.

"But what I can say is this. I promise I won't let you down.

When I went into this, I didn't really have an ambition beyond being the best-dressed reluctant defender of good over evil, which—no offense, Darqmoon, you've got your own lap-dancer-esque style—I think I achieved. But now I want more, a lot more. Now I want to be the best Los Angeles–based superhero ever!"

Alison held out a clenched fist. David was the first to touch his knuckles to hers. Then T. Then Dorinda. Then Kellyn. They were something. Maybe they were a group. Maybe they were a gang. Maybe they were a disparate band of misfits brought together by their complicated feelings for one special girl. But they were something.

They remained, united in that position, enjoying their solidarity, apprehensive but exhilarated about the future, until the heat emanating from Alison's fist got so intense that they all yanked their tender hands away and shook them until the pain subsided.